FACTION PARADOX:
THE BOULEVARD
Volume One

Edited by Stuart Douglas

THE BOULEVARD: VOLUME ONE

ISBN: 9781913456337

Published by Obverse Books, Edinburgh

Cover Design: Cody Schell

Cover Artwork © Lawrence Burton

First edition: June 2022

10 9 8 7 6 5 4 3 2 1

A CIP catalogue record for this title is available from the British Library.

Cousin Ravensbrook named by Matthew Kresal.
Cousin Gaval named by @Obliviscatur997

The Boulevard

(Faction Paradox: Location Unknown)

More formally, The Boulevard of Alternate Brutalities, the Boulevard is a Faction Paradox prison.

Physically, the Boulevard is, as the name suggests, a single broad street, stretching for an unknown distance in both directions, and lined on one side with a dense forest of oak trees.

Facing this forest is the prison itself, comprised of buildings lifted from throughout history at the moment of their destruction. This lifting extends to the street immediately outside each building, giving the Boulevard a patchwork appearance, and leading one drunken, time-travelling visitor to describe the Boulevard as a 'funky Frankenstein's Monster of a place'.

Behind each doorway on the Boulevard there is a cell, containing a single prisoner. Each cell can extend to encompass anything from the traditional square concrete enclosure with barred windows, to an entire planet. It is believed that the Boulevard is controlled by an appointed Godfather and a cadre of Cousins, assisted by guards taken from certain of the more aggressive Lesser Species.

Although there has never been any formal proclamation regarding the true purpose of the Boulevard, it is believed that the environment of each cell is tailored to the punishment – or, possibly but implausibly, the rehabilitation – of the individual imprisoned.

[from *Apocrypha to The Book of the War*]

Table of Contents

A Reasonable Man

Gareth Madgwick

The Boulevard. Now.

He had seen a lot of these places. Some in retrofitted red brick Victorian monoliths, some in asbestos-ridden, poorly designed concrete blocks. Some were even in low earth orbit or on the surface of new worlds.

Most things remained the same, like the bright lights; the collection of knives, scalpels and mirrors; the surgical masks and, most of all, the inert human lying on a table in the middle of it.

He didn't like them . The lights were too bright and too low and caused a glare on his glasses. The darkness made it hard to read his newspaper, a good broadsheet with a big cartoon on the opinion page. Nothing too controversial, just the issues of the day seen through a prism of domesticity: a family arguing at the breakfast table, crushing national and international controversies into a bite sized witty remark. It was a comfort.

He crossed his legs, one ankle over the knee, and leaned back on the chair in the corner of the theatre to read it, keeping an eye on the proceedings.

It didn't take long. The surgeons were chatting and joking, their eyes on the figure in front of them, their minds elsewhere. Talk drifted across the room of revues and pub crawls from their student days, weddings just a few years ago and a squash match that evening. A rematch for an embarrassing defeat last week, apparently.

'Shit,' said the lead. Blood started to drip from the table onto the floor of the theatre, turning into a steady stream. The anaesthetist scrabbled for drugs near the patient's head. All small talk was over, instruments were called for, a nurse ran, shouting for more blood. Slowly, the stream settled into a steady trickle, then simple drips. Steady drips that landed in the pool that had grown across the tiles and washed against the shoes of the men around the table.

The medical staff worked on, barked commands and instructions only, their faces grim. The damage had been done.

'That was careless,' the man in the corner muttered, as he turned the page to check the pools results.

P v Anon

In the Central Criminal Court

Eleven Day Empire

4th day of September 1752

Sentencing Remarks

1. *Would you stand please. Oh. I see. You already are.*

2. *He's shorter than you would think, isn't he?*

3. *I would say that the verdict has been passed on you by a jury of your peers, however, you were a mistake that we were not going to make twice, let alone thirteen times. Nonetheless, a verdict has been rendered and it is now my duty to pass sentence.*

4. *We have heard testimony before this court of this Faction's experiments with conceptual entities.*

5. *What? Why should I explain? Everyone knows what they are. You'll want me to call them a popular beat combo next.*

6. *Fine. For the sake of the record, conceptual entities are sentiences that exist solely as a memetic concepts. The War powers, particularly the Celestis, are well practiced in the reduction of a physical form into simple cultural concepts. Entities such as the Anarchitects and Shifts are well known. We are rarely entirely safe from a Shift suddenly appearing in a document we are reading with their smug commentary. There's something about not having a physical form that makes them utterly insufferable.*

7. *Will that do?*

8. *A group of Faction Paradox members decided on a different approach. The group was referred to by many names, but I shall choose one which best describes their nature and objectives.*

9. *They were idiots.*

10. *What these idiots decided to do is to reverse engineer concepts that had never had any physical form, but which had power despite this. The intention of this reverse engineering was to give these concepts that very physical form sufficient that they could be deployed as weapons in a war that uses Culture as a front.*

11. *Like I said, the idiots really should have thought this through.*

The Boulevard. Now.

This was rather more exciting. The smell of hot tar and burnt rubber, mixed with the fumes of petrol, told him where he was.

9

The smoke from a cluster of food stalls promised a meal. He folded the newspaper and put it under his arm.

Hopefully, before everything went wrong, there would be a chance to at least get a sandwich. He could hear the engines revving over on the starting grid, punters dashed for the trackside to watch. Excellent, less of a queue.

The sandwich wasn't a problem. He got a good bit of beef, cooked all the way through. It was always good to check. Horseradish sauce as well.

The problem was that every stall had only got ginger beer left to drink. He took the bottle and peered through the glass. It was dark, but he could just see the spiral shape floating within. Very funny.

Rotting arthropods were not something that he particularly relished.

The Eleven Day Empire. Then.

He was alone, ignored by the fathers, mothers, cousins and little siblings. An embarrassment. He walked the streets, idly exploring to pass the time. He had no real place, no part to play now they had finished with him.

The City itself seemed to maintain a shape like a shadow on the water, an idealised version of the real London. A place he knew so well without having ever been. Like him, the City that made up the Empire was constructed from London's experiences across the ages, not of the moment of its creation. Like the Square Mile in the 21st century, food stalls opened briefly to feed the few workers of the Empire. The meals were extinct meat, mammoths, smilodon, woolly rhino. Trilobites and chips were his favourite.

Unlike the stall keepers, he had no such job. A man whose existence was owed to commuting had nowhere to commute to. He had been given a minder of course, Cousin Bran, a barrel chested giant of a man not given to much chatter, wearing a fur cloak and basic leathers. Not the sort of fetish gear that some Faction members enjoyed wearing to annoy the Great Houses, but simple, loose fitting clothes topped by the ubiquitous skull mask.

He had no idea where the Cousin came from, how he had been recruited to the Faction or what his role was in the Empire. They had been introduced in the Vauxhall Building, when it was explained that Bran was to be his protector. Since then, the man had followed. It was never done oppressively. Doors would be held open, spare change provided and directions given in short, curt sentences. He had complete freedom in the Empire as long as he was happy to be followed.

He walked under the red sky, its silence boiling across him. Once, he had reached the edge of Tower Hill. Bran had grabbed him by his jacket. Shook his head and, in a few short sentences, explained what the Unkindnesses were. Since then, the man had no intention of returning.

He knew what the Empire was, of course. That it was stolen from the British Empire through ritual. Eleven days lost from the calendar in 1752, the 3rd to the 13th of September, signed over to the Faction to use as their home.

It was rubbish of course. Deep down, he knew that. It was just a change in the calendar. Just a way of counting. No one could seriously think that there were any actual lost days themselves. It was ridiculous. There was nothing for this shadow London to be built on.

He wanted his London back. The one he had inhabited without visiting. He wanted the grey skies, the smog that cloaked the town, the holler of the market stalls, the press of the other passengers on the commute. He wanted the rudeness, the stall holders telling lies on every street corner the out of towners looking confused, the tourist groups being led by umbrellas. He wanted normality.

The Boulevard. Now

This racetrack was close to normal. The bustle of people, mundane humanity, made him feel something, an ache that things would not be like this for long. The crowd gathered around the railing, next to the track, watching the cars as they started down the home straight.

He munched on his sandwich. Maybe this was finally a break in his torment. A chance to relax, watch a race, enjoy a snack. He settled, hearing the roar diminish as the cars rounded the track away from him. It was hard to place an era. The newspaper he carried was no help, it stayed the same. Mostly it was full of stories that painted various rich and powerful figures in a bad light, based on some imagined and unprovable indiscretion. Very expensive chip paper for the publisher.

The clothes were very early 20th century. None of the drab colours and cost cutting that came with wartime and austerity. A time of hope and excitement. It was a romantic age he supposed. The kind of time when people were drawn to the thrill of watching and hearing the speed and thrill of internal combustion.

The cars were returning now, large engines at the front, open wheels, single seaters, small and narrow. Highly unstable.

He heard the clang of metal as two of the leading cars connected, the loud thump as one rolled. He could see it now, the car itself was a spinning axle, spiralling through the air, occasionally hitting the ground at an angle. The crowd leaning on the barrier seemed to move slowly; in reality, the panic of observers suddenly realising their own tragic role in what was happening.

He watched the car hit the ground once more before reaching the railing. Surely it must now simply slide into the iron, denting it, killing the driver, but no more.

Of course, it then took a strange bounce and leapt into the air, its arc taking it over the railing and towards the bewildered spectators. He tried to look away, to avoid seeing the end of the lives of those men in their flat caps and women in their cloches.

The car crashed into them, turning panic into shock as metal buckled against bodies.

'Well,' he said to himself. 'I'm pretty sure that no reasonable person could have predicted that.'

Sentencing Remarks continued.

12. *After the experiment, they let you loose. They didn't know what you were for. They thought that a fussy, bald headed man wouldn't cause any problems and that, eventually, a use for you could be found. They watched you, of course. You were an important asset. It is fortunate that they did so, because that is how they found out what you were.*

13. *That was how we all found exactly who you would be of use for.*

The Eleven Day Empire. Then.

Blue sky was what he missed in the Empire. The constant red glow filled him with dread. Not of anything in particular, but the basic fear that things were just a bit more uncertain.

It was a thought he hated. The basis of the place was so false, so ridiculous. It defied logic.

The anger rose in him one day, while he was idly kicking his heels in Parliament Square, waiting for a bus that would never arrive. While Bran was leaning on his shadow staff, bonded to his arm, the man saw something he had longed for since he had emerged from the research laboratories in Vauxhall.

Small, but unmistakable, in the midst of the red glow, turning the light slightly purple by its presence, was a sliver of blue sky, just like had once existed over London itself. Through that gap a single shaft of sunlight stretched into the Empire.

The people around him were confused. They had stopped where they were fingers pointing at the sky and faces unreadable behind their masks. They weren't superstitious, of course.

Well, they were superstitious. You can't live in a pocket dimension protected by voodoo spirits and not be a little superstitious. But they weren't scared of a new shape in the sky on its own.

They had been, however, very concerned about what it meant for them.

The Boulevard. Now.

The man waited. He was still there. Presumably some appalling negligence would now be visited on the poor victims of the crash. He settled down as ambulances howled in the background. They had been parked a long way away from the sharp curve where the accident happened. No doubt some future judge would have to ask why.

Another day would have been a perfect one. The soft grass beneath him and the blue sky above, the sun baking the earth under the grass around him into cracks.

He watched from his spot on the hill overlooking the trackside to get a better view. Below him was the chaos of humanity, where each person knows something must be done, but has no idea what. He saw stretcher bearers running for the site of the wreckage. Lying on the floor, men slapping her face, waving smelling salts, was a young woman. Her dress in disarray, her hat long gone. Her legs held at a strange angle. As the stretcher bearers approached, he heard a shout. Emerging from the crowd, an older couple, the man loud, frantically waving, the woman holding her arm, obviously broken. Walking wounded.

The bearers ignored the young woman on the floor, heading straight for the older couple. It was an obvious choice he supposed. Completely unreasonable of them, however. He wondered how long the young woman lying on the floor would be for this world. Not long perhaps, those ambulance staff dooming her to a lingering death by running for an easy option amid the chaos.

Then, he was in a new location. A bedroom. He knew it well, a young woman's bedroom at night, with the window open, but empty, for now. They liked to put him here so that he could get some rest sometimes. He would be able to get a few hours in before he was woken by a young man climbing in through the window wearing nothing but a pair of socks and a bone mask with a large, protruding, beak.

He was aware of the inspiration, but didn't think much of the sense of humour.

Ennui. That was his punishment. It made sense. He wasn't here because of anything he had done. He was here because of who he was and the risk that he posed to the Faction. That's why they allowed him to rest. That's why he was nothing more than an observer in the realities they sent him to.

He liked the clothes at his last location, he mused, settling into bed. So much of his life was spent looking at people either in suits or in surgical gowns. People dressed for a day out was something different.

It was the bright clothes that had first tipped off the Faction that something was wrong with the Eleven Day Empire. Or, more accurately, with him being in the Empire. Men in tight pantaloons and walking canes, women in layer cakes trailing children in white dresses and coloured sashes. Almost all wearing powdered wigs.

He couldn't sleep. He picked up the newspaper. Began to read it. The law reports might help.

Sentencing Remarks continued

> *14. These people had no business in the Eleven Day Empire, of course. Some were ghost-like figures that drifted through walls that didn't exist in their real location. Some were rather more corporeal and confused.*

16

15. *The worst of it came when two Cousins sparring in Hyde Park were interrupted by two gentlemen settling a score over an insult to some maiden aunt or other. It descended into a melee of four men, including seconds, fighting both each other and also Little Sisters Claudia and Arian who they had suddenly surrounded.*

16. *It turned out that pistols were all very nice, but for a truly devastating duel, one really needed shadow weaponry.*

17. *It did not take long for our elders to notice that all of these ghosts and physical manifestations came from the 18th century. Or, to be precise, 2nd September and 14th September 1752. I should not have to tell anyone in this courtroom the significance of those dates.*

18. *It appeared that the Loa had failed us. That they had let people simply walk into our Empire from the time on either side of it.*

19. *The truth was, however, more sinister than that. The Loa, and the ritual that held the Empire together, were crumbling. The Gregorian Compact itself was being torn apart by basic rationality and reasonableness that said it should not exist.*

20. *It was being torn apart, in short, by you.*

The Eleven Day Empire. Then.

The London of the Eleven Day Empire was not the London of 1752. It drew on all the Londons that had ever been, sucking them to it, a smorgasbord of whatever elements had taken the fancy of the architects at the time of its creation.

That was why his birthplace, the location of the insane experiments to reverse engineer a conceptual entity, had been the Vauxhall Building inhabited by MI6 in the 20th and 21st centuries.

It made a pleasant walk, as pleasant as anything in the Empire could be. He had often wandered that way, almost ignoring where he was, his mind drifting to the many lives he'd lived before his creation, in dusty pages that nonetheless spoke of the life of humanity and portrayed its darkest moments. He stayed clear of the Tate, of course. Modern art had enough fear for him without the added complication of its being created by a group that routinely used Culture as a weapon.

He stopped outside it, however, and gazed across the river towards his birthplace. Somehow, here, amidst the requirement of total irrationality that was almost the very basis of the Empire itself, it seemed less incongruous than it did in its native time. Like a true temple to the sheer paradox of its own existence.

Bran leaned against the railing too, comforting in his silence. His mask, a simple one of pure white bone, giving nothing away.

'You must be bored of this place now,' the man said to him. 'Nothing to do but follow me.'

Bran had shrugged. 'It won't be forever.' He tensed then, leaned forward, looking across the river. The man followed his gaze. The building that faced them, its stepped walls soaring up into the clouds, was shrouded in mist all the way down. The buildings on either side, still crystal clear.

'Some sort of gas?' he said. 'They cook up all sorts in there. It's best not to look too closely. We had better move on.'

Bran shook his head, his posture that of a cat watching a mouse's nest.

Then the man saw why he was concerned. The building wasn't being covered by cloud. The cloud was showing through the fabric of the building. The entire edifice was slowly fading away.

Within he could see small figures, panicked and moving fast, tripping over their own coats as they pushed each other out of the way.

'We need to help,' the man snapped, about to run for the nearest bridge, before Bran snapped his arm out. He ran full pelt into the shadow of the wooden staff which was the large man's shadow weapon, and doubled over, gasping for air.

'You need to stay away,' Bran said. 'You've done enough for them right now.'

With that, he strode towards Vauxhall Bridge himself, leaving his charge staggering to pull himself up to the railing again, to look out at the building. Floors were, by then, even less substantial. Some figures were simply falling through them, to land below in a mess of limbs and white masks.

The building faded. It didn't collapse, there was no spectacular explosion, no cloud of dust, no mushroom cloud hovering over the city, it simply drifted out of existence and the occupants trapped inside fell to earth.

In its place, was a garden. Neatly lined with rows of trees, ideal for young ladies to parade with suitors while chaperones looked on from benches and young children played with boats in fountains.

That was probably exactly what they had all been doing, before the Faction's research department had fallen out of the sky on them.

Bran stopped on the bridge, gazed at the onslaught, at the many people running to help, their natural inclination to compete overridden by a desperate rush to preserve their civilisation, such as it was. Bran turned back to the man and grabbed him by the scruff of his neck, pulling him along, down the river. He remembered shouting, gasping, 'Why...?'

'To give them a chance to get back to where they should be. To give the Loa a chance to seal the breach. You need to be a long way from here.'

It was when they reached the entrance to Pimlico station that they stopped. In terms of the Eleven Day Empire, this was no access point to the underground trains on which he had spent so many imagined hours sitting to get to his destination. Instead, beneath here were the Stacks, a repository for anything the Faction wanted to keep safe. Or anything that they wanted everyone else to be kept safe from, strange items plucked from a thousand timelines

He had felt it. Even behind the mask, he knew that Bran was terrified. Something was pushing from below, felt, not seen or heard, but definitely there. A force, straining at reality itself.

'What's happening?' he had said, staring. From the depths, came snarls, shrieks and roars.

'The Empire is ceasing to exist.' Bran's voice had been calm, level, but it rose now. 'The London of 1752 is taking it back, absorbing us back into the timeline.'

'So what's down there?' the man had said, pointing down the steps leading into the darkness.

Bran had taken a step back, cocked his masked head to one side.

'In 1752? Nothing but loam. So where do all the things that we have put down there go if the city reverts to 1752?'

The man was dragged away again, down streets in which terrified citizens mingled with confused people of 18th century London. Bone white masks and bone white powdered faces. Black robes and hands covered in soot. Finally, they reached the Old Bailey, now drifting in and out of existence, as its walls formed and reformed around Newgate Gaol.

There Bran stopped. Figures descended from all around, Godmothers and Godfathers, their masks true representations of the horrors that would have befallen the Great Houses had they lost the wars at the start of their existence.

And the ritual had begun. But at the same time, a further ritual was carried out. One that he had only found out later was completely necessary.

'I arrest you on suspicion of undermining the entirety of the Eleven Day Empire and attempted unravelling of the Gregorian Compact,' Bran had intoned. 'You are not obliged to say anything but anything you do say may be given in evidence.' Just as anachronistic as everything else that was happening, but, with its heavy wording, so much a part of culture in broadcast media, and its complete lack of the fingers-behind-the-back double crossing of the later versions, it was as binding as anything could have been.

And so, he had landed in Newgate Gaol itself, the Eleven Day Empire's version. Awaiting trial for something he hadn't done, of course, simply for what he was.

Sentencing Remarks Continued

21. *When deciding to backwards engineer a conceptual entity, it was incredibly tempting for the idiots to turn to the law. The law courts of England, such as those we now stand in, were themselves the very epitome of power through culture, and power through ritual. They*

even liked dressing up for their roles. It is no coincidence that when they dispensed with their silly robes and wigs, the power of the law over the people of the nation started to wane. But that power had held for hundreds of years, not least through the legal fictions created in the courts themselves.

22. *Those characters were created by judges and lawyers to give weight to their decisions. These people, like the 'moron in a hurry' and the incredibly boring 'person having ordinary skill in the art' have a power already. Their views can change the fortunes of an inventor or ruin an entire company, all from the dry and dusty pages of a law text book. By creating them as a physical entity, their powers could be unconstrained.*

23. *None are so famous as the Man on the Clapham Omnibus. A reasonable man, a paragon of virtue. A man who is neither too cautious nor too reckless.*

24. *And so, they created you.*

25. *But they forgot the most important thing. The Man on the Clapham Omnibus is an observer in many of his cases. He considers what is reasonable and what is not and his views become reality. By releasing that man into the Eleven Day Empire, a place that runs on irrationality, on culture, on what is thought to be, rather than what is, they dropped a bomb under the Faction's very existence.*

26. *We had no way to stop you from destroying everything we hold dear, simply by watching us.*

The Eleven Day Empire. Then.

The cell was bare. Brick walls arched above him, only a wooden bench folded from the wall to sit on.

There were bars, high, near the apex. He had tried to jump up, to get a view of the city out there. He wanted to see if he was still in the Empire or the London of 1752. It was impossible to tell simply from the cold walls, this old building had existed for centuries, the city had grown around it. The law had grown around it.

Out there could be the ordered world of Georgian London, or the heart of the Faction restoring itself after his destructive influence.

In the silence of the cell, he was cut off, had no idea where he was, when he was and what reality he was now in.

He stood, walked to the heavy iron door and thumped it several times. There was no movement on the other side.

'I would like my solicitor please,' he called. No answer.

He sat, legs not quite reaching the floor, kicking his heels together as he waited. He didn't feel alone here. There was a presence in this room, a large space by the standards of most cells, with room for many more prisoners than its solitary occupant.

It was movement, out of the corner of his eye. Another figure in the room with him. When he turned, it was gone, faded to just the bare brick walls, shadowed by the red light through the bars of the window. Then, another, out of his other eye. Clearer now, he caught sight of them stood by the door. Again, when he focused, they were gone.

But more than that, the door itself was fading Like the bricks and the mortar of the Vauxhall building, it was drifting out of this existence. One second a solid sheet of iron, blocking his way to freedom, the next, it was swung open against the wall. Shadows drifted across it. The shapes of prisoners, mixing.

No high security wing this. Not with these big roomy cells. This block was for the less risky prisoners, like the white collars, the petty thieves and the rent boys. Free association when nothing else was needed and so the door stood open. He darted for it. Its shadow stood across his escape route but was as substantial as a cloud.

Outside, he was in the block, his floor near the top, a balcony that looked down on the floors below. Around him were warders, prisoners, both from the Empire and from the London that the Empire had been stolen from. As the prisoners became more corporeal, the panic in the Faction's wardens grew.

He knew what was needed. This was a distraction; he could escape. He ran for the stairs, taking them two at a time. As he reached the bottom floor, he glanced both ways. One direction was clear. In the other, he saw two skull masked guards pushing their way through the prisoners and wardens, shadow weapons slashing out and striking those that resisted.

He turned, shot down the nearest corridor, with no idea of direction. At each junction, he glanced round, looking to see what might follow, desperately trying to avoid the Faction and its guards. Searching for a way out. He went deeper and deeper, down corridors that twisted and wound through the maze of the prison, until he found himself darting down a single corridor. Then, at the end, two Cousins appeared, their masks, with their grinning teeth, seeming almost amused at him. He turned back, behind him was another pair; he could see the shadows of their swords dancing in the gas lights.

There was one door, one chance. He sprinted for it, pulling it open and slamming it behind himself.

He stood at the foot of a short set of steps, leading to a higher platform. Behind him, he heard the lock turning in the door he had just stepped through, a fatal clunk.

Above his head, the roof of a larger room, panelled in wood. He ascended towards it. At the top, he was unsurprised to see a further skull mask waiting for him, this one topped with a policeman's helmet accompanied by the blue uniform and shining buttons of an officer of the Metropolitan Police. The Cousin nodded once as the man joined him in the small dock.

Before him lay the courtroom. Two more Cousins, in black robes with their masks topped by horsehair wigs, sat looking bored at the tables in the middle, leaning back with legs crossed. A clerk scribbled in a ledger at a slightly raised desk, and behind him sat a bench, and high chairs. Instead of the royal seal, a skull hung from the wall.

'All rise,' muttered the clerk. As he did so, the jury filed in, twelve faces more inscrutable than any other behind their masks. They were followed by the judge, bowing to all those present before settling himself down in his chair.

'Right,' he said. 'Let's give this a go shall we?'

Sentencing Remarks, continued

> 27. *It was not reasonable to imprison you without a trial. Therefore, with your observation of reality implicitly affecting that reality, we couldn't. If it is unreasonable, if it defies reason, as understood by the little bald man on the omnibus, it now ceases to exist. We were therefore forced to set up a trial.*

> 28. *Twelve good Cousins and true, a judge, even lawyers. We found them all and we have held this trial. You, as one of the foundation*

parts of the English Legal System must be bound by the same rituals that cause it to function.

29. By those rituals you have been found guilty and it is now my duty to pass sentence.

30. You cannot remain here. Your very presence destabilises the entire basis for the existence of the Eleven Day Empire.

31. We cannot allow you to leave and enter the Spiral Politic. You have a power that functions incredibly well against us and could easily be used by those that seek to cause us harm .

32. Yes, I know that's nearly everyone else.

33. We can only imprison you in the Boulevard of Alternate Brutalities. There we must ensure that you are sandwiched and contained within an alternate reality. I have the duty to decide which.

34. It seems only fair that you should play the role you always did before the idiots conjured you into this reality. You will therefore be merely an observer to all of the events in which you were later summoned to pass judgement on in court cases throughout the ages.

The Boulevard. Now

The was movement at the window. That was rather unfair, he hadn't managed to sleep yet. He turned over in bed.

A figure sat crouched at the window, the moonlight was behind it, but he could just about see the white bone of the mask it wore. The effect was somewhat spoiled by the paisley patterned socks on his feet. The Man From The Clapham Omnibus sighed and pulled himself out of bed. He crossed to the window.

The figure cocked its head to one side.

'Any part of your body protruding into the room,' said the Man. 'That's sufficient to get you potted for burglary.' With that, he reached for the catch on the sash and let it come crashing down. The figure now behind the glass howled in pain and dropped down into the shrubs outside with a clatter of limbs.

The Man returned to his bed and reached for the paper again, picking up from where he had left off:

35. *So, in conclusion, the only effective sentence that I can impose would be indefinite detention in the Boulevard of* **We're coming to get you, be ready** *as long as it can be maintained.*

36. *Take him down. Or up. Or whichever way you* **You are vital for us.** *get the hang of quantum directions.* **Keep an eye out.** *you to both Counsel.*

Finally. It sounded like help was on its way.

Body and Soul

Paul Hiscock

February 19, 1955

Joe stumbled up the stairs to the street. Behind him, the lights went out as the club finally shut for the night.

His set had finished hours ago, and the rest of the band was long gone. He had turned to a bottle of bourbon for company, but even that had run out on him. All he had left was the trumpet in his hand, and a lot of good that was doing him. The audience tonight had barely noticed the music. Too busy talking to care about the musicians pouring out their souls in the corner.

He lifted the trumpet to his lips, and tried to play *Round Midnight*, but his fingers felt sluggish as he fumbled his way through the opening bars.

"Shut up that bloody racket!" someone yelled from an apartment nearby. "Don't you know what time it is?"

"Sure, I do," Joe shouted back. "Didn't you hear what I was playing?"

He heard a window slam shut.

"I guess he's not a music lover."

Joe considered playing a bit more, but the instrument felt heavy in his hand, so he let it fall down to his side. He'd had a case when he arrived earlier—must have left it in the club. He stopped and turned back to get it, but he was already halfway across the street, and he wasn't sure he could manage those steps again. It would still be there in the afternoon when he woke up.

He heard the sound of a horn from nearby. He must have woken a fellow musician, keen to play a duet. He raised his trumpet to join in, and something knocked into him, sending him flying onto his back. He watched as a truck rushed by, inches from his feet, the sound of its horn lowering and fading as it sped past.

"He almost got you. You're lucky I was here."

Joe looked up to see a man standing over him. He wore a dark green zoot suit, and a matching pork-pie hat with a black feather sticking out of the band. The gloved hand he held out to help Joe up was bone white. It matched the mask he wore—some sort of animal skull with horns that curled up around each side of his hat.

"I must have hit my head."

"Maybe so," replied the stranger, as Joe stood. "Do you remember your name?"

"Sure, it's Joe, Joseph Barker."

"The trumpet player, right?"

"Yeah that's right, I…." Joe looked down at his empty hands. "Hey! What did you do with my trumpet?"

The man in the mask pointed at the road.

"I didn't do anything to it, the truck did. I saved you, but your instrument wasn't so lucky."

All that was left of his trumpet was a sorry pile of crushed metal in the middle of the street.

"That's just fucking great! I guess that sorry excuse for a gig tonight was my last bow. Seems about right. Nobody wants to listen to me anymore."

"I'm sorry to hear that," said the stranger. "I thought you had a lot of potential. *Well You Needn't* is a work of genius."

"My record? I'm surprised you've even heard of it. Record company claimed they could barely give it away."

"Well, I'm a fan. In fact, that's why I'm here tonight."

"If you came for the gig, you're too late, and as you can see, I'm not going to be playing any more encores."

"Not for the gig. I came for you. Let me introduce myself properly. I'm Godfather Mephistopheles, and, as I said, I just saved your life."

"Godfather? Is that like some kinda fairy godmother shit, but for dudes?"

"Something like that. You should have died here tonight."

"You might as well have let me. My career's over. There's no way I can afford to replace my trumpet."

"I could still let you die, if that's what you want? It would be easy enough for you to join your instrument under the next truck."

Joe shivered. Suddenly it seemed a bit colder and darker on the street. But then Mephistopheles continued, and the moment passed.

"I came here to offer you a second chance. All you have to do is accept a small gift from me, and you can have the life you've dreamed of."

"What do you know about my dreams?"

"Just listen."

30

Mephistopheles cupped his hand at the side of his head. At first the sound was faint, but it quickly grew louder, and soon Joe could make out someone playing the trumpet. Not just someone, but him—a little flourish here, a note held slightly longer than other players would there. All the ways he would wring every drop of emotion out of a piece. And then, at the end of the solo, applause. Not the half-hearted tapping of the bored audience that night, but genuine, heartfelt appreciation for his art.

"That could be you," said Mephistopheles. "Just accept this gift from the loa, and they will take your old timeline, your old timeline where you die, and replace it with that."

He lifted up his hand, in its bone white glove, and now it was holding a black case. Joe didn't know where it had come from. He could swear it hadn't been there before. Godfather Mephistopheles held the case out flat.

"Open it," he said.

Joe undid the clasps and lifted the lid. Then he smiled.

February 20, 1955

"So let me get this straight," said Charlie, the drummer. "You get drunk, drop your horn under a truck, and a guy wanders up and gives you a new one?"

"Not just a new one. A better one," replied Joe.

"Maybe I should throw my bass under a bus," laughed Lou. "I could do with an upgrade."

Joe laughed, but it didn't feel funny. He'd had to tell them all about the trumpet, of course, but he hadn't mentioned his own brush with death.

"It doesn't look that special to me," said Art, the pianist.

"It's a good instrument. After all, if a Conn trumpet was good enough for Bix, it's good enough for me."

"Shouldn't there be a second N?" asked Art, studying the engraving on the bell.

"It must have worn away, or something," replied Joe. "Besides, what matters is how it plays, and it plays like a dream."

"Now's your chance to prove it." Henry pointed to the stage, where Mike, the club's owner, was beckoning to them. Then he picked up his tenor sax. "Looks like we're on."

The band made its way over to the small stage, as Mike began his introduction.

"Ladies and gentlemen, welcome to the Crossroads Club. I hope you're enjoying your evening. It is my pleasure to welcome back the Joseph Barker Quintet to perform for you tonight."

He could not have sounded less enthusiastic if he had tried, and the ripple of applause from the audience was similarly lacklustre.

Most of the club's patrons didn't even look up.

"*Stardust* in A minor," Joe said to the band and started playing, without waiting for a response. The selection caught them off guard. It was a slow number, not the sort of thing they'd usually choose to lead a set with. Yet, it seemed to capture the audience.

As Joe played the opening notes, silence spread across the room. The conversations stopped and everyone turned to give the stage their full attention.

Joe played on. He had his eyes closed, and seemed to be lost in the music. He didn't open them until the piece ended, at which point the room erupted with applause.

He turned to the band. "I told you, this is our second chance. Things are going to be better for us this time."

October 10, 1955

"Art's dead!"

Everyone turned on their barstools to face Lou, standing in the doorway.

"Of course he's not dead," said Joe. "We saw him yesterday. He's on his way to New York to record with Miles Davis."

"Lucky bastard," said Charlie.

"What's Miles got that I haven't?" Joe asked.

"Charisma, fame, fortune," said Henry.

Joe reached over and slapped him lightly around the back of the head.

"We'll all be famous soon enough. Trust me. Miles is old news. I'm the next big thing."

"No," shouted Lou, "you aren't listening. He never made it there. There was an accident. It was raining hard, and Art's car went off the road. He died!"

Charlie turned grey. "That's not possible," he said, before dashing to the bathroom. Through the thin wooden door, they could hear him throwing up.

"How do you know?" asked Joe.

"His sister told me. The police turned up at his ma's house this morning."

Henry led the shaken bass player over to the bar and put a drink in his hand.

"There you go, you need that. Hell, we all need one." He gestured to the bartender to pour another round. "It's terrible. I mean, he was younger than any of us. I can't even imagine."

Charlie staggered out of the bathroom. The big man still looked unwell, but he gratefully downed the shot that had been poured for him, and it restored a little of his colour.

"We should go pay our respects to his ma," said Henry.

They all stood, except Joe, who stayed on his stool, nursing his drink.

"You go. I just need a minute."

Henry patted him on the shoulder.

"Sure thing, Joe. You take your time. We understand."

They left him, sitting alone at the bar.

"It's tough, losing someone you care about."

Joe turned to see Godfather Mephistopheles sitting at the end of the bar. He was wearing a zoot suit, like before, but this one was midnight blue.

The bartender placed a whisky sour in front of Mephistopheles. If he noticed the mask, he chose not to comment.

"I don't care. The kid walked out on me. Didn't believe we could make it. Didn't believe I have what it takes. You know what the last thing he said to me was? 'You're good, but you're no Miles

Davis.' Well fuck him. Serves him right for running off to New York to play with Mr. Big Shot."

The room was going blurry, and Joe realised he was crying. He wiped away the tears with the back of his hand.

"He was a damn fine pianist though. Don't know how I'm going to replace him. It takes time to get a tight sound like that, you know."

"You could stop now," said Mephistopheles. "Hand back the horn and call it a day. It's a hard road to the top. Maybe it's not for you."

Joe picked up his glass and gulped down the last of his drink.

"I'm not a quitter. I'll make it to the top, without Art—for Art. You just watch me."

"I certainly will," said Godfather Mephistopheles, as Joe rushed out of the bar to catch up with his bandmates.

August 23, 1957

"What the hell?"

Joe jumped up in shock as a pint of tepid beer hit him in the face.

"What do you think you're doing?" he shouted at the man standing next to the booth where the band was sitting, holding a now empty glass.

"What am I doing? I'm not the one who left a suitcase on the floor."

He bent down and picked up Joe's trumpet case, which he threw on to the table. Lou quickly snatched up his drink as the rest of the glasses went flying.

"You owe me another drink!" the man shouted.

"Well, you now owe us all drinks, and new suits," replied Joe.

He clicked open the trumpet case and checked the instrument inside. He sighed with relief when he saw everything was safe.

"At least you didn't damage this," he said.

Henry stood up.

"Let's all calm down," he said. "No real harm done. Why don't I get us all another round, and we can sit and have a drink together?"

"I'm not drinking with the likes of you, boy. They shouldn't even be letting your kind through the door."

"Well, screw you," said Joe and grabbed the glass out of Lou's hand.

"Wait, Joe!" shouted Henry, but it was already too late.

"Wake up, sleeping beauties."

Joe groaned and tried to open his eyes. One of them appeared to be swollen shut, while the other struggled to acclimatise to the light.

"Where are we, and why does it smell of piss and stale beer?"

"We're in the county slammer," said Henry, "after you decided to start a bar fight."

"What about the gig?"

"What about it? Do you think they'll be letting us play anywhere looking like this?"

Now his vision was clearing, Joe looked around the cell. Henry was standing in the corner, and Lou was sitting on the floor. Charlie was lying next to Joe, still out cold. Their latest pianist, Karl, was leaning against the wall, trying to avoid making eye contact. Joe doubted he'd stay with the band once they got out.

"Where is he?"

"Where's who?" replied Henry.

"The guy who attacked us. Him and his friends."

"Leaving aside the question of who attacked who, obviously he's not here."

"Why not?" Joe reached up and touched his swollen eye, immediately regretting it as he winced in pain. "I don't remember much, but I'm certain I didn't do this to myself."

"It went like this," said Lou. "They were white, and we weren't, so when they tossed the coin they won a slap on the wrist and we won this lovely accommodation for the night."

"Well, it looks like it's morning out there. Now I'm awake, can we see about getting someone to let us out."

"Why do you think I woke you up?" muttered Henry.

Joe reached over and shook Charlie by the shoulder.

"Rise and shine, big guy."

Charlie didn't stir.

"How much did he have to drink?" Joe asked Henry.

"No more than usual."

"So, plenty." Charlie would drink them all under the table most nights.

Joe shook him again, then he felt something sticky. He held up his hand, only to find that it was covered in blood.

He scrambled away from Charlie. Henry started yelling for a guard to come, but Joe already knew that it was too late.

September 30, 1962

"You're doing well for yourself. Life in the Big Apple suits you."

Joe finished snorting the line of coke before he looked up. Godfather Mephistopheles was wearing a scarlet suit and hat that day. The lapels were wider than ever, but everything else was still the same as usual. The same bone white gloves. The same freaky mask.

He had become used to Mephistopheles's surprise appearances. Always when his bandmates weren't around, and always with the same question.

Mephistopheles stared at the trumpet case in the corner.

"Have you achieved enough yet? I could take it back today— conclude our deal."

"Have you seen all this? I'm riding high. The next album, it's going to be the one that goes down in history. It will put me up there with Miles, Bix, and Brownie. Why would I want to stop now?"

"Very well. I'm glad you're getting what you wanted."

"Sure. Say, did you want a line of this? There's plenty to go around."

"I really must be going, but don't worry. I'm sure your bandmates will be along to help you enjoy it shortly."

December 15, 1963

"It was a nice service," said Henry.

"It was boring as hell," Joe replied. "Lou would have hated it."

"You're right. He would have."

They watched the snow fall into the open grave. The coffin was already covered in a layer of white powder. Joe pointed it out to Henry.

"Seems appropriate," he said.

Henry didn't laugh.

"We should have played something," Joe said. "Given him a proper send off, the way they do it in New Orleans."

"Too late now."

"Well, I've got my horn. Do you have your axe?"

"Sure, over in the car."

Joe walked over to the funeral car that was waiting for them. The undertaker opened the door for him, only to be disappointed when instead of getting in, Joe pulled out two cases.

"Just a few more minutes."

The undertaker mumbled and stamped his feet in an attempt to stay warm.

Joe returned to the graveside and they took out their instruments. He started playing, and a few moments later Henry joined in.

The *Saint Louis Blues* wafted across the graveyard.

"I'm getting out," Henry said in the car on the way back into the city.

"Here?" asked Joe. "It's the middle of nowhere."

"Not out of the car. Out of the jazz scene."

"Why?"

"Do you really need to ask that, when we just buried Lou? We started out as a quintet—now look at us."

"Lou always overdid it. You and me are more careful. Hey, give up the drugs completely, even the booze if you feel you must. It doesn't mean you have to stop playing."

"I'm sorry, Joe. I think I've got to put it all behind me, or sooner rather than later it's going to be my grave you're standing next to."

They drove on in silence, until they reached Henry's apartment building. He started to get out, but Joe grabbed him by the shoulder.

"Are you sure you want to do this?"

"Never been so sure about anything. You should think about it too. This life, it ain't healthy."

April 30, 1965

The pianist was in the middle of his solo, and Joe was tapping along with his foot. It was a good sound tonight. Not like the old quintet, of course, but not bad. He might be able to do something with this crew, if they stuck around.

However, one thing was bothering him.

"Do you know the chick at the table down front?" he whispered.

The bass player looked over.

"Nah, Joe. Never seen her before."

"She's been staring at me all evening."

"Guess she must be a fan."

"I guess so."

The piano solo drew to a close, and he raised his trumpet, ready to take the lead.

As soon as the set was over he jumped down from the stage. He waved at the bartender, then sat himself down at the table, opposite the girl who had been staring at him.

"Hi, I'm Joe. Can I buy you a drink?"

Before she could answer, a waiter appeared at the table with a bottle in a wine bucket and two champagne glasses.

"It looks like you already have," she said, as the waiter popped the cork.

"May I know the name of the lovely lady I'm drinking with then?"

"You may, or rather I'm May."

Joe laughed.

"Then maybe we could get to know each other better," he said, raising his glass.

July 8, 1969

Joe looked at the trumpet case, gathering dust in the corner. For the first few months after he'd stopped playing, he'd expected Godfather Mephistopheles to turn up at any moment, and reclaim his gift. But it was three years now, and the mysterious man in the zoot suit and the horned mask hadn't appeared.

"All that booze, all those drugs, they messed with your mind, baby," May told him. "Men wearing skulls on their heads don't wander the streets at night handing out musical instruments. He was all in your head, but now you're clean—now you're free."

She leaned in close to him, and placed his hand on her slightly rounded stomach.

"You don't miss it, do you baby?"

"Of course not." He hesitated before answering. She noticed, of course. She always did.

"You don't have to go anywhere else to play. Your biggest fans are right here. In fact, maybe you should get that old horn out. Practice playing some lullabies."

"Sure, babe," he murmured. "Maybe later."

January 16, 1970

"I told you, it'll just be a couple of weeks. Boston, New York, then back down to Philly to join you at your parents' house. You said you wanted to be there when you had the baby."

"I wanted us to be there."

"And we will be. There's still plenty of time. I'll be there with two whole weeks to spare."

"Why are you doing this?"

"It's easy money, for us—for our family. The record company says there's a whole new generation discovering my music. They might even consider a new album, if there's enough interest."

"Right? And it isn't just an excuse to go around drinking, and partying with your old buddies, getting up to who knows what?"

"It's not like that at all. You know none of the old band are still around. It's just a bunch of kids they've put together to back me. I'd much rather be with you."

"Then don't go."

He picked up the trumpet case, then leant in to kiss her, but she turned away.

February 5, 1970

They ended the set with *Groovin' High*. At the beginning of the tour, it had been *Get Happy*, but they'd switched it up. Never mind that it meant ending with a sax solo, or that the reviews focussed on the boy playing it—Marty Taylor, the rising star whose name seemed to get larger on the play bills at each venue they played.

The applause started to fade and Joe turned to pack away his instrument. His lips tingled—even after all these weeks he could still feel the years without practicing properly. Time was that he could have kept playing all night, but he didn't have that stamina any more.

"Next stop, Pittsburgh," said Marty, slapping the drummer, Ben, or was it Ken, on the back.

"No, it's Philadelphia next," Joe said. "Last stop on the tour."

"Nah, man. They added in some extra gigs. Our adoring fans, they can't get enough. Great, ain't it?"

"I need to get back. May is waiting for me."

"That's right, you're expecting, aren't you. When's it due?"

"Just two weeks."

"Well, this is just four days more. Plenty of time."

"Yeah, plenty of time," Joe replied, but he didn't think May would agree.

February 19, 1970

May's father answered the door. He looked older than Joe remembered—his short hair whiter and his strong shoulders slumped.

"You're not welcome here, boy."

"Mr. Davis, sir, I know May is angry. I'm later than I promised, but I'm here for her now."

"We couldn't reach you. Those fancy executives in New York only ever seemed to know where you'd been yesterday—fat lot of good that was to anyone."

"They added a few more stops on the tour. I didn't have a choice."

"You always had a choice, boy. I told May not to marry a no-good jazz musician, but she swore you'd quit."

"I did. I have. I'm home now, and all I want to do is see my wife, and be with her when our child arrives."

"We couldn't reach you." The old man's voice cracked and there were tears in his eyes. "You weren't here three days ago when she went into labour early."

Mr. Davis pushed Joe backwards.

"You weren't here when she was screaming your name."

He pushed Joe away again.

"You weren't here when my grandson didn't start breathing, or when my daughter bled out on the bed."

He pushed once more, and Joe stumbled off the porch, falling on to his back.

"You weren't here yesterday when we buried them both, so why would we want you here today when there's nothing left. Go back to your fancy musician friends, because you're not welcome here."

A bouquet of lilies lay on the freshly filled earth, in front of the small wooden cross bearing her name. He put his flowers down

45

next to them, but the bright carnations seemed out of place. He'd bought them as an apology, not to mourn her.

He knelt on the damp grass and wondered where he should go. He had no family left in the city, no friends. He'd outlived them all—even May, even his son.

He could go back to New York, but all that waited there was an empty apartment. All he had left was the trumpet in his hand, and a lot of good that was going to do him. When the tour had ended, the record company had sent a nameless executive to thank him. It had been a great valedictory tour—the perfect way to pass the torch to the next generation.

If it was all over, then he knew where he needed to be. He stood up and turned towards the city.

It was around midnight when he reached the old Crossroads Club. The building was derelict, windows broken and boards barring the door that led downstairs.

He took the trumpet out of the case and fitted the mouthpiece. Then he started to play—not one of the standards that had built his career, but pure improvisation filled with all the loss and pain of the last fifteen years. He blew it all out, until his lips were numb and his breathing was laboured. Then he squatted down on the pavement and cried.

He did not notice the man on the other side of the road, until he started clapping—not the rapturous applause of a fan, but slower, and more deliberate.

"Bravo! That was truly inspiring. With playing like that, there's no telling what you could still achieve."

Godfather Mephistopheles was dressed all in black, from the feather in his pork-pie hat to the tips of his gloved fingers. Only the hideous skull that he wore as a mask broke the darkness, shining brightly in the moonlight.

"However, I think it is time, don't you? The human mind is fragile, it can only take so much pain. I don't think you could stand to lose any more, not that you have any more to lose. It's time to hand me the trumpet and call it a day."

"They're all gone," cried Joe.

"I told you it was a hard road to the top. Not everyone can make it. It was you or them."

Joe stood up and stared into the black orbits of Mephistopheles's skull, but deep shadows concealed the face behind the mask.

"Me or them?"

"New timelines aren't built from wishes and fairy dust. It requires manipulating an intricate web of cause and effect—finding just the right sacrifice to please the loa. Take your friend Art. Poor old Arthur. Never destined to be the frontman, or achieve great recognition, but everyone would have heard his playing on some of the greatest albums ever—if he'd just made it to that first date with Miles."

"You killed him, you bastard."

"Nobody killed him. It was just a random car accident. Just like it was just a bar fight that killed Charlie, and just an overdose that killed Lou. Nothing special or noteworthy—that's the point."

"You didn't manage to kill Henry though. He got out before you could work your magic on him."

"I told you, we don't kill, we sacrifice. Without you, Henry would have become one of the greatest bandleaders of his generation."

"You let him waste his life?"

"No, Joe, you let him waste his life. Fading away into obscurity to give you a little longer in the sun. So much potential, so much energy. I admit that we only gave you a little bit. After all, it takes a great deal to feed the loa. But I promise you, we didn't waste anything."

Mephistopheles held out his hands.

"Now it is time to hand the trumpet over. I don't think you have anything left to give."

"Give?" shouted Joe. "I never gave anything. You never told me what it would cost. You just took without asking."

"I kept asking. I offered time and time again to end our agreement and take the trumpet back. You could have stopped at any time, but you were addicted to the applause. You could never give that up, even when it cost you everything."

"May," whispered Joe.

"You know, for a time I thought I'd misjudged you, but it pays to be patient."

"You took my wife. You took my son."

"No, you walked away."

Joe stared down at the trumpet in his hands.

"I wish I'd never seen this cursed thing," he said.

"Just hand it over then."

Mephistopheles reached out for the trumpet, but Joe stepped back, away from his grasping hands.

"If I give it to you, you'll just pass it on to some other gullible fool. I won't let you do that."

Dodging around Mephistopheles, Joe ran out into the street. Just like fifteen years before, a truck bore down on the tired trumpet player, its horn blaring. At the last second, Joe threw the trumpet onto the ground, into the path of the oncoming vehicle.

As the tyres of the truck crushed the trumpet, a cacophony of sound erupted from the instrument. Joe thought he could hear a phrase on the piano, a crash of drums and cymbals, the deep thrum of a standing bass, and the wail of a tenor sax. The music of all the friends whose potential he had squandered. And above all the music, most painful of all, the crying of a baby boy.

As abruptly as it started, the noise ended. The truck rumbled past, leaving the flattened remains of the trumpet lying on the road.

Mephistopheles ran over and knelt down next to the broken instrument.

"What have you done?" he shouted. "It's all gone."

"You'll never use that cursed instrument to tempt anyone ever again," Joe said, smiling.

"You foolish boy. That trumpet wasn't special. I could pick up another one in a pawn shop tomorrow morning. But the energy, all that lovely potential energy you'd gathered, wasted. The loa will be furious. It will take me centuries to regain their trust, and meanwhile I'm left with nothing."

"Then I can die happy," said Joe.

"Who said anything about dying? You deserve far worse than that. We have a special place, where you can continue forever."

Mephistopheles paused, and for a moment the shadows made it look like his awful skull was grinning.

"However, first a little something for you to think about for the rest of eternity. They are barely going to remember you. You'll just be a footnote in jazz history. But you could have been so much more. They would have rediscovered your album after you died. When we first met, I told you *Well You Needn't* is a work of genius. And it is. The only recording by a man with so much untapped potential, who died too young."

Godfather Mephistopheles grabbed Joe roughly by the wrist.

"So much beautiful energy," he said. "What a waste."

Then the two of them disappeared from the street, leaving nothing but a broken trumpet lying in the road.

A faint sound can sometimes be heard wafting across the Boulevard—the mournful tones of a trumpet.

The player wrings every drop of emotion out of his music, but when the piece ends there is silence. The club where he plays is empty. Nobody is ever there to appreciate his performance. Nobody to call out his name. Never even the tiniest ripple of applause.

After a moment, he starts again—playing his soul out into the void.

The Boy Who Couldn't Stop Aging

Tim Gambrell

As soon as Cousin Sophia entered the house, she knew that the experience would not be a pleasant one. The Boulevard contained any number of individual 'experiences', but there was something about the interior of this house that sickened her. Yet, it wasn't the peeling, waxy wallpaper, fluttering in the draught. Nor the patches of mould flourishing in the corners of the ceiling. Neither was it the fusty carpet, threadbare in places, its ancient pattern now indistinguishable beneath years of dirt and grime.

It was the air, the atmosphere. It was somehow... *wrong*.

The *wrongness* had infected the fabric of the building—which meant it had corrupted the mathematical matrix within which that particular prison cell operated. It allowed the dilapidations to show. It suggested entropy was at work. But one thing it didn't do, *couldn't* do, was release the prisoner. No matter what, he remained trapped, held there to see out his sentence.

The mewling of a child behind the door to her left caught Sophia's attention. She had an expectation of what she would find within. She moved to enter. She would be there, in the house, a while.

Cousin Sophia's insides lurched as she stepped through the doorway. Displacement. As if she'd been transported elsewhere. But all she had done was step through from one adjacent room to the other.

The sense of wrongness was stronger here. The data she had reviewed, in preparation, suggested this environment had not always been that way. As with the entrance hall, Sophia felt that the base code had somehow become corrupted. It was, no doubt, due to the occupant.

Across the room, on an over-stuffed chair, sat a boy of perhaps eight or nine years old. At least, currently he was a boy, but Sophia didn't anticipate him remaining that way for long. She knew what to expect. The floor creaked beneath her step and the boy looked at her. His eyes were constantly blinking. He was whimpering in terror and he paused only to wipe his nose on his sleeve. She waited to see what would happen next.

'Can I get you anything?'

The words took a moment to process. Then a further moment passed before Sophia realised they were addressed to her. She turned to see a square-jawed, firm-set, middle-aged man. He was seated across from the prisoner. Although he spoke to Sophia, his gaze never wavered from the young boy. Like any good jailer. Any good guard. Any incorruptible AI.

'No. Thank you,' Sophia replied, genially.

The guard nodded. Slowly. 'You wish to sit?'

She took a moment to appraise the rest of the room. Moth-eaten curtains hung at the windows. The walls and ceiling were festooned with spider webs and thick dust from decades of disregard. She could make out a sunken chaise longue, an occasional table and a cabinet filled with trinkets. Faded splendour, tarnished further by the unpleasantness of the occupant.

No, the room was not inviting. For want of a mouldering wedding cake, only Miss Havisham could have been content there. Sophia was many things, but she drew the line at cosplaying Dickens.

'Please yourself.'

She realised the guard had got fed up waiting for her to answer. She felt a momentary twinge of annoyance. She wasn't used to being dismissed. She wasn't there to be dismissed. She was there in an official capacity.

'Thank you. I will sit if I want. I will sit where I want. And I will sit when I want. Don't let me intrude upon your duties. I am here merely to observe the routine.'

'Is that all?'

The strength of the boy's voice took Sophia by surprise. She looked at him with earnest intent. He had suddenly changed from whimpering pathos to confidence. The boy smiled and the immensity of the situation at once crowded in upon her. If all the evil in the universe could be poured into one single moment, it was there in that smile. And it was aimed solely at her. Sophia shuddered.

'He doesn't take his eyes off me,' the boy said. 'Like the three Judges of the Dead all rolled into one.'

'You know of such stories?'

'I had an education,' he replied.

Sophia found she was unwilling to take her eyes from the boy, also. She felt the springs of the musty chaise longue groan judgmentally as she seated herself. She would not recline. The boy continued to stare back at Sophia, and for a moment his face changed, altered. The boy fleetingly became an old man, his soft blond locks hardening to steel grey. Then it was over; he was a boy again.

'Are you comfortable, here?' she asked.

'Very, thank you.'

'You know why you're here, of course.'

'I do,' the boy replied.

'Good. Not all do.'

'I am here so you can help me get better.'

Sophia paused. She hadn't expected the prisoner to look at it that way. She glanced momentarily at the guard, then back to the boy. 'Who told you that?'

'I am getting better. One day, you can release me.'

'Is that so?'

'Yes. I think that's why you're here.'

'You seem very sure.'

'I am. I deserve the chance to appeal.'

Sophia took a long breath and sat back into the corner of the chaise, trying to affect a relaxed, perhaps even nonchalant, demeanour.

The boy slowly inclined his head.

She waited for the Pandora's Box smile to appear again, but it never came.

'How's the food?' she asked, after a moment.

'Enough,' the boy replied.

'Enough?'

'Yes. Enough to keep me alive, but insufficient to garner any joy from my continued existence. I often wonder why you didn't just kill me in the first place.'

Games. This situation was dangerous, that was a given.

'You are an unstable space-time event. To end your life prematurely may cause an instability. Much safer to allow you to exhaust and expire naturally.'

'They always said it would kill me, in the end.' He took on a frantic, concerned look. His demeanour seemed to change with the same speed and unpredictability as his age. Sophia watched him, looking for clues, searching for truth behind his face. Was this an act, or was it really an affliction over which the prisoner had no control? The whimpering returned. 'Please, I can't control it. You have to help me.'

'I can't. No one can,' Sophia told him, stony-faced. 'That's why you're here.'

Gradually, the boy seemed to calm himself. The whimpering subsided. His eyes clouded over from time to time. Sophia sat and watched him, the poor schizophrenic wreck.

'Tell me what you remember,' she said, after a while.

He looked worried. 'I remember everything, all at once.' Over a few fleeting seconds, his form aged from that of a young boy, through teenage years, into adulthood, middle age, on into old age and decrepitude and finally beyond death to a rotting corpse and crumbling skeleton. Then, just as quickly, it all reversed, playing backwards to a baby, before settling once again on the small boy of school age. 'See?'

'Yes. Can you relate it in a linear chronology?'

The boy didn't respond immediately. Instead, he brought his legs up onto the chair and crossed them, his elbows resting against the sides of his knees.

'I had a happy childhood,' he began. 'My family had great things in mind for me. As I grew up, I developed a strong aptitude for biomechanical engineering. I did well at university, and stayed on as a research student, until I had enough patents to my name to be respected independently of my alma mater. By this time, of course, I was married with a young family. I continued in that line, with moderate success, while my family grew up and eventually entered the world on their own endeavours. As a happy middle age led into a comfortable retirement, my wife and I took joy in our grandchildren and sought a more pedestrian way of life. Eventually, as is the way with these things, I grew frail and unwell, and finally died, leaving my wife a widow for some years until we were once again reunited in the afterlife.'

The boy finished his story and looked at Cousin Sophia, as if expecting a round of applause.

She raised an eyebrow, archly. 'How sweet. Except that's not what happened at all, is it?'

He was suddenly a decaying corpse. 'You tell me.'

'It's possible that what you've told me was how your life was *supposed* to run.'

'Anything is possible.'

'Why don't you tell me, instead, of all the people you drove insane. The damage you wrought as your timeline played out before them within the space of a few spoken words, blowing their poor minds.'

The boy said nothing, merely smiled again. As if that was answer enough. Sophia gave an involuntary shudder. It was indeed answer enough. For there was no hint of regret.

At Cousin Sophia's request, the prisoner and the watchful guard had left the living room and ventured out to show her around the rest of the house. Like the hallway and sitting room, the whole house exhibited corners of decay, as entropy ate away at the programming.

'How far does it extend?' Sophia asked, gazing up at what looked to be an infinity of balustraded landings.

The boy turned to her from the top of the stairs. She paused, as did the guard who was three steps behind.

'It goes on and on,' the boy replied, gesturing above. 'You can see that.'

'Our environment has a great impact upon our state of mind.'

'I can walk for days, should I choose, and still only be two rooms away from the hallway.'

'That's convenient—assuming you're not keen on a long walk back.'

'However, I think my state of mind is defined less by my ability to wander, and more by my guard, who, as you see behind you, cannot let me from his sight even when I am supervised by another.'

Sophia glanced at the guard for comment. He said nothing, his gaze remaining fixed on the boy.

She sucked her teeth and picked some strands of spider web from the side of her robes. 'In fairness to your guard, I don't believe he has any choice in the matter. It's all part of his programming. Part of your prison.'

They walked on in silence. In and out of rooms, some mere shells, others furnished in a variety of styles, all past their best. As the boy led, Sophia saw his regular changes from behind. He aged up and became young again. Twice he degenerated back into a foetus, and she had to be careful not to tread on him. The same when he collapsed into a pile of dried bones.

After what seemed an aeon of landings, stairwells, rooms and more of the same, they found themselves back on the ground floor, in the hallway outside the sitting room. The boy turned once again to Sophia.

'Like something by Escher, isn't it?'

She nodded. 'And with good reason, after all.'

There was a plate of food for each of them, waiting when they returned to the sitting room.

'You wonder why the guard eats, too, no doubt?'

The boy had presumably noticed Sophia's slightly raised brow.

'For effect, I assume,' she replied.

'Being able to share mealtimes is possibly the only joy I have, here.'

'Do you sleep, much?'

'Sleep?' He turned his full attention to her. 'Sleep induces dreaming. Dreaming is where all the victims live. All those you referred to earlier, driven insane by my inability to hold a conversation without aging up and down my timeline. And let's not forget what you didn't mention: my extra special ability. Psychically projecting the aging process onto others. Making them change in the blink of their own eye. All the good people I drove into madness, or desperation, and death. The early innocent few. Friends, family. My parents. Then there were the ones who tried to help me, or from whom I sought help. In dreams, I can see the moments their minds flipped, or their hearts gave out.'

He sat back and folded his arms, before continuing.

'And then there were the people I went after, deliberately. When I knew I was forever cursed and could never walk innocently among my fellows again. Politicians who failed. Gangland leaders, murderers, criminal masterminds. I took them all on, like some kind of superhero. I destroyed them all.'

Again, the boy paused. Sophia knew not to interrupt. He licked his lips.

'In my dreams I get to re-live all those events. All those horrors. Over and over again. You're right. I do sleep. And I dream. And I *love* it!'

Sophia found herself backing further into her chair at the boy's vehemence. At the gleaming intent in his eyes.

'But that's only half the story,' she said. 'You didn't just kill those gangland leaders and criminal masterminds. You took their place. You created a criminal empire for yourself.'

She found herself looking into the rheumy eyes of an old man, his deeply lined face writ large with stories of a life lived hard.

'I brought *peace*. I ruled. If only my rule had been accepted by all, there would have been no further trouble.'

'The plaintive cry of all megalomaniacs.'

The boy, a boy once again, howled in anger and cast his food viciously to one side. Sophia noted that it pixelated and vanished into nothing before it could land and make a mess. She tried dropping her plate. It did the same.

'And you, Faction Paradox,' the boy spat. 'You should have kept your noses out of my business.'

'Your business?' she scoffed. 'It was never your business. It was our business. Always. Everything about you says to me, lack of respect.'

'Hmph!'

Sophia leaned forward, elbows on knees. 'You will show me,' she growled. 'Show me the *you* taken in by Faction Paradox. Show me the *you* who underwent the initiation ceremony.'

The boy looked at first like he was trying to resist the change. But any control he had over the process was insufficient to defy the strength of the request. He aged from a shiny-faced schoolboy to a moody teen, with collar-length hair, the suggestion of post-pubescent facial hair, and eyes ringed with the shadowed remnants of sleep deprivation.

He gave a snarl. 'Satisfied?'

She was. 'Tell me about it.'

'You must have read the reports, transcripts and all that, if you're here to check on me. They wouldn't send you in blind. It wouldn't be safe.'

'This is true.' She steepled her fingers and rested her chin there. 'But I prefer to consider first-hand evidence, not third-hand reportage. So, indulge me. Tell me what happened. Tell me what you did that no one else in the history of Faction Paradox has ever done. Tell me how you became you.'

'I don't remember much about my initiation ceremony—'

'That's the same for most of us.'

The boy paused, as if he found it difficult to start again. 'What I do remember, distinctly, was being fascinated by what was going on. The sheer *theatricality* of it all. It seemed ridiculous, and yet at the same time incredibly dangerous, powerful.'

Again, Sophia interrupted him. 'That was because it was. Although I draw the line at ridiculous. I think that, there, we have the first inkling of your lack of suitability. You must have concealed it well.'

'I'm not an imbecile. I knew enough not to turn around and point out how ludicrous I thought the whole ceremony was.'

Sophia felt her bile rise. A few steady breaths brought her temperament under control, once again. The rituals were sacrosanct. To hear the boy speaking such heresy was an affront to her whole system of beliefs. But she couldn't show him. That would be taken as weakness on her part, and an advantage to the boy.

'Go on,' she instructed him, her voice low and controlled.

'I had a friend. I confided in my friend that I had undergone initiation. He had not had the kind of broad education from which I benefitted so much. He didn't know of Faction Paradox. Until I told him.'

'In breach of your oath.'

'I know.'

'And?'

'He liked what he heard. Thought it sounded exciting. So, I told him I could get him initiated.'

'Which, potentially, you could, via the established route. But I believe that wasn't what you had in mind.'

The boy smiled that evil smile again. 'Those beneath our contempt are easy to take advantage of.'

'So, you used him, this poor *friend* of yours?'

'I arranged for him to come to the place of initiation at a time when I knew the area would be clear. I wore my robes and gathered together such as I could find of the necessary trappings to perform the ceremony. When my friend arrived, I undertook the ceremony as best I remembered it, just the two of us.'

'You did not even stop to think how dangerous this might be?'

'Blood rituals, nonsense and suchlike. No, of course not.'

Cousin Sophia stood and screamed down at him. 'It is *not* nonsense!'

The boy sat there, meekly looking up at her. 'I admit I had no idea of the power contained in the rituals. I believed it was all symbolism. Mumbo-jumbo.'

She seated herself again, conscious that she had allowed her anger to get the better of her. 'I understand from the reports I've read that you quickly discovered otherwise.'

'Again, my memory is hazy–'

'An inbuilt safety mechanism.'

'Yes. Such things are not to be pondered on. I know that now.'

'It's a shame you were not so circumspect at the time.'

The boy paused before proceeding. 'You are making the mistake of believing I may now regret my actions.'

'You talk in contradictions. You indicated, shortly after I arrived, that you felt an appeal would be just, and that you believed this was the purpose of my visit. Now you are saying you have no regrets.'

'I certainly do not consider that I would do anything different, should I be granted the opportunity to re-live that period.'

'But, *why*? Why not save yourself all… this?' She wafted her hand around the room, expansively. The guard was still seated opposite the boy, his gaze unwavering.

'Because, at the end of the day, one has to remain true to who and what one is. Don't you see that? Without truth and integrity, what are we but puppets, dancing to the tune of some greater authority?'

Sophia realised she had no immediate answer to the boy's philosophy. The only course available to her was to ignore the heresy.

'Tell me more of the false initiation over which you presided,' she said.

'As I mentioned, my memory is hazy. But very quickly I realised that things were amiss. The blood. So much blood. I don't know where it came from, but it kept on coming. The chamber was flooded with it. And time energy. I could feel my skin prickling with age. In a moment of weakness, I tried to scream for help. But I could find no voice. Nor could I hear anything above the flooding of the blood and the screams of terror from my friend, who was totally unprepared for what he was witnessing.'

63

'And what exactly was he witnessing?'

The guard spoke. 'His soul was being torn inside out, and he was watching his best friend age indiscriminately before his eyes.'

The voice took Sophia by surprise. She looked at him.

'You were the first victim?'

The guard nodded, his gaze remaining steadfastly on the boy.

Sophia turned back to the prisoner. 'And, so, his image was used as a permanent reminder to you of your crimes.'

The boy gave no acknowledgment. 'I fled, of course, before anyone arrived. I presume my friend was found and treated. I don't recall, now.'

'No. He died in dreadful pain and fear,' she told him.

'Ahh, yes, of course,' the boy replied, matter-of-factly. 'I remember now.'

'And what do you remember of your new-found abilities?'

'Only that it took me a little while to fully understand how I had changed. What had been given to me. My mother aged to death before me. My father's heart gave out as he pleaded with me for an explanation I could not provide. All I could do was bounce back and forth through my timeline, honing my skills. I am grateful to them for at least providing me with the opportunity to do that.'

'You clearly felt no remorse. But what occurred—did it not make you respect the rituals in any way?'

'In all honesty? No. All I could see was that there was a power there, potentially untapped by others too frightened to venture further.'

'Yet you were leaving a trail of damaged time in your wake. Rends and rifts. It was a logical eventuality that you would be found out.'

The boy shrugged. 'I thought only of my new powers. Who wouldn't?'

'I think you received the answer to that when you were eventually taken in and tried.'

'Honestly,' he said. 'Seeing them all there like Lords. The bunch of stuffed shirts. They claimed I had brought shame upon their order. Said they couldn't handle rogue units like me. Too right, they couldn't.'

'I assume that's where you found that your abilities had no effect on other Faction Paradox members?'

'They held me in check, yes. That was impressive. I wish I'd learned how to do that.'

'And you expected to die?'

'What fear had I for death, when I could advance myself to that stage of—well, it's hardly life, is it? Existence, then. I could do so on a whim. They knew this. Perhaps if I'd known about the Boulevard before, I might have altered my attitude.'

'Remorse?'

'Annoyance. I didn't realise that somewhere like this existed, where I could be left to sit out eternity. The mindless tedium. It's enough to drive anyone beyond sanity.'

'Death was problematic. You had become a complicated time-space event. I have seen the judgment documents. Incarceration would allow the timelines to settle and mend. It would also allow you to appreciate your errors, maybe atone for your sins.'

'Empty rhetoric and techno-babble,' he said, scowling.

'You have to learn respect for the rituals. Understand why wild cards like you can't be left to run amok. I sense this has still to happen, even though you have been on the Boulevard for a very long time.' Sophia illustrated this by fingering some of the dust and cobwebs along the back of the chaise.

'So, what? Once I tell them I'm genuinely sorry, will they allow me to die?'

'I'm not here to make that decision.'

'Then, why are you here, Cousin?'

'It was noted, at the time, that your mental abilities were considerable.'

The boy shrugged at this apparent non-sequitur. 'I believe that was why I was able to survive the concocted ritual and harness the abilities of my own timeline.' He demonstrated by once again bouncing up and down along his own timestream as she watched.

'I told you when I arrived, I have come to observe your routine.'

'A smokescreen. I see through you. The parole board do home visits now, do they?'

She rolled her eyes. 'Your facetiousness does you no favours.'

'Really? It's being so cheerful that keeps me going, you know.'

Sophia stood and began to pace the room. 'You've been here a considerable time already.'

'As you said.'

'Yet, I find you still a boy.'

'Flatterer,' he giggled. 'I moisturise.'

'Younger than you were when you entered the Boulevard.'

'This is inconsequential. You know I can move along my own timeline.'

She turned to him deliberately. 'But despite that, you have a resting age which should increase. You are not immortal. You will eventually grow old and die naturally. The long way around. The shortcut version, thanks to your self-inflicted curse, will always bring you back to the 'now'. So, why is your 'now' perpetually a young boy, not yet into double figures?'

The boy dismissed her. 'A side-effect of my sentence,' he told her.

'There are no side-effects of your sentence. Your sentence is your sentence. That is punishment enough.'

'Can we stop playing games, then? I'm tired of this.'

Sophia agreed. She took a long, measured breath, before speaking again. 'Answer me this. Do you remember how long you and your guard have been here?'

The boy looked away, somewhat petulantly, then seemed to reach an internal decision. He shook his head.

'Yes,' said the guard.

'That's because you're programmed to,' said the boy. 'You can just review your data.'

Sophia glanced from the guard to the prisoner. 'A different question, then. How long have I been here?'

'You?' the boy replied. 'Today. A day. Half a day, maybe. Long enough for a chat and a long walk and another chat.'

She shook her head. 'I've been here a year.'

He gave a splutter. 'Never.'

'It was a very long walk.'

He looked flabbergasted. 'But... that's... that's ridiculous.'

'Is it? Perception is a very tricky thing, here on the Boulevard.'

'No!'

The boy was suddenly in her face, and just as suddenly no longer a boy, but a snarling, mouldering cadaver, its breath a noxious cloud of decomposition. She stood firm and shoved him in the chest. He staggered back to his seat, becoming younger as he went, until he collided with it as a small boy once again.

'Search your memories,' she told him. 'Think it over. You will see that I'm right.'

The boy was clearly not used to receiving orders—or, perhaps more particularly—finding it made sense to follow them. As he sat, Sophia could see the thought processes flit across his face. Eventually he began to whimper again, in the same way he had when she first arrived. He looked up at her with fearful eyes.

'Help me,' he said. 'I am... I am terrified of myself.'

She nodded, stepped up to the chair and crouched down before him, taking his cold hands in hers.

'I am going to the control panel by the rear window, over there.' She indicated the wall just above the dusty upright piano.

'There is no control panel,' he replied.

She smiled. 'There is if you know what you're looking for. I'm going to deactivate the AI.'

The boy looked up immediately, his face brightening with amazement. 'You're going to release me?'

Sophia nodded. 'Yes,' she said. 'I'm going to release you.'

She stepped over to the piano. Above the row of dusty knick-knacks displayed on top, there was a control panel within the leaf-print wallpaper. It was only visible from one angle and only accessible from another, as a security measure. Sophia reached out and dexterously input the override code, before flicking a switch.

The boy disappeared.

The general sense of wrongness about the house lifted.

The guard, suddenly released from his monitoring duties, blinked his dry eyes and looked at Cousin Sophia.

'What's going on?' he said. 'What's happened to the prisoner?'

'Don't,' she replied, shaking her head slowly. 'Enough of the pretence. The prisoner is still here. You are the prisoner.'

He didn't deny it. He cleared his throat. 'How long have you known?'

'I knew as soon as I entered the room,' she told him. 'You are the right age, after all. I just had to work out exactly how you'd corrupted your AI guard. You'd managed to distort the visual matrix for a start, so he didn't look like the poor lad you tried to initiate.'

'I realised early on it was the only way to escape from here.'

'There is no escape.'

'All right then, to negotiate my release. To be able to control my affliction, understand my crimes. You've not seen me pass along my own timeline the whole time you've been here, have you? Only the corrupted AI. I've cured myself.'

Sophia took what had previously been the boy's seat, directly opposite the prisoner. She watched him carefully the whole time, never removing her eyes from him.

'The AI had been programmed to replicate your actions,' she said. 'To help you counteract them. Perhaps even give you a taste of your own medicine. But somehow you used that to your own advantage.'

'You said yourself that I have considerable mental abilities,' he couldn't hide the smugness in his voice.

'I did. And I perceive that, over time, as you found control of your abilities, within yourself, you managed to project onto the AI the belief that it was the prisoner instead. It had none of the control you had learned, and it was unable to adapt. It still exemplified all the actions known to have caused you to be incarcerated here. Perhaps it even convinced itself that it was you? And you just had to wait for your opportunity, then you could try to escape.'

'There is no escape. You said so.'

'True. But that's never stopped inmates from trying.'

The prisoner held out his hands, in a pleading gesture. 'Look, I don't want to escape. I want to be released, legitimately. I've changed. I've seen the error of my ways.'

'Then why the pretence? Why not come clean with me when I appeared?'

'Because I knew I'd need to prove I'm no longer a threat; that I have self-control. What better way than by just being with you for all that time, never changing? I know I can never be healed, and I can't undo the wrongs I committed, but at least you have seen the fruits of my endeavours.'

'While you pretended to be a programmed artificial intelligence.'

'But you've told me you knew I was me, regardless. So, the point is surely moot? I've proved to you my level of self-control.'

'I cannot deny that,' she confirmed.

'I've come to respect the Faction rituals. I believe I deserve a second chance at freedom, a second chance at *life*.'

'I agree.'

The prisoner paused, mid action, clearly believing he'd mis-heard. 'You agree with me?'

'I do.'

He looked at Sophia with suspicion. 'You can't possibly mean-' He cut himself off, the words failing him.

She said nothing, only smiled.

'I-' He tried, again, and failed.

71

This time, Cousin Sophia simply nodded.

The prisoner seemed to physically shrink in his seat, as if the relief that had started to flood across his face was somehow emptying him. Sophia watched as his breathing steadily increased, which seemed to inflate him again. Relief was becoming delight. The prisoner's face lit up. Fleetingly, there was the slightest impression of him aging, then it was gone. No doubt a minor loss of control, caused by her apparent acceptance of his argument.

He finally managed to speak, his voice catching slightly in his dry throat. 'I don't believe it.'

'Your AI guard should now be more representative of the progress you've made, not simply a reflection of who you were when you were sentenced. I've reprogrammed the guard, in light of your appeal.'

'An appeal! Oh! I never even dreamed… And will you be part of that appeal, Cousin?'

'I will be with you the whole time,' she confirmed.

'The things I could do, with my freedom.' The prisoner glanced at her. 'Good things, of course. Positive things.'

'Of course.'

'I must… I must…' Thoughts were clearly flowing too fast for him to put into words. He raised his hands to his mouth. They were shaking. His whole body was trembling. Yet his age remained remarkably under control. Sophia could see tears glistening in his eyes as she continued to watch him closely.

The prisoner gave up on words and resorted to laughing. The laughter became whoops of joy as he skipped and frolicked around the room, jumping and bouncing on the furniture with child-like glee. He tumbled inelegantly onto the chaise longue, which gave a crack and collapsed beneath him. The prisoner lay there, spread-eagled over the flattened chaise, and laughed some more.

Eventually the laughter gave way to a deep sigh of satisfaction. He shook his head, as if disbelieving what was happening.

'And I thought there was no recourse to appeal once you were on the Boulevard!'

Cousin Sophia didn't reply. She simply continued to stare at him, the way she had been ever since the boy had vanished.

The prisoner looked across at her. 'I said, I thought there was no recourse to appeal, once you're on the Boulevard.'

'We are not monsters,' she replied, flatly.

'No.' He gave a mischievous grin. 'They always said the only monsters lived here.'

'And they were right.'

'Ha! So, when is it? My appeal?'

Sophia crossed her arms. 'You've not queried the ease with which I deactivated your AI guard.'

'Should I have?'

'Nor the fact that I was aware of what you had done, and who was who, before I appeared.'

'Isn't that why you came?'

'Yes.'

He sat up, eagerly. 'So, come on then. When is my appeal?'

'I am.'

'I am what?'

She fixed him with a steely gaze and waited for the realisation to hit. It took a few seconds.

'You are?' His eyes grew darker, more intense.

Sophia nodded.

'You are my appeal?' He stood.

'Was,' she quietly replied. 'The appeal has now ended.'

The prisoner's mouth hung slackly. Saliva glistened on his bottom lip as he rocked slightly back and forth in time with his breathing, which had become more laboured. He was clearly struggling to maintain control.

'Why didn't you say?' he whispered.

'That is not part of the protocol.'

'But that isn't fair!' the prisoner burst, like a petulant child. 'I mean, I would've...' again the words seemed to fail him. He looked helpless for a moment, then became gripped by a thought. He approached Sophia, a bright gleam in his eye. 'How did I do, though?'

She didn't respond immediately. Words continued to tumble from the prisoner.

'Can you tell me? It's not like I haven't been open and honest with you. It's like a journey, isn't it? A lot can happen in a year. I mean, at the end of the day who decides?'

'Report reads as follows,' Sophia announced, cutting him off. She paused for a fraction of a second—an eternity for the prisoner, judging by his expression. 'The prisoner completely lacks contrition.'

'Bitch,' he spat, his lips immediately curling in anger. 'Not true!'

'The prisoner shows an unacceptable level of self-entitlement; has no respect for authority–'

'How could you?'

'–rules–'

'You led me on!'

'–or rituals. Despite what he claims.'

He leaned his face in close to hers. 'I will *kill* you.'

She continued, regardless of the intimidation. 'Therefore, the situation–'

'The situation,' he burst, shouting her down, 'remains the same.'

'It does not.'

'Surely the appeal failed?'

'*You* failed.'

'Then what has changed?'

'Me.'

'You?' The prisoner leaned back slightly. 'Have you changed?'

Sophia took a step back herself, appreciating the space between them. 'I am the change. I am your incorruptible replacement AI. The new guard. Your appeal made it clear that an upgrade was necessary.'

'I'm stuck with you?'

'You are,' she told him, matter-of-factly.

'Forever?'

'The terms of your sentence have not changed.'

'A constant reminder of my failed appeal. The appeal I never officially asked for. The appeal I didn't know was taking place until *after* it had happened!'

She allowed herself a smug smile. 'Have you not noticed that my gaze hasn't left you since the previous AI was deactivated?'

It was clear from the snarling, primaeval hatred on his face that he had not.

'How's the self-control doing now, Prisoner?'

He roared with passion and rage. Cousin Sophia stood and stared at him, as she was programmed to do, her vision filled with an ever-changing maelstrom. The prisoner manically yo-yoed in age from corpse to foetus and back again, screaming tearful heresies and tugging at his own flesh as he did so. Any semblance of self-control now long since discarded.

But Cousin Sophia was safe in the knowledge that, no matter what the prisoner did, no matter what he subjected her to, she was incorruptible and could not be harmed. The Boulevard would not make that mistake again. Not with this prisoner. She considered the background of the room, as she watched her charge wail and writhe.

I must redecorate, she thought. I could be here a while.

Marticide

Robert Shepherd

Why was Godfather Cococyte consigned to these red-dust streets of the Boulevard?

For Marticide, the records of the Faction show.

Most new initiates assume this is a typo.

But it is not.

Murder is complicated. And so too is manslaughter: Mars-slaughter, rather. Once there were many versions of the planet Mars, lost droplets of blood on the timelines. Later, after? We all know that something went wrong. There's an outline sketched in chalk of all the realities that were purged. There's a planet that's more than dead, and in that there's a crime.

But that was a long time ago, and it never happened at all. Cococyte never thinks of it, never knows that he's even in prison. He no longer has any idea of what he's done, or what he is.

Maybe he even thinks that he's in paradise. There's red grass and there are trees, there's the Martian sea lapping against the shore. There are the underwater houses where the aliens live, and he hasn't even noticed that they're empty. All will be well for our prisoner, if he never sees that there's anything wrong. But he will, of course; it's inevitable. Deduction is something he does.

We are watching him now with our artificial eyes, as he walks down his waterside road. Watching as he walks down away from the sand, walks into the sea beyond. We watch as the water soaks up through his blackened clothes. He is looking down at the rows of empty houses, that stand absently regimented, stern as the tuft of white hair that extends from the top of his head. We are watching him as his eyes watch the light catch the water, those piercing, harrowing eyes, those lamps from nightmares.

We know what it means for a world to meet that gaze, and so we know that we must keep watching. We are not built to know fear, but still we feel mechanical dread. Our circuits twitch and pulse, calculating ways to escape. Within our plastic bodies, the binary floods us like hormones.

We've seen so many things. It's hard even for us to remember.

But we think that we all may have been watching him when—

—the man he once was awoke from his frozen slumber, heaving in the dry, cool air of Mars.

He was broken, then, mangled in his mind and his body. His brittle skin had burst over cracking bones, his brow was covered in blood and blackened bruises. And his ship was ruined, of course, smashed over the vast Martian plain.

There were bodies strewn around his, and those ones were no longer alive. It didn't make sense that he was the one who'd survived. He was old, after all. Frail. He'd always been a man of the mind, and never the body. Images were flashing through his mind, of younger men panicking. Saying metal could never repulse gravity; that it had been insanity to ever think otherwise. That they'd built a ship that could never work and now it was going to be their tomb, and it wasn't long after that when the screaming of men and metal had blended into one.

It had worked once, though, a small part of his mind insisted. Hadn't he travelled to Mars already, sometime long ago, and hadn't he used gravity repulsion to do it? Back in what he'd once thought of as the past: his adventures with Fred and with Denis,

78

his work on the Grand Line that would travel between Earth and Mars.

All those images were bright and clear, just like memories. But as his wits returned to him, he saw that they must have been dreams.

After all, the Mars in his mind had been vivid, bright. Rock formations gleaming in so many colours; bioluminescent life that lit the ground.

There was nothing like that at the crash site: only red dust, stretching forever around him. Endless and tedious, he observed. Unalive.

A lightbulb went off in his head. The trees here had crumbled to dust, hadn't they? He remembered something like that, though perhaps he'd imagined it too. Red dust that would cover up the colours of the Martian plain, their blues and their greens and yellows all smothered, old paint hidden under rust. And everything was dusty, here, too, on the Mars that he'd woken up to. Like a library full of tedious books, that hadn't been visited in an age. Perhaps that's all it was, then. There was something that had happened to the trees—

But. They'd aimed for the sea. Hadn't they? They'd hoped to land in the depths of the Martian ocean, far from where trees could have grown. And that was also ludicrous, of course. It was much too cold here for oceans. Perhaps the temperature could have dropped suddenly, catastrophically? So the water could have frozen in a matter of years? But then there'd be evidence of erosion left behind, not a flat and irregular plain. . So, there was never any water, nor any trees. There had only ever been the dryness and the dust.

Yet there was still life here, just as there was in his dream. And it seemed to be thriving, even without liquid water. Here was a

79

creature, now, feasting on red clumps of dust, heaving great scoops of it into a toothed waterwheel mouth. There was a thing like a man with thin, long hands, lugging a great chunk of ice on its flattened head. And over *there*—

–his heart jumped into his mouth–

—was the face a giant snake which he'd seen before. In his mind, the adventure on Mars he'd remembered. The one that he'd thought was a memory, and which now he knew must have been a dream.

But the snake was dead, like everything else he remembered: it was only a head, it was only a skull. And standing behind that skull was none other than a man he knew all too well—

"Helvetius!" he cried. "Whatever are you doing on Mars? And what are you *wearing?*" he added. "Are bones now the fashion in England?"

He saw his acquaintance smile behind the skull, although not in so pleasant a way. Professor Helvetius was known for having many theories about the universe and no friends at all to tell them to. Every part of his brain was dedicated to the pursuit of thought. He wasn't the sort of man who would waste any effort on charm.

"Bones will be the fashion across the whole Earth, soon enough," the Professor said. "But that's all by the by. Circumstance has forced unusual choices on me. New ways of seeing, and a mask to see everything through. Even my name itself has had to change. I don't go by *Helvetius* anymore. They call me Godfather Avenir now."

The old man scoffed. "That's a very French name for an English gentleman."

"It's a name that looks to the future," said Avenir. "Just like my mask."

The old man laughed. "I suppose a skull is what comes in all of our futures," he said, "if you take a certain pessimistic view."

Avenir scowled.

"It's a realist view," he said. "And a future that's approaching quite rapidly. It can't have escaped your attention, can it? France and England and all of the rest of them. The powers you call Great are marshalling for war. Ypres, the Somme, Verdun-sur-Meuse. So many Frenchmen will have skulls for faces soon."

He glanced at the charred corpses in the wreck of the spaceship behind them. Neither of them were men who cared much about collateral damage.

"But none of that's why I'm here," said Avenir. "My thoughts are with a greater war now. It's a War that needs recruits. New alliances. And as it happens, well... We have a proposition for you."

The old man spluttered. "*We?*"

"There are various factions that I'm associated with," Avenir said. "The Bolsheviks speak of causes that may one day be realised. I prefer those that cannot be. We wear the skulls of the creatures that never were. The spectres of possibility, if you will."

It was already so cold around them, and still the old man felt a chill.

"That doesn't sound like something any scientist would be interested in," he said, trying to sound haughty.

"Perhaps," said Avenir. "But then you're not just *any* scientist. We've been watching you for some time," he went on. "Because of what you are, and what you can do. You're someone we can use; that's the truth of it. We're always looking for someone we can use."

The old man frowned. "You are referring to my abilities as a scientist?" he said.

"Something like that," Avenir said. A strange smile loomed behind the skull.

Some would think it odd to cling to science at a time like this. The old man knew that far too well. They'd told him many of his discoveries were closer to fantasy than reality, once. That was never the case, not to the superior mind. Anything could yield to logical analysis. Even the skull of a snake that never was.

"You understand that I am a rational man," he said, remembering Avenir's talk of creatures who never were. "Possibility's scope may be great, but it is not limitless. I've no time for rash science fiction."

"You're referring to the war?"

"I'm referring to what you're wearing! You say it's a possible creature. But it's one out of my own imaginings"—

"It is from an eradicated version of this world. Or do you think that I'm spinning you a tale?"

"You must see how implausible it all sounds. Easy to make it all up. You could have heard me recount the creatures in my dreams. Perhaps I made a thing of it; wrote them down. Indulged in some

82

science fiction of my own! A story of a snake too large for the gravity of Earth. Its bones as weak as a paper maché mask"—

"And yet here we both are on Mars," said Avenir. "And only I remember how I got here. And right now, only I know how to get out while remaining alive. It seems to me you have no option but to speculate."

That chill again, cold and bitter. Like the shock that comes when suddenly waking, jolting one bolt upright back to the world.

"They *were* only dreams," the old man said, sharply. "They had to have been."

"Perhaps," said Avenir, distantly, "a dream can shatter as easily as a skull."

The old man fell silent, hearing that.

The strange creatures around them chirped and grunted. They were nothing like the ones that he'd once seen. What the man who had once been Helveticus was saying seemed quite impossible. But still—

"I don't really have a choice," the old man said. "Do I? If I want to survive. I'm going to have to join your merry band."

"It's not very merry. But that's about the size of it."

"Then let me be *Cococyte*," the old man said, as firmly as he could.

"I'm sorry?"

"That will be my name. A Martian name for a Terran gentleman! Then at least I'll be a bit more worldly than you."

He paused, squinting over the dry distance of the world.

"You speak of factions and wars, Helvetius," he said. "The Cococytes were once a faction; and one that fought. Here. On Mars. I did see that, I saw it with my own eyes. There was so much death. It feels like that couldn't have been a dream."

Avenir nodded.

"But now I sense they were never here at all," the old man said.

"It is a strange time for this world," said Avenir. "Only recently there was panic in the Martian Embassy. It seemed that all the canals that were once here had disappeared."

Cococyte frowned.

"But there's never been a Martian Embassy," he said.

Avenir nodded.

"You're quite right," he said. "Of course, there hasn't."

He sighed.

"*If you succeed, you'll have many friends,*" he said. "*But if you fail, you'll be alone.* Ovid said that, once, and you did. But with respect, I would disagree. Some kinds of success are the loneliest you could imagine."

"I did say that of you, long ago." said Cococyte. "But how could you have known that I did?"

"The Faction was never about explaining mysteries," said Avenir. "Perhaps you'd do well to remember that. Especially now that you're a part of it. Godfather Cococyte."

But there were now more mysteries than ever before, Cococyte thought. The creatures in his dreams that never were and had left their bones, the water that had flowed here warmed by volcanoes

84

that never had been. He was a harsh man, and quite unsentimental. Still, an overwhelming sorrow filled him when he thought of that great world he had explored so long ago.

And then everything was hazy around him and he was drifting into a dream, and he imagined his tears filling up all of the dead lakes, making places for all that life to exist again. And feeling the pain fill up his mind and his cracked-in body, Godfather Cacocyte felt himself fall deep into sleep—

There is a face below Godfather Cococyte, here in the Boulevard. But that face is not like us; it does not watch. We are staring at its unblinking eyes, hewn out of sand. An enormous sculpture of a woman's head—a human woman, for a human-centred world—gazing up hard at the Godfather. It looks a bit like a judgment as he walks down a long, winding road.

There are pyramids, too, which he passes as he keeps on walking. Enormous buildings, hewn from great bricks of sand. Graves for the dead, of those who are held to be Gods. And yet if those Gods had awoken from their deaths and found themselves trapped in those tombs, they might feel they were in a prison...

...we know what you're thinking, of course. Don't think that we're stupid, just because we have plastic for brains. We know what people say, when they hear that there's a Faction prison. That our cult is defined by the rituals of breaking laws: of physics, of people, of time. Imprisonment wasn't ever a part of the aesthetic. Isn't this place a paradox in itself?

Well, we'd say. Perhaps it is. Perhaps anything starts to seem like a paradox, once you really start to think about it. But no matter. There are far worse things than paradox; there's a lot more to fear than contradiction. Look closer, think harder.

Sometimes the thing we're most frightened of is what's waiting for us behind the mirror. And Godfather Cococyte has always been a paradox reflected.

He'd be reflected now, in fact, if that sand woman's eyes were really real. She'd be looking right at him, as the road he walks winds round and round, coming to a halt at a great height over her gaze. And that woman's only made out of sand, but then that's what we're made of too— heated and processed into silicon, into something that's able to scream. And she'd be screaming now, we expect, she'd be shouting as loud as she could, but Godfather Cococyte wouldn't even notice the sound. He'd be too busy looking, you see, he'd be peering right into her eyes. He'd be gazing into them—harshly, never lovingly—staring into the hard spheres of them, looking down—

The ground was flat and calm, and the dust didn't move. The Martian Zyln walked under a clear red sky.

There were no other Martians around him. Why would there be? There wasn't much that was useful on the surface. The real treasures of Mars were hidden, underneath. It would have been easy to stay a secret, if they'd ever wanted to be one.

And so he was alone—or so he thought—as he walked through the Great Dust City. But in another way, of course, he wasn't alone at all.

Although much of the City was hidden from human eyes, its Great Face had been built to honour them. Mars had wanted Earth to see it, once it was time. They should know as soon as possible that theirs was a planet with neighbours.

But perhaps there was at least one Earthman who already knew all about it. Zyln was by that Face when he saw a hazy figure, far too tall and slim to be a Martian. Just there under the curve of that smooth, sand chin, resolving into someone who seemed to be human. A man in an astronaut's suit, his helmet a strange square skull.

"Why are you here?" said Zayn. "You shouldn't be. They say that it's still too early."

"On the contrary," said the man, with no obvious emotion in his voice. "It's already far too late. My name is Godfather Avenir. And I'm afraid that your City is doomed."

Zayn felt himself tense at that. The chemical that flowed through him was not adrenaline, the reaction in his body wasn't like a man's. But there are things that evolve over and over again, and the first of them is always primal fear.

"You're here to fight?" he asked the man. "To destroy our people, even though we welcome yours?"

Avenir laughed. "I'm here to watch!" he said. "I don't have a quarrel with you. This is a noble city. And you are a very proud race."

Zayn didn't know what to say to that. He'd only been walking along the sand, minding his own business. There didn't seem to be much that was proud about that.

"We're just living our lives," he said. "In the same way that anyone does. We have no major foes. No one who wishes to harm us."

A thought occurred to him, and the chemicals surged again.

"Not Venus?" he said. "Are they coming for us again?"

Avenir shook his head.

"Nothing like that," he said. "It's my fellow cultist who's doomed you. Godfather Cococyte. A great man. Revolutionary, in his way. And French, of course; it comes with the territory. There are things that he sees that none of the rest of us can. Though he doesn't notice everything, of course. He didn't even see that he's come unstuck in time."

The wind was whistling around them, flat and low. It didn't feel to Zayn like the man was describing his imminent death. It felt like he was telling some impossible tale. A story of a faraway world.

"They've given him a great telescope back there," said Avenir, waving his hand at the sky. "On Earth, where they call it the 1970s. They have photos of what you've built, you see. The Pyramids, that great face. The emoji you've scrawled on the edge of the Argyre Planitia. And old Cococyte? Well."

He shook his head with regret.

"He's coming to take a look."

The fear in Zayn's body dissolved away, replaced by a minor irritation.

"That's all?" said Zayn. "Why would we be worried about that? We want your world to find us, when it's finally time. He'll just see everything that we've built to show you. It's really here."

Avenir sighed.

"Not when Cococyte looks, it won't be. He'll see that none of it was really there at all. That it's all just a trick of the light, a human tendency to see what one wants to see."

"But it's *not*," said Zayn.

"No. But when he's looked? That's exactly what it will be." Avenir shrugged. "Your species has heard of quantum physics. An observer can induce a collapse in possibility, in the right circumstances. A cat is alive and dead, until someone thinks to take a look. And that's what this is, you see. He's the observer. And Mars is the cat in the box."

"The cat's fate rests on a single point of light," said Zayn. "A planet is far more complicated than that."

"It is," said Avenir. "But then Cococyte's quite the observer."

"But *I'm* an observer, too," said Zayn, feeling the anger wash over him. "All of us are, here on Mars. You people from Earth, with all your visible skin. You think that it's only what's on your world that counts."

He bared his teeth at Avenir, as best he could. "Why should it matter what he sees; what you see?" he cried. "I know this City is real! I've lived here for years! Maybe it seems fantastic and mysterious to your friend. But it isn't to me. It's just where I happen to live."

Avenir was silent at that, for a while.

"Perhaps there are things in this universe that don't quite fit," he said in the end. "And perhaps he is one of those things. If he can put all of creation into its proper place, then he might find the place he belongs. He'll never realise that, of course. Men like him look outward, never inward. They destroy the world around them if it means they don't have to change."

"Then he is only special because he's insecure?"

"He's special because he can never accept his specialness. So he is drawn to making the pieces of the world fit together. And it means something if he finds out that they don't."

"Then you're saying that none of this was ever real?" said Zayn. "That *I* wasn't real? Because of him?"

"Oh no," said Avenir. "You're perfectly real, right enough. But a few moments from now, you'll have never existed at all."

The fear finally slammed into Zayn, then, the intensity of it making up for the time it had taken to get there. What it would mean to *never have been*, for everyone he'd known and loved to simply *go*, forever. He thought of tiny, stupid things. The flavoured ice that they'd buy from shops, a stupid tune his mother had said was just noise. All the tiny things that made up a life, which just wouldn't be. Not anymore.

Panicking, he tried as hard as he could to look up at the Face in the city before him, at its clearly human features, as if by staring at it hard enough he could will it to keep on existing. But even as he looked it was shifting and dissolving, like any face would do if you looked at it for too long, until it was only a mass of lines and shapes that signified nothing at all—

—underneath his helmet that was a skull, Avenir blinked. And when his eyes opened, there was no Zayn or City at all. There was only himself, standing on a rubble-strewn plain. There was no longer any reason for him to have come here. There hadn't ever been, not at all.

Alone in the lifeless sand, Godfather Avenir sighed.

And then he turned his gaze to the vast red desert beyond—

He's walking down a tarmac road, now, down through the dead dust of Mars. A makeshift human settlement behind him, disappearing. They've finally landed on Mars, though it's taken so much longer than it did back in Cocoyte's dreams. The building is shoddy and ugly; a concrete and tinfoil dome. It doesn't look like a structure that anyone would ever have dreamed of.

And Cococyte's step is heavy, conflicted, even though the gravity's so very light on that road. His thoughts are weighing him down even more than his primitive spacesuit. He looks imprisoned, we conclude. And he doesn't even know that he's in jail.

"What could be worse than a paradox?" people say when they hear of the Boulevard. And the truth is almost anything is, if ever you really stop and look at it. Sometimes the universe tells you it's best not to think too hard about something. And always, when it does, it's very important you listen.

He's not listening, he never did. There's nothing he won't look at very hard. Except his decisions, or his choices. The idea he might go down another road.

But you can listen; we know that very well. We're watching you, right now, just like we're watching him. So believe us when we tell you: always watch out for the observer. If someone shoots their own grandfather, the universe has ways of working it out. If your grandfather starts asking too many questions, it's maybe best that you shoot him yourself.

For if you don't you might find yourself like Godfather Cococyte, and his is not a road you want to follow. Look at him now, at his staring, wild blue eyes. Look as he gazes out into the void—

He was on Mars: that much he knew, at least. But he no longer entirely remembered why. His breath misted against the inside of his helmet, the world bone cold. There was the tiny grain of the planet, and the endless nothingness beyond.

His mind whirled with what he'd assumed must be memories. The landing, the cramped conditions. Other people. Humans. There must be a connection between those images and where he was right now. It all needed to fit together. Or else he might really have gone quite insane.

There'd been an expedition. Hadn't there? But it was always going to be a perfunctory one. Every serious astrobiologist knew that there'd never been life here on Mars. People still clung to it, even so. They wanted to believe. But there was less and less evidence there was much to believe in at all.

And yet there was still faith among the public, and so there was funding for now. And so there had been a job, a *real* job with a contract and a pension, at a time when those might as well have been extinct. And maybe there was even a chance he'd do some real science along the way.

That was a convincing story. It all made sense.

He no longer had any idea if any of it was true.

In truth, he didn't know what he was even expected to find. There were instruments in the pockets of his spacesuit. Complex nonsense. But how could he know what to search for here, looking for the origins of life? They didn't even know how it started on Earth, after all. There'd been so many theories. Sulphur vents, and clay. But one by one, they'd all been shown to be impossible.

Perhaps it had only ever been a coincidence, after all? Or God, of course. But he seemed to remember disproving God long ago.

A thought was forming in his mind, terrible and unbidden, and as it filled his brain, his stomach filled with dread. He felt light headed, although he had quite enough oxygen. He fell to his knees, and he hardly even noticed.

He knew he was given to delusions and strange dreams. What if that was all it had ever been? That there'd never been an expedition, and never an Earth to send it. That there'd never been anything, not really.

There'd never been life on Mars, because there'd never been life anywhere at all. Something as complex as deoxyribonucleotides, assembling out of nowhere! Only so much science fiction. It was as much of an impossibility as a rocket that repulsed gravity. Mars, the Earth, all of it. It had always only been a shade in a madman's dream—

"Godfather," said a cold, firm voice from above him. "You have to stop this now."

Cococyte looked up at the figure, who was wearing no spacesuit at all. His gaze seemed quite undisturbed by the cold, by the lack of oxygen. He was dressed in the fine clothes of an English gentleman, with something impolite upon his face.

"Avenir," Cococyte said, his voice seeming some distance away. "But whatever are you wearing?"

"I told you once before," said Avenir. "Our Faction wears the skulls of the creatures that never have been."

Cococyte frowned.

"But that's a *human* skull," he said.

"Then you appreciate how serious things have become," said Avenir.

There was a lifeless silence around them, extending forever.

Cococyte was not a weak man, nor a sentimental one. But it was still all he could do not to cry out in despair.

"I've led everything I've seen to ruin, haven't I?" he said quietly. "What must you think of me?"

Avenir laughed. "I think you are a Frenchman!" he said. "A follower of Laplace, wanting the universe to go on like clockwork.

But then clocks break, and worlds do. And so do men. There's a lot more than mere determinism in the world."

He looked down at the quivering wreck below him.

"And that does mean," he said, more softly, "that free will really does exist. And so, you really are able, Godfather. To make a choice."

Cococyte looked around briefly, at the dust, at the rocks, at the world. Remembering the oceans that had been here, such a very long time ago.

"It's too late for Mars," said Avenir, "or at least all the versions you've seen. But life can still be saved, and humanity. People can. All I need from you is to accept you've committed a crime."

Cococyte laughed bitterly.

"And what crime is that?" he said. "Exactitude? I have only ever meant to further discovery."

"I expected some resistance," said Avenir. "It's in your name, after all; the one that you once had. But also, that name signifies an ending. Let that ending be *yours*, Godfather. Not that of the universe you once tried to understand."

"Understanding is all I wanted," said Cococyte. "I bore no ill intent."

"Not all crimes require intention," said Avenir. "Especially when there are so many lives that were lost. Theirs was a fate worse than death, and so yours is a punishment worse than a killer's. Perhaps it isn't just. But it's the closest thing to justice we can make."

The man on the ground was silent then, for a very long time.

94

Then, almost imperceptibly, he gave a tiny nod.

And he stretched out his arm to meet Avenir's outstretched hand—

It is said that there are those who must always keep watching. And it isn't always explained why that always has to be true. But there are things that even the Faction can never allow to happen, there are pots that none of us should ever see start to boil. There are observers who might come to observe too much. And so here, in the Boulevard, we now keep them under observation.

The cat is alive and it's dead, and that's good enough for the cat. It was good enough for us, in the end. But there are always people who would try to open the box, to make sure the cat's only dead. Godfather Cacocyte was the very worst of them all. So now he's in a box of his own.

We're watching him now, as he walks with that dim, fickle light. Red as the furnaces he once fired, cold as a glance from his eyes. He's been walking for a long time, and he'll walk for a long time still.

The road that he goes down is long, and it is demanding—he would have said it was his calling, that science was his duty. Like so many prisoners, he was only ever really looking for an answer. But perhaps at the end of that road there was never really anything there.

Around that small red light there is a darkness, and at the centre of it he's walking still, and he is screaming. For the darkness has consumed him, but we will not let it consume all the worlds, however sensible or logical that may be. We are built by the Faction, and the Faction is many things. But it is not a thing made from that darkness, no matter how deep into it we stare.

For Godfather Cacocyte is an ending.

And there are things that we can never allow to end.

The Sisters of the Little Moments

(or Hyparxis House)

(or The Senator and the Parasite, a love story)

Kelly Hale

Between everything changing and staying the same lay temporal treasure, a steady harvest of half-measures gleaned from Humanity's tendency toward two steps forward and one step back.

This drip drip drip of stolen moments, like imprest funds in an office petty cash drawer, fueled the smaller engines of those who favoured Chaos, and patched little holes in the mechanisms of Order. Like any office petty cash drawer, it required regular replenishment. Unfortunately for Sister Agnostina, her current source of replenishment was proving morally unassailable.

Senator Andrew Jacob Skrelli, U.S. Senator for the great state of Pennsylvania had, thus far in his career, avoided any number of common scandals. There had been no inappropriate touching or texting with subordinates, no youthful date-rape incidents to dredge up. No racist, sexist, homophobic language caught on video. No secret donations to fascist organizations or funnelling of charitable contributions into election campaigns. He paid his taxes on time and had never—not once—taken a photo of his genitals, let alone transmitted said photo to a young male intern.

An obsessive attraction to an underling, a blowjob beneath the executive desk, a discretely funded abortion—any little thing would have been useful. Her team could swoop in, pluck the buds of seething bitterness from his wife's publicly broadcasted forgiveness, scratch the surface of the pundits outraged histrionics to find the smirking schadenfreude beneath. And, of

96

course, there was always the quiet but persistent moments generated by a weary constituency losing hope and trust as they slowly surrendered to increasingly familiar, jaded resignation.

But the man would not submit. Would not succumb. Would not lie down on that hotel bed with that transsexual sex worker. Instead, he shook her hand and promised to do everything in his power to address ongoing discrimination and bias towards both sex workers and transgendered people.

Sister Agnostina was at a loss and the other sisters knew it. Didn't even bother to whisper their complaints behind her back anymore.

'Has her guy done the thing yet?'

'When's that thing gonna be done?'

'I can't do my thing until she takes care of her thing.'

'Has she even started the thing?'

'See, this is why I hate group projects.'

Under a literal Time Crunch, Sister Agnostina assured them she'd have it all taken care of by week's end then discretely outsourced the task to a specialist.

Over the course of millennia, Dyzeps had developed an unfortunate romantic longing for the concept of true symbiosis. Synchronically and harmoniously entwined with Host Body seemed dreamy. Sublime. A closed circuit of perpetual contentment. A spore cloud drifting forever in the winds of love. Exotic. Alluring. Idyllic.

Sadly, impossible.

The closest Dyzeps has ever gotten to romantic ideal is an exquisite *tension*. Engulfment delayed and delayed again, right to the edge of the precipice, then pulled back and pushed to the edge again, and back and to the edge and back—

Each time the pedicel finally bursts and spore cap blossoms from the skull, casting seed to the whims of the cosmos, Dyzeps hopes at least there will be one precious moment of shared ecstasy before the host's inevitable dissolution.

It is a vain hope. This host will be no different.

As per protocol, a surge of norepinephrine is released upon infiltration. Dyzeps then presses the latest acquisition to leave the safety of its nest and ascend a nearby tower.

This is ideal. The hour is quiet, twilight dim, dew-drop cool.

Unfortunately, the tower proves to be the host's work nest. Heedless of the gloaming hour, other humans gather in the nest, flitting in and out, hammering their many digits on little devices, flapping their tongues on chitter-chatter. There is much consulting and advising going on, so many earnest discussions and grave concerns. The drafting of forms and official positions. The taking of stands and signing petitions. All interspersed with shared consumption of nutrition for conversion to energy. Energy pointlessly expended on more of the same. The host is never alone for more than a few moments.

This is *not* ideal. Quiet isolation is required to unspool hyphae into the space between muscles and organs, and push into the limbs. Spelunking the cavities of a host body requires finesse. It would not do to raise suspicion before control is established. Other Dyzeps have been lost to poisons when discovered early in the process. But then, good fortune. The host needs to expel solid waste and enters a confined space to do so. Dyzeps sends hyphae threads out from the initial entry point to burrow into fasciae and entwine with nerve fibers. By the time waste elimination is complete, Dyzeps has made Host Body's leg twitch.

The Mundane Order of Sisters of the Little Moments had once been known by another name, back when they were acclaimed artisans of embroidered Time, their work commissioned by all the Great Houses. Mostly for heralds and devices and such. Or sentimental keepsakes. Patches. Appliques. Whimsical counterpoints to inherent paranoia. That was before the War of course. Before paranoia grew monstrous. There were rumours the sisters could unravel eras, or even entire Houses, with a single unpicked thread.

The Order had negotiated for neutrality, but that lack of affiliation came with a price; their timeless mortal existence reduced to harvesting 'inter momenta' for use by both Faction Paradox operatives and agents of Great Houses alike. For not every task needed showy rituals or sombre ceremony. Sometimes they only required proverbial pin money for the pocketbook, so to speak.

Abbess Anin still had her sewing kit, though she kept it well hidden. After her favourite scissors disappeared from it one afternoon and reappeared two days later pierced straight through top of her left hand and out the palm, well...it seemed best. There's not much left in the kit anyway. A spiral needle, a bone awl, a zippered pouch with a few sparse, hopelessly entangled quantum threads, and the old lucet fork she'd used to braid those threads for passementerie work—work she could no longer do even if she wanted to. Fine stitchery required flexor tendons. Sensation in the fingertips.

She never knew which side had done the damage.

This morning Cousin Nefanda of Team Faction made an appearance. Tiny rodent skulls nestled in the bows on her jaunty hat. The stabby tip of her umbrella made a small indent in the linoleum.

'I'll trouble you for those b'tweens now.' She lifted her pointy little chin, bared her pointy little teeth. 'Thirty units should do the trick.'

Brought up short by this apparition in the middle of the corridor, the Abbess was unable to school her expression quickly enough. She managed a suitably cool response, nonetheless. 'We don't have them to spare just yet, I'm afraid.'

And she was. Afraid.

'But I've been waiting for *years* and *years*.'

'It has only been four days since last we saw you, Cousin.' The corridor wasn't wide. Nor as narrow as it felt when she attempted to slide past without physical contact. 'If you'll excuse me—'

She reached the swinging door of the lavatory and plunged into the promised sanctuary on the other side.

'Still," Nefanda said, following her in, "does it usually take this long? Whatever is the hold up?"

Abbess Anin moved quickly to the row of stalls on her left. If her need to use the facilities appeared urgent, perhaps her need to get as far away from Nefanda as possible wouldn't seem so obvious.

She pushed open a stall door. 'Occasionally we must toss a stick of dynamite into the river to catch fish.'

Cousin Nefanda hummed her intrigue at the statement. 'That sounds wonderful. And messy. Local idiom, I presume.'

The stall farthest from the lavatory door was still not far enough. Abbess Anin could almost feel the teeth snapping at the back of her neck.

'I allude to a crude method by which detritus from the bottom of a temporal puddle gets stirred up. It isn't literal.' She turned in the open stall, hoping the partial view of a toilet would provide a clue.

Nefanda's moue of disappointment was even more disturbing than her teeth.

With a bump of her hip, Abbess Anin slammed the stall door shut. 'Sister Agnostina is in the field tossing the metaphorical dynamite even as we speak.' She hiked up the skirts of her habit. 'I believe there is a politician, hush money and a prostitute in play—'

She saw the broken lock, hissed through her teeth, and thrust her hand out to bar the door. The curly-horned tip of an umbrella pushed it open, scraping the edge of the door across her bared knees before exposing her completely.

'I heard she was trying to get a fellow to post pictures of his junk on Instagram.'

Apparently, comprehending local idiom was a problem that came and went.

Abbess Anin locked gazes with her. Then proceeded to urinate. Loudly.

Cousin Nefanda turned away. Not because she'd taken the hint or was embarrassed or had suddenly become polite. Bored most likely. Or feigned boredom. It was no doubt confusing to decide what one was feeling when none of one's feelings were *genuinely* felt. Caught by her own reflection in the mirror over the sink Nefanda tipped her head one way then the other, blinking slowly.

Irregular scrawls of oxidation marred the edges of the mirror. Behind the glass, the silver backing was spattered with more oxidation, little black dots like stars, constellations flung across the surface, a universe containing her face. Cheekbones too high, too sharp. Eyes too wide, too black. Her hair, an indiscernible shade of brown with a sticky synthetic sheen—like a Kanekalon doll's wig sewn onto her skull. She patted the curls.

'I could have got you a credible accusation of consorting with foreign adversaries. It would have filled the coffers for months.' But her voice rustled like cellophane, hinting at a deeper distraction.

'We generally prefer gleaning from existing events and situations. Mustn't tax the system too much. It's not best practice.'

'But you should never have let stores get so low in the first place. I can't think what could have depleted them to such an extent.'

That would be you, *Cousin.*

Abbess Anin finished her business and went to the sink to wash her hands. Cousin Nefanda stepped aside, watching with a mixture of disgust and fascination. The Faction wore their quaint perversions on their sleeves (or hats in Nefanda's case)—blood, guts, bones, organs. But the actual day-to-day biological functions of organic beings repulsed them. They were much like their 'enemies' in that regard.

It had taken the Abbess quite some time to get used to it herself. Until scissors through the hand brought reality to bear upon her situation. But that was ages ago. She hardly remembered what it was like before this.

She flicked a glance at Nefanda in the mirror. Whatever temporal scheme the creature had cooked up must need to appear low-key, without the usual showy rituals and extravagant bloodletting of which the Faction Cousins were so fond. Was she secretly building a new kind of paradox device? Switching sides? Plotting a coup? Had she developed an addiction to little moments, and now practised the ritual of liquifying *inter momenta* in a spoon over a candle flame before injecting it into… whatever was analogous to a circulatory system?

'I shall find Sister Agnostina and give her the benefit of my advice,' Nefanda declared, and before the Abbess could suck in a breath to protest that plan, the lavatory door was already swinging shut onto an empty corridor.

She raced to her office suspecting she'd be too late.

The senator had been complaining of a headache off and on in the hours before he disappeared, leaving word with his staff that he intended to hike the Appalachian Trail for couple of days to 'get his head on straight.'

When Sister Agnostina finally tracked them down, Dyzeps had them holed up in a Super-8 motel off Interstate-10, halfway between Jacksonville and Tallahassee. Nowhere near the Appalachian Trail, but also nowhere near where the man was supposed to be. News crews armed with anonymous 'tips' were even now on their way to Playa del Carmen to catch Senator 'seems genuine' Skrelli with his pants down in a posh resort hotel at taxpayer's expense.

The senator, paralyzed and laid out on top of the bedding, was still in his politician's uniform. He strained his gaze askance to see her, pleading wide-eyed as tears rolled down the sides of his face and dampened the pillowcase. He could blink but could not turn his head. The muscles in his neck were taut ropes against the collar of his shirt. His Adam's apple kept catching on the knot of his red, white, and blue striped necktie. She could just make out the garbled 'help me' and maybe something about calling 911—

Independent speech should not have been possible at this point. Or those darting eye movements. She ignored the senator's distress, addressing instead the thing inside him.

'What are you doing in Florida, Dyzeps?"

The senator's body spasmed. A low keening at the back of his throat battled with fricatives and lateral consonants trying to push their way out. No vaguely intelligible words made it past his lips, however. She realized, with growing trepidation, that he must be fighting Dyzeps efforts to use his vocal apparatus to respond to her.

She scrambled for her mobile phone, typing emphatically—*What the hell? Mexico! Supposed to get him to Mexico!!!* She left her thumb on the exclamation point until the dialogue bubble was just an endless scrolling field indicating the rageful quality of her anxiety.

It took twelve long seconds after she lifted her thumb for the hyphae vibrations to transmit a response through the Dyzeps mycelial interface. A semblance of speech erupted from her phone's speaker—like the tines of a fork scraping a plate. So much worse than the man's efforts.

'Host does not comply.'

Her brain stuttered on this error message, unable to adjust for a moment. "But– but that's your specialty."

'Host does not comply.'

'You *make* him comply!'

'More time. Need. More ti-eem-a.'

'Time is what I don't have! That's the whole point!' Her mobile vibrated in her hand suddenly, then began to trill—

'Is that your Abbess Anin?'

'Shit!' The phone jumped from her hands and tumbled to the carpet, bouncing a few times. But she made no move to retrieve it.

Cousin Nefanda stood silhouetted in the door frame with an aura of sunshiny blue-blue Florida sky behind her head. Humid heat quivered in the air around her. Traffic from the Interstate highway whooshed and whined in the distance, and closer by, a motel room door opened, closed, hushed voices in call and response, reminders about chargers and keycards. Sandals and plimsolls shuffled along the walkway, down the metal stairs, luggage bumping the rails, a bland but lovely universe walking away—

'Sister! Sister, are you there?'

Cousin Nefanda snatched the mobile from the floor, silenced it and put in the pocket of her blazer.

'I think she wanted to let you know I was coming.'

Sister Agnostina closed her eyes, attempting to steady the churn of fight or flight hormones.

The Abbess had always been careful to shield the sisters at Hyparxis House from exposure to the War and the myriad comings and goings of its operatives. But those operatives were slippery creatures and sometimes slipped between the house wards. Sister Agnostina's first encounter with any of their kind had been with this one.

She'd come up from the cellar with a bag of rice and there in the refectory kitchen stood a zombie schoolgirl Lolita with a band of rat skulls decorating her straw boater. Sister Agnostina's immediate thought was *oh well, somebody's trying too hard,* but then she noticed how the other sisters, in the process of preparing the midday meal, had stopped moving. Things were boiling over on the cooker, the fridge door was making that little beeping noise it made when you left it open too long, and Sister Heather Tesseris was bleeding all over the chopped carrots, seemingly unaware she was missing the tip of a finger. Abbess Anin had swept in then, all business and good sense, hustling the strange creature out of the room. But as they passed, the Cousin turned to look over her shoulder at the kitchen's occupants, and for a moment, at Sister Agnostina specifically. 'I just love nuns,' she'd said, her voice breathy, grin spread wide. 'They're crunchy with the Lord.'

Although the Sisters of the Little Moments weren't *those* kinds of nuns, it hardly mattered here and now. War was at the door of this cheap motel room flashing its teeth.

'What do you have there, little Sister?' The Cousin's voice had a balmy, stroll on the beach quality to it, as if addressing a dog who'd dragged some interesting bit of jetsam out of the water. She took another step into the room. The door closed behind her. 'Has your fishing expedition gone all caddywhompus?'

'I don't—' Sister Agnostina began. She took a breath, tried on a smile, touched her lips to feel the shape of it just to make sure. 'I'm afraid I don't know what that word means, Cousin.'

'Caddywhompus. Sideways. Tits up. Out of whack.'

She walked over to the bed and stood, knees bumping the edge of the mattress, looking down on the twitching man, teeth catching at her lower lip in winsome contemplation. 'I think this

106

one's good for nothing but chum. He's all in bits now.' She flicked a side-glance at Sister Agnostina. 'Shall we throw him back?'

The senator's body arched off the bed dramatically and fell back again, his legs wheeling, making accordion pleats in the floral duvet. There was no way to tell if the frantic actions were the Dyzeps trying to run from Cousin Nefanda's threat or the senator trying to outrun the Dyzeps inside him.

'He's *fine*,' Sister Agnostina said, her voice sharp-edged. Then, mostly to reassure herself, added. 'It'll be fine. Really. I've got it under control.'

Cousin Nefanda was eerily still, unbreathing, unblinking, watching, waiting.

So, more words were necessary, words that kept coming, tripping over each other to get out of the way of the next one. 'As soon as I get him to –when we get to Playa del Carmen, everything will be fine, it'll be fine, fine, perfect really. The press will be there, the press does most of the work, anyway. They love this kind of thing, politicians in motels.'

On the opposite side of the bed from Cousin Nefanda, she set about straightening out the bedding and the senator's tie. 'Well, maybe not *this* motel, too cheap, too sad, too … *fremdschämen?* At any rate, wouldn't rile the masses nearly enough for our purposes. But a Mexican resort hotel with a mistress or mister? He'll be hot for eight to ten news cycles at least. We just follow in the wake of his misfortune and collect the leavings. We'll be reaping *inter momenta* for months. All the b'tweens you could possibly want or need. Trust me. It's fine. Fine. Just fine. We do this all the time.'

They didn't though. They rarely had to. It was only because of Cousin Nefanda's increasing demands that it had been necessary.

Sister Agnostina reached up and pinched her lips together to stop her mouth from saying that.

'But what if his head explodes in front of all those cameras?'

Explodes?

'What? Why would it –? What?'

Cousin Nefanda gave her a look of indulgent, mild reproach and tsk-tsked like a disappointed nanny. 'Oh dear. You don't know how it works *at all*, do you?'

A queasy realization altered any further attempt at self-assurance. True, she hadn't asked a lot of questions about the process. Only '*Can you do it?*' and '*How long will it take?*' She hadn't wanted details, only results.

'Your Abbess used an intriguing, quite colorful metaphor to describe this type of field work –' Nefanda leaned over the senator's body, her back parallel to the planes of the bed, knees locked, legs and torso at a perfect right angle—'but I was under the impression she hadn't mean it to be literal.'

Her gaze roved over jerky limbs and contorted features like a detective's magnifying glass. Maybe it was. Maybe she had augmented eyes for that very purpose. After a long minute, she straightened. The tops of her stockings disappeared back under the hem of her skirt. She tugged and smoothed the pleats in front.

'You have engaged a Dyzeps parasite to do your dirty work, little Sister. It is currently colonizing the host, weaving its hyphae into *all* the tissue, fine-tuning chemical secretions in real time. Once the host's body has done whatever performance art you've got in mind, the colony will begin digesting the host from within, and before you know it, a huge bulbous spore cap will burst out the

108

top of his head. Possibly live on camera, in front of a global audience.'

She brought her hands up palm to palm, bumping the knuckles together before flaring her fingers out like a combustible blossom—

'*Boom.*'

Dyzeps is aware of the external threat. They had been dealing with the warring powers for eons and eternities, wet work commissioned by every side: High or Low, Remote or Entwined, Static or Tumult, it is all the same to Dyzeps.

But this *host*, this glorious Host Body, it is *treasure* crying out for interfusion. More exciting, it wants to be taken, wooed. Plays a game of *come closer/go away.*

It torments and teases, challenges, frustrates, stimulates, makes hyphae shiver. Oh, Host Body knows full well what it is doing to them.

That is why this chance for romantic entanglement must not be wasted. There is no scenario Dyzeps will accept where complete union with Host Body is not the result.

They have communicated this fact to the agent of mayhem and come to an agreement.

There were rumours about other sisters of the Order being written out of their own lives, out of the timestream, out of continuity—people Sister Agnostina should have known or might have known or never knew now. The possibility that she could be … *unremembered* put a fine edge on her awareness, dragged her

109

attention back to the only person in the room capable of making that happen.

Cousin Nefanda said, 'Head explosions would stretch well beyond the average news cycle, don't you think? Not to mention billions of spore seeds shooting out all over everything, infecting others. A spreader event like that could alter the trajectory of this little planet's future history. It is why use of Dyzeps is contra-indicated except in highly controlled environments.' She paused, winked. 'Well, for most people, anyway.'

She removed a small drawstring pouch from a blazer pocket (not the one with the confiscated phone) and bounced it gently in her hand as she looked about the room, seeking something in particular or something that would do.

A cockroach. A large one, spotted, and scuttling behind the television on the pressboard credenza. Five steps around the bed brought her to it.

'I mean, personally? I'd love to see where this all leads.' She thrust her arm behind the darkened screen and withdrew it again, the roach caught in the cage of a fist. 'There, there,' she said to it. To Sister Agnostina she said, 'But you do understand how it might appear to those outside looking in. How it might seem that the Mundane Order had compromised their neutrality. Picked sides.'

She put the drawstring bag on the top of the credenza and placed the cockroach next to it. The roach made small clicking noises but otherwise didn't move. A ridiculously long, blindingly sharp hairpin was pulled from a hat that seemed not to need one. She put one hand over the insect.

'I couldn't possibly let a neophyte like you do something so extravagant. That's my thing.'

She plunged the hatpin through her hand and into the roach beneath, burying the tip in the fake oak veneer. If there was pain, she made no sound, didn't show it, only a trembling scramble with the stabbing hand to grasp the pouch and tease the strings open.

'I'm going to help you out. Patch up the holes in your plan. The Mundane Order of Sisters of the Little Moments will be spared any judgment for your misdeeds.' With the opening of the bag widened, her fingers pressed across the maw like teeth. Nefanda turned to her and grinned. 'Brace yourself. This will not be pleasant. At all.'

Sister Agnostina never saw what was in the bag, unless all that it contained was pure fury and a cloud of hydrogen sulphide.

He doesn't know where they are, what this place is, except that it's probably Hell. The thing inside him has devoured every dating site cliché and vomited them onto a ludicrous landscape—an uncanny valley of *its* delusions and *his* constant excruciating pain. Cosy nights in front of a fireplace. Long walks on a beach.

The cosy nights in front of the fireplace even include wine though the parasite can't always coordinate his arm and hand to get the wine to his mouth. Not that it matters. He's never thirsty. Never hungry. He doesn't seem to need sustenance. The parasite occupies most of his interior spaces. It's wrapped around his organs and propping up his bones. The only part not under its control seems to be his brain.

Maybe not the *actual* brain, maybe only whatever is left of his mind, the part that makes Andrew Jacob Skrelli unique unto himself, the part that's so pissed-off about all this. He'd done stupid things in his life, sure, but always tried to make it up to the people he'd wronged, always tried to do better, *be* a better man—respectful, compassionate, a champion of justice. If this is hell, he's certain he doesn't deserve to be here.

That his mind is still his own at all seems moot at this point. Sometimes it feels like he's asking and answering his own questions with the parasite hovering in the background, just a creature of instinct, stretching millions of tiny poisonous limbs into the deepest regions of his body. But then it whispers to him, muttering inchoate desire. It *wants* something from him. Something it hasn't gotten yet.

So, it takes him for long walks on a beach where the sky is always blue, the clouds are cotton puffs, the waves lap at his feet, and there is sand between his toes. He walks past driftwood, shells, dead starfish. Hears the roar of the ocean, the cries of swooping gulls. Smells the brine in the foam, decaying fish and the stink of kelp. Can almost taste the saltwater taffy from a shop on a boardwalk they never quite reach. Because, despite the sense of distance ahead, behind, and out to sea, the beach is nothing more than a scrolling backdrop. A continuous looping illusion of forward momentum, like in a Hanna-Barbera cartoon. A stroll along a short stretch of reality.

Sometimes, on this treadmill death-march version of a parasite's ideal date, somewhere between the gulls and the wind and the whoosh of the waves, he hears gunfire, explosions, people screaming. But he can't turn his head to look. The parasite won't let him.

Sister Agnostina opened her eyes. A distraught woman thrust something into her arms. 'Please, please. I'm begging you. Hide him. Protect him. Save my baby, please!'

The baby, a lumpy noodle shape swaddled in a pale blanket, radiated warmth, smelled pleasant. She tightened her arms around it instinctively, pressed it closer to her chest to keep it from slipping to the floor.

She and the woman and the baby were crouched between the pews in a darkened church. *No.* Crouched between rows of wooden folding chairs in what was *meant* to be a church, one of those ad hoc places of worship, an empty store front in a failing shopping centre perhaps. The chairs faced the back of the store. There was a narrow altar with the cross of Christians affixed to the front and what looked to be a gooseneck microphone on top, ready for a preacher's sermon.

Above their heads, through high-set narrow windows, a murky blueish light scanned the ceiling and slid back and forth across the walls. Outside, the sounds of indistinct shouting, the rattling of doors then glass breaking. The woman's terror was like a sucking chest wound, her tear-streaked face a beacon drawing the danger closer.

'What's your name?' Sister Agnostina asked, her own voice oddly calm.

'Amber.' The denim pinafore dress and triangle scarf on her head gave a distinctly sister-wife kind of vibe. She touched the blanket covered shoulder her infant. 'And this is–'

'Don't tell me.'

A shout sounded. Amber jumped, looking over her shoulder at the door then back to Sister Agnostina.

'Quick. Give me your veil.'

Sister Agnostina reached up, not entirely surprised to find a veil there though she hadn't been wearing one in the motel room. She

113

pulled out the bobby pins holding it in place, her other arm pressing the baby lump to her chest.

Amber wrapped the veil around a 10 lb bag of rice, folding and tucking it in so it resembled the blanket around the baby. Sister Agnostina thought it odd she hadn't noticed the bag of rice. Had Amber been carrying a bag of rice and a baby this whole time?

'You head for the sanctuary,' Amber murmured. 'I'll lead them away. Fool them as long as I can. You know what to do after that.'

Sister Agnostina placed the baby on the seat of a chair. 'I don't— I don't know—'

Where is sanctuary? That's what she tried to ask, but Amber seemed to think she was vacillating on some prearranged agreement and grabbed her by the arms, fingers digging into her biceps through the heavy fabric of her cardigan.

'Listen to me! I wasn't being *paranoid*, okay? It wasn't paranoia like Joe kept telling me, gaslighting me. I found his internet searches, all his emails with those groups on the dark web. I know what he is. What he's doing. What *they* do. He's radicalized beyond salvation. My husband's soul is lost, but our son's isn't. You *know* what *democrats* do to innocent babies. I won't let him sacrifice our child to some unholy alliance with the Clinton cabal!'

Her statement implied a proper *holy* way to sacrifice a child and Sister Agnostina stifled a rising laugh of hysteria. What surreality was this meant to be? Was this a parallel universe? A bubble in hell? Why did she still exist at all? Or did she?

A lot of questions and no time to ponder answers, which was surely Cousin Nefanda's intention in sending her here.

Amber rose from her crouch, holding the swaddled bag of rice. 'I'm trusting you to save my child, Sister.'

'Oh, please don't.'

Pounding on the door, fists first, then something heavier, a makeshift battering ram.

'Go,' Amber hissed. Her terror and desperation had solidified into something hard. Sister Agnostina caught it like a ball and ran toward the only other door she could see.

Drunken sex. That's what it's like. Dorm room drunken sex that goes on and on and on—not because you're some nineteen-year-old I-can-go-all-night stud, but because you're too shit-faced to get off or keep it up or you've blacked out in the middle of it. After three or four (or however many) hours trying, all you've got to show for your time is a limp raw dick and a bored, frustrated girlfriend who breaks up with you a week later.

Only in this situation *he's* the bored, frustrated girlfriend and the only way he can break up with the parasite is if he's dead. And it doesn't want him to be dead. Not yet. He almost wants to die out of spite. But he'll be damned if he's going to let the parasite decide his fate. He'll take the thing down with him.

The entire colony trembles, barely withholding completion. Dyzeps has never lasted this long before. No Host Body has ever lasted this long before. The urge to unfurl pedicel and thrust into soft, yielding brain tissue is exquisite torment. Their spore cap swells, thick and heavy with the need to push out and burst open.

Yet, if they complete the act, Host Body dies.

If they unwind all hyphae and withdraw, Host Body dies.

To lose Host Body is *unbearable*.

This. This is *true* romantic tragedy.

At Hyparxis House, they counted time in the manner of the locals—seconds, minutes, hours, days, et cetera. Sister Agnostina had been missing for two days, twelve hours, thirty-six minutes and however many seconds were tick-tick-ticking away. Though Abbess Anin could not be certain Sister Agnostina was still alive, she knew by the very fact of her worry, the young woman still existed in some reality or other. She had not been erased or unremembered.

'You haven't managed that at least,' she muttered to Cousin Nefanda's back.

Nefanda had just finished replenishing all the little-moments and in-betweens she'd taken from the stores, plus a bit extra. She brushed her hands together in a job-well-done. 'No need to thank me.'

'I would not presume. Just as I would not presume to question your reasons for needing so much extra ... pocket change—'

'That's wise.'

'—nor why Hyparxis House is now located in West Palm Beach, Florida.'

'Oh. I thought Florida was a preferred location. Ah well. Confounding variables and all that. Your method for catching fish is not without risks.'

'That's why we're reluctant to utilize it,' Abbess Anin said, then more carefully, 'Did you catch something useful?"

'All sorts of things! And look—' Nefanda pointed through the office window (there was an office window now)— 'you are but

116

a stray golf ball away from the new southern White House. Isn't that exciting? See? You can just make out the gold glittering on the ramparts.'

The sudden appearance of a window looking out to a philistine's concept of 'classy' was the least of Abbess Anin's worries. But her concern was misinterpreted.

'Oh, come on! It doesn't affect your work in the least. In fact, it should make it much easier from now on.'

'Did Sister Agnostina get caught in the fallout?'

'No. I merely set her to one side. She's… safe enough. You should have every confidence she'll find her way back. Most things that don't belong there eventually do.'

'Where, Cousin? Where is she?'

'Here's her phone. Give her a ring.' And then she popped off.

After Nefanda left, Abbess Anin tucked the phone into the sleeve of her habit. She'd have use of it later. Her desk was in a different part of the office, but the rolodex looked to be the same and she set about contacting a few friends. They in turn sent messages through the continuum web—up, down, and across the strands, informing all relevant parties that Cousin Nefanda of House Paradox had replenished the *substantial* funds (she was careful to stress that detail) she'd drawn from communal stores. *Inter-momenta* were once again available for the use of all.

The mistrustful nature of Nefanda's associates would uncover whatever whimsey of destruction she'd wrought. Let them deal with her.

It seemed it would now be necessary to bring the sewing kit out of hiding.

Sister Agnostina huddled behind a row of bins in an alley spying on the service door of a pizza parlour, Amber's swaddled infant in her arms. People, laden with boxes, bulging backpacks, and shopping bags rounded and heavy with what she hoped was whole prosciutto hams or salamis or wheels of cheese, pressed the call buzzer and were admitted inside. So far no one had come back out.

This was *not* sanctuary. Of that she felt certain. But she didn't remember *why* she was watching this door, these people. Didn't recall how she got here but had the odd sensation she'd done this before. The same feeling, she realized, that had tickled her senses with Amber in the church.

The muscles in her legs burned like she'd run hard and fast for a long time. Her heart still pounded too, and her pulse throbbed at her throat. It was fear though, not exertion. *Fear.* Of this place. Of these people. Of the woman in the bloody apron who opened the service door to them.

She heard the bike before she saw it—a swish and soft click click click coming from the far end of the alley. She ducked lower and scootched farther out of sight. The skinny older man in cycling gear dismounted near the service door and leaned his bike against the brick wall. He poked a finger at the call bell. The door opened and the woman in the bloody apron greeted him. They exchanged pleasantries as the cyclist reached into the panier and pulled something out, something squirming and flailing.

Sister Agostina clapped a hand over her mouth to stifle a gasp. Too late. The woman in the bloody apron tensed, eyes squinting like she could just make out Sister's eye squinting back through the dark slit between the bins. Then just as suddenly the woman stilled. Her face relaxing into a smile.

118

'*Gotcha!*' someone said behind her.

Sister Agnostina lunged forward, the imprint of her attacker's breath hot and wet on the back of her neck as she shoved a bin hard, sending it rolling into the middle of the alley. Fettered by the infant in her arms, she couldn't get her feet under her to take advantage of the cleared path. She stumbled to her knees, one arm out to keep from crushing the baby when she hit the pavement.

She never hit the pavement.

The man's hands were huge, thick fingered, sinking into muscle, ready to crush bone as he dragged her across the alley to the wide-open door and down a set of cement stairs and into a brightly lit hell.

Abbess Anin looped a thread onto the lucet fork, working quick as her hands would allow and fashioned a tether anchored to current reality. That done, she retrieved Sister Agnostina's mobile and pressed her thumb to the centre of the phone's screen. After a moment's examination she sighed. 'Foolish child.'

But there was no time for worry or remonstrations. She tucked the sewing kit beneath her wimple for safe keeping and followed the shadow links on the phone to the Dyzeps at the other end.

As they walk, Skrelli's head keeps drooping. The parasite sends a jolt to lift it up again. He's been walking with his eyes closed anyway. The sights of the beach are distracting, annoying. He needs to appear submissive, ready to surrender. It makes the parasite so mad! Hence the angry little jolts. Like that one, forcing his eyes wide.

He wouldn't have seen the nun otherwise.

Off the Boulevard, Abbess Anin follows the boardwalk to the Venice Beach Massacre. The beach is a nightmare. But it's not her prison so she walks past the flailing, screaming, sobbing, begging, scatter and tumble of semi-naked humans. Survivors claimed no one knew where the bullets were coming from (not even the navy tactical response unit dropped down in the middle of the mess). It was the first known use of quantum stealth technology by Christian terrorists. The fact that they also managed to kill each other (it was *really good* camouflage) didn't make anyone feel better about it. Especially after a series of explosive devices demolished most of the Venice boardwalk.

She can't imagine why the parasite would choose such a place where its host would be at high risk for slaughter, but then she spots a quiver in the air some distance down the beach close to the waves—waves that were not in sync with the rest of the Pacific Ocean. A flash of rainbow light like off a soap bubble tells her it is a pocket of looping time. Within it, a barefoot man with trousers rolled up strolls the loop, his gaze on the damp sand beneath his toes, seemingly oblivious to mayhem all around him.

As she approaches his head snaps up, spots her moving purposefully toward him. There's a brief flicker of hope before his feet start walking him backwards. Arms wheeling, he leans forward fighting retreat. It's like he's at war with his own legs, twisting his body, arching his back, knees stiff. He falls back onto the sand scuttling away until his back connects with the barrier in a jelly-ripple.

She slides between atoms and marches over and pulls him to his feet, giving him a little shake like a naughty child.

But up close it's clear the only thing keeping him alive is the parasite thriving within him. His skin has a powdery coating, and the sclerae of his eyes are a violent red from burst vessels. He looks surprised then angry. His mouth opens, and words come screeching out.

'*Go. Away.*'

'If you wanted the man to last forever you needed a stasis field, not this…' She gestures vaguely at the container they're in, hiding her deep distaste.

'*Romantic. Cosy. Ideal. Love. Ecstasy.*'

The man bends an arm, aims it up, palm rigid and flat like he's trying to slap his own face.

'Transitory notions. Nonsense. What is it you truly desire Dyzeps?'

'*Want. Want. Union. Host. Want*—' The man's head tips back, neck arched, face to the sky— '*Sym-bee-oh-sisss!*'

Ah. That she could do. She removes her sewing kit from beneath her wimple.

'Man, if you hear me, listen close. I can pull the Dyzeps from your body. You will die, and it will live, but your suffering will end. Or I can fuse it *to* you. It will live inside you, you will be in constant pain, but your body will be yours to command, and when you die, so will the Dyzeps.'

The man's body seizes, spasms violently before collapsing. The bulging muscles in his neck, the fury in the garbled 'NO' are enough to confirm the *man* has chosen option number two.

Sister Agnostina squeezed her eyes shut. But she couldn't shut out the odors, the sounds. A low moan starts deep her in chest, her own contribution to the keening and whimpering of infants in varying states of dismemberment. They tear Amber's infant from her arms, lay it on the prep table and pin it to the cutting board with long chef's knife.

Instead of a squeal and the wet squelch of brutalized flesh there's a crunchy sound and a dry hiss.

'What the hell?' The blanket is pulled away. It's the veil she gave Amber!

'Is this—? Is this rice?' The hiss gets louder. Acrid smoke curls up around the blade.

'Oh shit,' someone says. A flame blossoms out of the spilled grain. 'Oh, shit shit shit.'

A second of stunned incomprehension before the bomb goes off.

Inside the man's body Abbess Anin catches the Dyzeps' single pedicel along with its connecting hyphae and winds them together around a spool. She knots the spool to the senator's atlas vertebrae with a quantum thread leaving one long end that she pulls through his body to the surface of his flesh. Here on the back of his neck she stitches a pattern—a quick brutalist work, none of the artistry she once employed, but her hands won't manage more, and this lattice of long stitches will get the job done. Once finished, the ideogram sinks back into the man's neck, quantum locking the two entities together.

'I haven't the power to return you to your world exactly as it was when you were taken,' she tells him. 'You will have to fight much harder now to correct your country's course.'

Sister Agnostina regains consciousness still screaming inside her head. She may be screaming out loud, but the explosion has damaged her eardrums. It also blew the basement to smithereens and sent her flying, up and out, into the alley where she now lay amidst toppled and scattered bins. She can't feel her legs. Can't move to see if they're still attached. When Abbess Anin finds her, her throat no longer makes sounds. The spiral needle in the Abbess's fingers begins quilting her parts together, there in an alley behind a pizza parlor off the ruins of Connecticut Avenue Northwest in the patchwork remains of Washington DC.

When the Abbess has done enough to get Sister Agnostina up and moving, they make their way over crumbled sidewalks and fallen power lines to what was once a stop on the Metro Red Line. There they ride the tether cord back to Hyparxis House.

Senator A. J. Skrelli returned from his sojourn on the Appalachian Trail a changed man. The first change was to his political party affiliation. Much to the horror of his former colleagues and the delight of his former opposition.

His wife was surprisingly unbothered by the political shift (she'd been secretly disturbed by his growing popularity with the transgendered community) and though his new aggressiveness in areas of their domestic life bothered her enough to establish a separate residence, she agreed to play the proper politician's lady in public.

They adopted two children from third world countries (though *not* from South America and the Caribbean), contributed to Christian charities, attended fundraisers, and hosted their own at five thousand dollars a plate.

He was very pleased with his new campaign volunteers, particularly Addison who often stayed late or came in after her classes at Georgetown. (Public Policy with a minor in Economics.) Tonight, she offered to pick up dinner on the way over. One of the other volunteers, Kelsey, had to leave early so it would just be the two of them. 'Lobster mac and cheese from Morton's' he told her, 'and whatever you want. Don't worry about the cost. Put it on the campaign credit card.'

She'd never had lobster mac and cheese before. 'Try some of mine,' he said, offering a bite from his own fork. When she tried to take the fork from his hand, he insisted she open her mouth for it.

Her eyes went big-eyed Bambi huge for a second. She looked down and away, her face flushed. 'Um…'

'Come on,' he said poking the sticky glob at her lips, 'one little bite won't hurt.'

She opened her mouth, pulled the morsel off with her teeth.

'Good, huh?'

She gulped. 'Mmm hhmm. That's—that is- is uh, good. It's really rich though. I shouldn't–'

'Stop. You're in great shape. College gymnastics, right? You can afford to indulge a little. I even think Kelsey left some beer…'

'Oh. No. Senator, yeah, no, I'm not twenty-one yet.'

'Ah well,' he said, headed for the mini fridge, 'we'll pretend we're in West Virginia.'

Dyzeps, jealous as usual, clenched hyphae around his heart, and *squeezed.*

You are the Absurd Hero

Kevin Burnard

Back to start.

The street is rough. Physically, that is. The tarmac is bumpy and jagged, it's digging into your back. It hurts. You should stop it doing that. You sit up.

There's a man standing over you. Did he push you, or is he helping you up? You reach for his hand, but yours passes through it, like he's a ghost from some crappy 90s TV show.

Neither then.

"Who are you?" you ask. It's a cliche, but it's the sensible thing to do.

"I don't have long," he pleads. "My name is Godfather Sisyphus. I need your help."

He looks the kind of man you'd avoid in the street, but feel guilty about later. Frail. Gaunt. There's muscle there, but it's the desperate survival kind, not the keto diet and personal trainer kind: the barest essentials of a body. Another day, you'd assume he's homeless and fishing for money. Today, your hand just went right through him, so the help's probably related to that.

"My body is trapped in another reality; the Boulevard," he continues. "Only you can free me."

Maybe you're just a sucker for an esoteric tale, because you're still here and looking for answers. "How could I even help?" you ask.

You climb to your feet as he explains. There's a book, a very special kind of book. It hasn't been in print in years. It's called

125

The Book of the War, and right now, one last copy is available on eBay. The fate of this man depends on it, in conjunction with some kind of ritual he's hazy about. "What's in it for me?" you wonder. Selfish git. But fair enough.

Sisyphus smiles, though it's clear he's in pain. He's straining with effort, and not only to get the words out. It's like he's struggling with an enormous weight, just out of sight. "If you follow the ritual and free me," he promises, "I can give you the power to rewrite time."

Well, sure, that would be great, but who believes in that? You laugh and turn away. That's more than enough time spent on this weirdness already.

A piece of paper blows into your face. Swearing, you scrape it off and look for a recycling bin. No, hang on. That's your handwriting on it. How is it your handwriting? The pen, even, you recognize the ink. It's one you own. The paper is that piece of junk mail you got the other day. How did this happen?

"I wrote this tomorrow," the writing says.

"A cheap trick," says Sisyphus, "but that's all I have the power for now. If you accept, and as you can see, you already have, go home. Sleep on it. And in the morning, write this down. I'll take care of the rest."

That power, to change things. To fix the things you've lost, stop your traumas before they happened, warn the people you love, stop the things that should never have happened… how can you say no?

You look up the listing and check the price.

Oh.

It's very tempting to say no.

*If you refuse to get caught up in this nonsense, continue to page **128**.*

*If you will write the note and serve the Godfather, continue to page **129**.*

Continued.

The street is rough. Physically, that is. The tarmac is bumpy and jagged, it's digging into your back. It hurts. You should stop it doing that.

You can't.

There's a weight on your toes, pressing hard. It's even rougher than the pavement below you. It keeps pressing, and you can feel bones shattering as it moves across your feet. Your ankles splinter, then your shins. This might be a good time to start screaming.

You blink madly, trying to wipe away the tears and blinding pain. The pressure rises past your knees, and you feel the tendons snap as it does. Your groin is similarly no match for the weight. That's especially messy. You see it now. You're being crushed by a boulder. It keeps climbing, past your stomach, past your chest. You're still screaming as your lungs pop and your mouth is subsumed by rock. You'd give anything to get out of here and try again. Wouldn't you?

The boulder rolls on.

*Go back to page **125.***

Continued.

You toss the pen away, looking at what you've written. It matches perfectly with page that blew into you, every smudge and awkward squiggle in the ink. Godfather Sisyphus may have been many things, but clearly he wasn't lying there.

So instead, you worry about the next step. You pace back and forth, the mind-boggling number burning in your brain. You've checked your bank. Whatever savings you've got, they're apparently not good enough for *The Book of the War*. Seriously, what kind of crazy person would spend that much on an old book? Well, clearly you're thinking about it, but you're a special case. Right? There aren't many other people with judgement that crap?

But you've heard him whispering. *Sisyphus, Sisyphus, Sisyphus*. The name worms through your head. You don't know this man, you have no reason to care. But you can *feel* him out there. He's hurting. He needs you. And oh, he will be so grateful. He will keep his promise. You'll have the power of time in your hands. It's an almost religious conviction burning in you, but you know it's true.

You're still pacing. You're at home, taking in your surroundings. You might not usually be one for pacing, but right now, it's working, and it's the only way to think. It takes you back and forth across the room, surrounded by your belongings: clothes and couches and trivial little things. What do they matter compared to a trapped ghost? Your little life has nothing compared to the magic you've found today, let alone the reward.

Time travel. The thought still makes you giddy. If you sell everything you own, you could afford the book, surely. Besides, one lottery ticket or horse racing cheat would be enough to replace it all. People could steal your stuff for all it matters now, next to what's to come. Steal... oh, that's another option, isn't it?

A feverish idea forms, whipping through the crevices of your brain. Oh, brilliant. The item's listed location isn't far. Not next door, but not unreasonable to travel. You could go there and get it. You could go there and *take* it.

The pacing stops. You don't even need to think about it, your feet just fall still because you can tell you're at a crossroads.

Which path do you choose?

*If you choose to steal the book, continue to page **131***

*If you choose to rob a bank to buy the book, continue to page **134.***

*If the book just really isn't worth a life of crime, continue to page **128***

Continued.

It felt like the mail would never arrive. The box is in your hands now, though, and everything's going to be alright.

It was a simple ploy, really, but you feel pretty clever for it. You placed an order from the seller, like any normal person would. It's not like *The Book of the War* is the only thing in their shop.

You don't even bother opening the box, just some old book of Greek myths. You don't need it, you just ordered this because it was cheap, and because it would tell you everything you need to know.

There it is, written on the box: a return address.

Now you know exactly where to burgle.

This is a newer experience than would be ideal, you realize as you pull on the ski mask. You don't even really know if ski masks are the best masks for burglary, or if you've just got that idea from TV and movies. But you've got it now, and there's no turning back.

Climbing the wall to the balcony took practice at a parkour gym, sturdy climbing gloves, and a good run-up, but you've just about managed it in relative silence. You drop onto the landing and congratulate yourself on a job well done. It'll be harder jumping down than climbing up, you know. There aren't many footholds, and it's a long drop. But one problem at a time.

The door is unlocked. Clearly, the owner never expected anyone to attempt anything like this. You slowly ease it open, wincing at every creak. What if the owner hears?

Don't be silly. You've watched this place for a week. The owner's always, always asleep by 11; it's total lights out, and it's creeping towards three right now. Besides, they're hardly likely to sleep with the book, are they?

The carpet is red, you can tell that even in the dark. You consider turning on the small torch you've brought but decide to hold off. The moon's bright tonight. Actually, it's full. And someone designed this place to make the most of natural light, so you're more than provided for.

It's a nice place, very old, but there's something forlorn about it. It's antique in the spooky, needs a repair way, not the home improvement magazine cover way. No wonder they need the money they're demanding. Tough.

Upstairs or downstairs? Where are you going to search first? You pause, ready to make that choice.

That's when the chanting starts.

"Grandfather watch me. Spirits suffuse me. Lay my time on your altar, so none may refuse me."

All lights are out, but silence has not fallen. And there's a whooshing scream through the air, like wind through power lines

"Once I had bounty, now only know strife. Grandfather, Spirits, I pledge you my knife."

The scream grows louder. It's rushing through the hall. It's rushing at you.

"Blood from my veins, and blood to the smoke. Let the Children of Paradox's enemies choke."

Choke?

Where has the air gone?

It's like a wall has been put up in the middle of your throat. Your chest heaves, but you cannot cough. You punch your neck, desperate to dislodge whatever's forced itself inside you. When that fails, you start to tear your flesh, anything to get it out.

Through the whumping rush of blood in your ears, your pulse reaching fever pitch, you hear footsteps approaching. A woman stands before you. You've seen her before from a distance, but never this close. Maybe it's not sleep she does in the dark.

She's the owner of the house, emphasised by the keys jangling at her hip. What's more, she's the owner of the book. And when you fix your horrified eyes on her, you meet only the gaping eyes of a skull.

The book is in her hands. Only your own blood is on yours.

With one last desperate leap, you pounce at the prize. She swats you away.

"Not another one," she sighs, as your oxygen-starved brain drowns in gray. "I hate criminals. That's all you are, aren't you?"

Not anymore. Now you're dead. But hey, you're doing this to get the power of time travel. Wouldn't you like the power to *go back to page 130 and try again?*

Continued.

"People always think it'd be easy to rob a bank," the man's saying. You try to ignore him, but he's very loud and lacks boundary awareness, so this is just your fate now.

"Do you know the kind of security these places have?" he continues. He's on a roll. "What are you going to do, point a gun at the teller and tell them to fill up a bag? They have metal detectors. They have armed security. Do you even *own* a gun? Have you ever pulled a trigger?"

You're standing outside the bank. It's a gray day, hint of drizzle, but not enough to make loitering too conspicuous. But to some people, the act of just standing in a street is an invitation to talk. He's probably some kind of security geek or something, too scrawny to be any use in the actual industry.

"Like, look through the window. There it all is, on display, just glass in front of the heavy-duty stuff. They *want* you to see how easily they could wreck you. That's how they avoid having to actually do it."

You've just gotta ask at this point. "Why do you care so much about bank robbery?"

The man smiles sheepishly. "I'm a screenwriter trying to plot a heist movie. But you just can't realistically do it anymore. Drives me crazy. You can call me Tucker, here's my card."

You pocket the card, with the intent of tossing it in the first recycle bin you see. He was probably crazy already. Who else would be a screenwriter?

What happens if you try to turn and give up? You consider it for a moment, but already, something's stopping you. A distant memory, perhaps? Or is it something clearer? Pain lies behind, certain doom ahead.

Maybe there's another option. You have an account with this bank, right? That's why it's the first you thought of to rob. Maybe you can just go in and withdraw everything, sell everything. The sum total of everything you've ever had is surely enough for one book, right?

Go on. Think about it.

*To sell your belongings like a reasonable person living peacefully under capitalism, continue to page **139**.*

*If your heart's really set on sticking up a goddamn bank, continue to page **136**.*

*But really, what's stopping you from throwing the towel in? **128**'s for you.*

*And there's still that other robbery option at **131**...*

Continued.

"So, what you're saying is, it's impossible to rob a bank in 2021?"

"Yep."

"So they just make a show of force to stop you even trying."
"Yep."

"So," you say, hoping Tucker's brain is as frazzled as you think it is, "if someone actually did try to rob the bank, unarmed and totally just winging it, it would be the last thing anyone would expect."

Tucker stares at you.

"I'm gonna do it," you say.

Oh my God in heaven, you actually did it.

The bag's in your hot, sweaty hand, full of cold hard cash. How the hell did you do it?

You stop to take a breath around a corner, pulling the mask off your head for air. The events of the robbery whizz through your head. The paperclip was much more useful than expected, but the novelty gun cigarette lighter significantly less so. You hope that man you bludgeoned with the plastic flamingo will be okay.

Tucker is staring at you. "You actually bloody did it. That was the dumbest thing I have ever seen."

He's holding a laptop bag under one arm. He furiously smashes it to the floor, electronic bits and plastic shattering across the pavement like his dreams. "I've spent years trying to get anywhere, anywhere with this and just go back to square one every time. You just waltz in and… you actually just went and… I give up."

There's sirens blaring on all sides. Oh crap, they've found you.

You search your pockets. The paperclip's still there, sticky with blood. So's the novelty gun lighter. What else? Your wallet? What are you gonna do, flash your driver's license at the cops?

No, hang on. Fake gun. *Fake gun.*

"Hey Tucker," you ask, "wanna help me with something?"

"Life has no meaning and it's all your fault."

"Life means something to them," you reply.

You turn to face a hirsute policeman, righteous conviction and a hint of barely disguised racism in his eyes—*why is that even there?* As you do, you raise one hand, the novelty lighter clutched tightly within. "Let me go or I shoot this guy."

The cop turns to his partner. She's bigger, less hairy, and probably more racist. You absolutely cannot take her in a fight, so try not to get in one.

"Nobody move!" you shout, just for emphasis. They don't. They're taking this seriously. Good.

But Tucker isn't. "Just shoot me already," he moans. "It can't get any worse."

This guy must have had serious issues, and now they're your issues. You can't bring yourself to shoot him, right? It's not even a real gun.

Behind the two cops are more cops, probably about five cars in all. They're fanned out in formation to block almost any exit.

What's more, like the gaze of a predator in the night, you can feel the sights of guns train themselves on your neck, chest, back, head, anywhere that could kill you in moments.

You see the smaller cop's finger twitch on the trigger. You have moments before he pulls it for real. The bank still stands behind you. The cordon of cars stands in front.

Think fast. Are you diving forwards, or backwards?

Bang.

*If you dove forwards, continue to page **149**.*

*If you dove backwards, continue to page **144**.*

Continued.

You need to check the order status.

"I'm sorry, but it's time to leave," the librarian tells you. Your fingers slip from the mouse as she pulls you away. It would have been hard work once, but starvation's made you very light. You're too poor to resist.

But you need to check the order status.

"The library computers are closed. It's time to go," she says again, more forcefully. She swats at you with a book of Greek myth, every blow stinging way more than it should, thanks to secret librarian martial arts techniques. Pages flap around you as she repels you from her Dewey Decimalled domain: Hades, Orpheus, Dionysus, Sisyphus…

Sisyphus?

Before you know it, you're on the street again. Questions can wait. You'll be asking him for answers in person soon enough.

You stumble through the cold, rain drenching your ragged clothes. You miss home. You had one once, but you threw away all the money you had. All your belongings. All your future rent. Your phone. Your computer. Anything you could ever call yours. It was still only barely enough.

It'll be there soon, though. The mail will come. Not to you, of course, but to the place you once called home. A place with warmth and food and clothes and a place to check order status.

It's a long way to home.

The rain is getting heavier now. Puddles are a thing of the past, it's now running in a thick, mucky river that sucks at your ankles.

In a frenzy, you wade across another street, drivers brave enough to weather the storm showering you in wet, grimy sheets as they pass. If you could only check your old mailbox, maybe you'd know the order status. Maybe you'd have the book.

You don't see the next car, and it doesn't see you.

It's not a collision, not really. It's just the whumf of air as it speeds far too close, catching you in its wake. You lose your balance and tumble into the runoff, brown, asphalt-y water filling your nose and mouth. The skin of your knees grinds away against the uneven pavement. Pain lurches into your head.

Can you get to your feet?

The next car comes. No, you can't. You've now had the pleasure of feeling your foot shattered beneath a wheel.

There's something familiar about it.

You stumble, falling back into the dark water. A big gulp of it goes down into your lungs.

It's not walking, it's not crawling, it's not swimming, but bits of all those things feed into your movement now, a writhing through the street in search of respite. It doesn't come. Cars batter you with water and wheels.

You're broken. You're drowning.

One more car passes to finish the job. It's a mail truck.

And somehow, somehow you just know your order status.

Oh well. Time to die.

*Try again? Go back to page **134**.*

"You're supposed to be dead."

Why aren't you? You're lying in the street, blood pouring from your shattered body and mixing with the rain, but you refuse to die. Is that all it takes? Sheer bloody-mindedness to keep going?

"Just die already," the voice says. She. You've heard her voice before, but where—?

An image floats through your mind: a house, a hallway, a woman in a skull mask singing a chant. It's not quite a memory, but it feels like it should be. And in it, she killed you.

She's strolling through the wet, the hem of her long, lacy red dress getting soppy and stained with mud. It's a beautiful piece, probably one of a kind, but it's the bundles of paper packages in her arms that she's clutching to for dear life.

"Who are you?" you hiss.

"Sister-in-waiting Annie, Faction Paradox. You're not going to stop me getting in."

Getting in where? You think back to the vision you had, days ago now. Godfather Sisyphus. Are these two family? Is she trying to get to him, too?

Well, screw that. She's not gonna take that time travel reward from you, even if she does have the ritual part now. You try to stand, but it's still out of the question. Instead, you kinda flop pitifully in her general direction.

"You're finished," she laughs. It's very annoying, so you bite her ankles. Her blood bursts against your tongue, thick with iron and magic.

"Ow! God!"

She kicks you to the hard ground, packages scattering to the wet floor, plus a faint plop of something heavier, metal maybe. The roar of water fills your ears, droplets running across your face and making you choke.

Before you can fight back, you feel a knife slide between your ribs. "Die well, die poorly, I don't care, just die," Sister-in-waiting Annie spits.

With a flourish, she sweeps up her packages and swoops away.

Seriously, you're dead. Go back to page 134. Or 128. Or 125. Just go.

The street is rough. Physically, that is. The tarmac is bumpy and jagged, it's digging into your back. It hurts. You should stop it doing that. Groaning, you roll over, pushing yourself to your feet. *Ow.*

Something metal just bit into your palm. As if the knife wasn't bad enough…

It's a key, the old-fashioned kind, with a long stem and flat notches at the end. Have you ever seen a lock that actually uses something like that? Probably not. There's a number on it, 169, maybe a hotel room number? God knows which hotel. It'd look cool as a necklace or something, though. You pocket it.

Huh, no, there's a thought. Hands drifting from your pockets, you pat your stomach, then your back. You were definitely stabbed, that's not something anyone forgets. But the skin is almost new, just the faintest ridge from a scar to tell the story.

How long has it been? The sun is shining now. Maybe you can finally check your order status…

Ignoring the serious stink-eye from the librarians, you pull up the public computer. It's arrived.

Time to break into your own old mailbox, right? Or do you want to wake up on the street again…

*You're alive. Don't screw it up. To proceed, go to page **153**.*

*To screw it up, continue to page **128**.*

Continued.

Now you know why they call it a hail of bullets. The roaring impact against the glass is like the worst storms you've ever seen, turned up a thousand, thousand times. Through it all, though, the glass is holding. Banks are built to last.

Police battering rams are built to fix that. You need to get out of here as fast as possible.

There's another door at the back. Run. Run. Run.

"Get on the ground!" someone shouts. Well, screw that. You dive through the door, and on you run.

And you run.

And you run.

The police are out in force. Helicopters buzz through the air, oppressive shadows slicing across the sun as your world falls apart around you. You have the money. You need the book. You need time travel to get you the hell out of this mess. Oh God, you need time travel.

A place to hide would be a good start. With every corner, you see flashing lights on police cars, and walls of uniforms. You're running so fast the street signs blur together, past intersections of something lane and nothing street, the letters just wisps of colour that pass you by. None of the roads lead to freedom. They've got you surrounded. Any closer and they—

A hand seizes your wrist.

You scream and punch the owner. He pulls you with him as he falls, and you both tumble to the floor. Tumbling, you claw and scratch and bite and let loose every violent animal impulse that might be triggered by a battle for life or death.

"Stop! Stop! Stop!" the stranger hisses. He's pointing down the way at police lights, the flashing colors moving closer with alarming speed.

They heard your screams and fighting. It's over now, unless—

"This way," the man adds. He ducks down an alley where none was before. Well, you've just gotta follow him, haven't you? It's not a choice.

The air is colder here. You shiver, and the man mentions something unhelpful about temporal folds draining energy from the air. Perk is, he says, the police can't find you here, not that they'll stop looking for a while. You'll have to lay low.

You get a better look at him now. There's a sort of ex-wrestler look to him, only with more scars and, conversely, more intact teeth. An ugly blob of blue ink has splattered itself beneath the skin of his right arm, a desperately lazy attempt to cover a tattoo. Somehow, though, you recognize the shape that once was, and that still lurks beneath. It was once a skull, but not a normal skull, one with strange spikes and indentations and a cruel, cruel jaw. A skull you swear you've seen before.

There's something more about him nagging at you, but it's just not clicking yet.

It's not the time to worry about it. You pull your phone from your pocket and confirm a *very* expensive purchase, express shipping and all.

"So you're the one screwing with Faction Paradox," the man tuts.

Come on. You know who they are, don't you? Admit it.

145

"Getting into some kind of time travel cult stuff, yeah," you admit.

"Cult? That's putting it mildly," the man laughs. His hand absently scratches at the blob of blue staining him forever. "Faction Paradox are fanatics for performative chaos. I've known agents who cut off their own past self's arms just to sew them onto themselves as a statement. Devotees who bathe in the blood of their own child selves to court eternal youth. They compare themselves to vodou, a resistance religion created by the enslaved. The Faction like that idea of freedom, but they're no slaves. They're a major power in the biggest War that ever was, and a fanatical one that thinks they're the rebellious little guys. All that righteousness and anger and sheer power is *not* something you want to screw with."

You nod, half-listening. Your phone's given you a little ping that your order is already on the way.

"And you took one look at these guys and thought, hey, I'm gonna break one of their worst members out of prison? Just think what it takes for *them* to think you've gone too far!"

Prison? That's not what Sisyphus said. He said he was trapped on some street. Looking back, it's clear how little you actually know about this Sisyphus, or the book, or the ritual that awaits you. How did you get swept up in this obsession? Did you ever really have a choice?

"Let me guess, you were promised time travel. And believe me, anyone who knows the Faction knows time travel. Especially their enemies. Oh, yes, enemies. There's a War going on, like I said, and the Faction are just the tip of the iceberg. You don't want to see what's lurking underneath."

146

There's something lurking beyond those words, not just subtext, but presence. Like a thousand writhing tentacled horrors trapped between moments, or a firing squad trained on you positioned between thoughts. Even the man hides something more. Or maybe less: there's something *missing* from him. You turn away in disgust.

"I'm trying to help you!" the man insists. He seizes your arm tight, uncut nails slicing a layer or two of skin off your wrist. "You bought that book from Annie, right? She's a fool of a witch. 'Sister-in-waiting', she calls herself. She'll never be a Sister of the Faction, but they tolerate her posturing and haphazard spellcraft because she amuses them. Occasionally, though, something valuable slips into her hands, like that book. She doesn't know its worth, to sell it like that. If she did, she'd have never touched the damn thing."

"So I got a good deal on it?"

"Nobody wants objects of power like people who already have more of them. And they won't hesitate to step right through you."

"Quite right, Little Brother Abel," a deep, posh woman's voice purrs, easing itself through the air with the same precision and impact as the sword that's suddenly pierced the man's chest. "Afraid you've made the same mistake at last. You never could run from us, you know."

"Camus!" he breathes. It's his last.

"Mother Camus, to you."

As Abel's body falls to the ground, it all becomes clear. His body tumbles to the floor, but there's no shadow swooping up to meet it. He never had one at all.

147

The woman beams up at you, pulling aside a familiar skull mask. She's middle-aged and twinkly, but bound in blood-red lipstick and a stark white suit. More red seeps across it moments later: the small burst of a man's blood, drawn with precision. "I'm afraid I'm not supposed to let you keep going with this, either. You're such a little person, it was hard to track you down, but Abel here did take you out of time, away from all the other confusing little signals. It's a bit conspicuous."

This can't be happening. You clutch for straws: "Sisyphus has time travel. We'll go back and stop you."

"You really thought you could break Sisyphus out, did you?" she laughs. "We have time travel, dear, and you don't have that luxury yet, do you? I'll just have to nip this one in the bud."

Hang on. Does that mean you've already—?

Before you can finish that thought, there's a sword cutting through your neck.

*But maybe she's wrong. Maybe you can go back to **136** and try again…*

Continued.

You charge into the bullets.

It takes all your strength to keep going for the second step, then the third, and so on. It's not because you've been hit—on the contrary, nobody seems to have expected you to be so reckless—but you can feel the rush of air being punched out of the way by whizzing metal projectiles, hear the scream as the sound barrier is torn apart in a thousand tiny ways. Every muzzle flash turns you into a deer in their headlights. The human body never evolved for a world of guns, but they're blunt and destructive enough to set off every defensive instinct ever evolved. None of them, unfortunately, are adequate.

Tell billions of years of evolution to shut up. Keep charging.

And you run.

And you run.

Until you aren't running anymore.

The door was open, you weren't even thinking when you dove through it and slammed it behind you. Barely cognizant, you've already slammed the lock shut. Fear won. Fear always wins. And maybe, today, it's kept you alive.

There's an angry policeman already hammering on the door; you can see him through the window. He's impossibly muscular, but his meaty fists barely make a dent. The glass is bulletproof. You knew that already, didn't you?

It's an unfamiliar window, but you recognise your surroundings soon enough. You are in a car. It's disappointingly empty of the useful stuff: no guns, no pepper spray, no handcuffs, all of that's been taken to apprehend you with. Some foolish policeman, though, forgot something a little more fundamental.

He forgot his car keys.

Maybe you're a great driver. Maybe you're not. Maybe you've never sat in the driver's seat of a car in your life, and only have the vaguest ideas how the damn things work from TV. What even *is* a clutch? Right now, it doesn't matter. You've been given a second chance.

Drive.

"Helicopter, 12 o'clock!"

"I know!" you hiss to your passenger, swinging a hard right. You careen through an ice cream cart, screaming kids dropping heaps of vanilla soft serve to the street.

"You didn't have to hit the ice cream cart!"

"Yeah, well maybe it was fun!"

And that's the truth, isn't it? There's so much you don't know: what the ritual is, who Sisyphus is, why *The Book of the War* is so important, and so on. But maybe you do know one thing, and that thing's why you're going through so much trouble anyway. You've been given a mission by a higher power, and you're taking the chance to live big, be special. It's kinda awesome.

The oppressive buzzing continues overhead. There's far fewer obstacles in the sky to hold the propellered menace back. In the shattered prisms of your remaining rear-view mirror, you see a gun turret slide out the side. Someone looks pissed off and very ready to end you.

"Cops!"

"I see them!" you snap. There's a line of police cars across this road, blocking your way once more. They've given everything they've got to this chase.

Hard right again.

There's an old church next to the road, great big stained glass window facing the street. Well, there was, anyway. You've driven right through it. A rainbow shower of glittering shards tumbles in your wake. Worshippers dive for cover behind pews. A preacher drops his mic and runs as fast as his little old legs can take him. You gun it, busting through the open doors behind him, flashing the lights and siren.

"Can I get out now? You're making me motion sick."

Seriously, who the hell is that in the back seat? You don't remember anyone sitting—

Oh for the love of Murphy's Law, it's Tucker the depressed screenwriter. This police car wasn't unoccupied when you stole it after all, and you weren't the only one looking for safety behind bulletproof glass.

"I'm on the run from the police, Tucker!"

"It'll only take a second!"

"So would a gunshot!"

Another hard right.

God, that windmill was close. At least the sheep got out of the way. Is it wrong that you care more about that than the priest?

"I'm going to be sick!"

You look around at the decently upholstered seats. "Try not to!"

Tucker retches a reply. You turn on the radio. That's quite enough of that.

So, are you going to run from the police?

"Hell yeah." **160.**

"I am a decent, law-abiding citizen who surrenders to cops." **128.**

Continued.

The mailbox is just around the corner.

"It's all to do with blood."

It's a familiar site, one of those places you walk past day after day without ever taking it in. It's just a thing you do, until suddenly it's over. Today, you suppose, is the day it's over. Or was it over yesterday, and you never realised at the time?

You hear his whispers now. He speaks the truth. You can feel the witch blood churn through your body, making you strong again. No, making you stronger. Blood is power.

Yeah, you sold the key with everything else. It was a dumb move. But come on, you've got that secret spot you hid spares in, everyone does. Failing that, pick the lock, that always works on TV. There's probably a good YouTube tutorial for any lock nowadays.

"Blood is just a fluid in the body, full of impurities and waste and viruses and, yes, biodata, but also full of symbology. The ancients saw how life stopped when blood stopped, or how draining it drained life. And where enough people believe in a symbol, there is magic. The vampires of old knew this, and they taught me. Blood is the strongest magic, and you've drunk enough to know true power. Now we can speak properly."

The lock won't open. God dammit.

"Why won't the damn lock open?" demands Godfather Sisyphus, King of Ephyra, trickster of the ancients, prisoner of Faction Paradox.

"I don't know!" you say.

"Make it open!"

153

You start to punch and kick the mailbox, desperate to follow Sisyphus' orders. He knows power. Power saved your life. He will give you more. The mailbox is in pieces. There's a policeman staring at you.

"Oh crap," whispers Godfather Sisyphus, King of Ephyra, trickster of the ancients, prisoner of Faction Paradox, into the deepest corners of your soul.

"I think I'm gonna need you to come with me," says the cop.

To go with the nice police officer, go to page **2AA**.

GODFATHER SISYPHUS DEMANDS THE LITTLE MAN'S BLOOD. **155**.

Continued.

You pick up a shard of the shattered mailbox. Hey, this is sharp. You could do some damage with this.

The policeman stares at you like you're crazy. He is, unfortunately, entirely right. This does not stop you from pouncing and slicing his neck open in a single leap, nor you drinking your fill from his veins.

Actually, it kinda tastes crappy. Vampires must have miserable lives. You're glad you're only a blood-sucking renegade cultist of a *completely different kind*, in training.

"Whoa, dude, you didn't need to drink *it. Come on now," says Sisyphus.*

"You want me to do a blood ritual to free you from a cosmic prison, right?" you ask. "Let me be the judge of what's weird."

"I chained up a god of death one time, so they made my life so miserable I wished I was dead. Even then I didn't resort to drinking blood *on the regular."*

"But you did drink it."

You feel the mental impression of a noncommittal hand gesture via brain whispers.

"You gonna finish that, bro?" some random guy asks. He looks ragged and dirty, but there's a gleam of power in his eyes. A too familiar power.

"What? Ew, no," you reply, having finally decided the blood drinking is indeed too weird.

"Cool. You da man." Ragged boy grins, showing fangs, and chows down on what's left of the cop.

"We don't have time for this. Collect the book from the wreckage and prepare my ritual!"

"What is the ritual?"

He tells you.

It's insane. It's bloody. But you're game to try. It'll take some work to get the sacrifice in place, and you'll want a chance to flip through the book to check it out, but you think you know how to—

"Whoa, hey, you aren't leaving, guy," ragged vampire bro continues. "I'm still hungry."

You stop. You know exactly what that means.

"Oh for crying out—"

You never get the chance to cry out. You're vampire chow.

*Go to page **157** and get in the god damned police car. Edgy prick.*

Continued.

Everyone has a Will. Statistically speaking, William was at some point the second most common name in Australia, the fifth most common name in the United States, somewhere up there in the UK, for royalty if nothing else, and while, admittedly, it doesn't even chart in China, there's probably a good reason for that. Basically, you probably can think of SOMEONE when you think of the name Will. Whoever you thought first, this is them. Your Will. Insert pronouns as applicable.

Your Will is not free. Your Will is sitting handcuffed in the back seat of a police car, next to you.

Oh yeah, you're also handcuffed. You struggle, not that it does much good. You're not Houdini. Unless… well, you do have a mysterious key, don't you?

"Hey Will," you whisper, "can you reach my pocket?"

Where there's a Will, there's a way, right?

Will shrugs. "What good would it do? The law's harsher if you resist, and you end up in the same place."

Helpful.

Out the window, you see trees pass. You're moving somewhere, whatever that place is. The police car cruises down street after street, the threat of bars lurking at the end.

"You don't mind if I put an audiobook on, do you?" asks the policeman. "Need to study, I'm going for a classics degree. Bunch of my coworkers are huge racists and I just can't deal anymore."

You make appreciative, concerned noises. The more he rambles, the less he hears you escape.

"Anyway," Will whispers, gesturing to the stereo, "you already know this story. You can listen again if you want, though."

"...even as the trickster king was chained in the pit of Tartarus, he was the consummate charmer. 'How do these chains work, oh great Thanatos?' he asked, as though impressed by the thoroughness of his imprisonment."

"Don't let them trap you forever," he whispers.

Never. You will fight your way out of anything. It takes work, but you've maneuvered in ways you never imagined.

"As Thanatos explained, Sisyphus seized his chance, binding the god within his own prison..."

The grooves of the key bite into your tongue. Nearly halfway there. So intent are you on the task, the story washes over you. Time races by, until...

"...his cheating of death was thwarted, but Sisyphus had other plans. He instructed his wife, upon his demise, to hurl his naked body into the street. When Persephone found his battered nude body in the river Styx, she..."

There. The grooves are lined up with your cuffs. It's time to slide it in.

You push. Nothing.

Will looks at you sadly. His eyes are somehow deeper than you've ever known Will's eyes to be, simmering with a knowing regret. Will knew this would never work.

"You're trying the wrong lock, it'll never let you out," he says. "But there's always more to the story."

You look to the chains around Will's wrists. It seems wrong to seem them tied up, almost as wrong as it is to be bound yourself. Maybe you could try another lock after all?

Will nods. "Sure, you're trapped. That's a fact. But you can still choose how to fight the inevitable."

"And so the boulder became Sisyphus' eternal punishment. He was forced to push…"

The boulder. How could they know about the boulder?

"What is this?" you demand of the cop.

"It's just my textbook! Sorry, myths can be pretty morbid. If you want, I can change it—"

"Attention, all patrol cars. Armed robbery suspect escaping in stolen police car via docks. Please intercept, over."

"Officer 260610 on it, over," the cop answers.

The car lurches into life with renewed purpose, pulling you into yet another strange adventure. Though you're no closer to your goal, you have to admit, you're enjoying the ride.

"What do you want?" asks Will, dragging you back to the terrifying now.

You have the power. You can finish the story of Sisyphus and rediscover your master's secrets. **160**.

Or, alternatively, you can let Will loose and see what happens. Either way, it's a new frontier. **171**.

Or you can just quit. **128** *awaits…*

Continued.

"Fish!" shouts Tucker.

You flip on the windshield wipers, fish guts slopping across the glass and tumbling into your car's wake. You know about the fish. Shut up, Tucker. You drove through the storage barrel on purpose.

Is this where you were?

Tucker is screaming. You remember Tucker, right? The annoying screenwriter with an existential crisis? You turn up the volume to drown him out.

"There once was a king named Sisyphus, ruler of Ephyra, later Corinth," explains the voice on the radio. "And while he was powerful, as any ruler inevitably is, his real power was in his wits. For Sisyphus was a trickster, and he set his sights on no less than death itself."

The docks are in chaos, and you're the cause. Tyres screech against wooden piers and crash over market stalls as you race along the water's edge. A faint gurgle behind you is all that's left of the closest pursuer. You cornered quickly. They didn't. They're getting a much closer encounter with the fish now.

But there's more. Always more. You zoom around a corner, tyres almost slipping over the edge. The water waits hungrily for you to screw up.

There's little time to scan the area for an escape route. You just see one outlet street after another, each full of flashing lights. There's no way inland. But maybe there's another option?

"After betraying Zeus' secrets to a river god, he was sentenced to an eternity in chains. But…"

160

SCREECH.

You race around a corner, tires drowning out the words. Even in the noise and the chaos, your brain fills in words of its own. It can't possibly be the same Sisyphus, can it? Are these the chains he needs your help to be free from? It seems wrong that a figure out of myth could be begging for your help via some pulp sci-fi book, but somehow, you just feel they have to be the same. It's like there's a piece of Sisyphus in you that's been urging you on, one there all along that you're only now starting to feel.

"...with the bestower of death in chains, great task on hold, all death stopped, including Sisyphus' own. In exchange, they made Sisyphus' life so utterly wretched and hopeless, he wished death would return."

"I know that feeling," says Tucker.

But these are old legends, surely. Where's the mention of Faction Paradox? What about time travel? What about the hovercraft racing towards you with some sort of giant cannon affixed to the front?

Hovercraft? Seriously?

"Stop the car or we will fire!" shouts a voice over a speaker.

You gun it. What else is there to lose?

"After the second time cheating death, Sisyphus was punished by the gods for his trickery. He was sentenced to push a boulder up a hill for all eternity. He believed his cleverness was loftier than Zeus himself, so he could never again reach those heights, despite always trying."

Oh god, you're trying.

Your phone beeps with a notification. Payment processed. The package is in the hands of the mail system now, and your fate is in the hands of the gods. Or of Sisyphus. Or of your own future self. Now would really be a good time for you to prove it all works out and you got yourself some time travel, right?

"And as a particularly spiteful punishment from the god of death, Sisyphus was cursed. Every time the boulder neared the top, no matter what new, brilliant scheme he devised, the great stone would slip away from him, and roll back to the bottom of the hill, crushing him along the way."

Ahead of you is nothing: it's the end of the pier, dark water waiting. The hovercraft races alongside you. Looking inland, it's a wall of cop cars. The whirl of rotors above is no help, either. You're surrounded.

"But maybe Sisyphus was too addicted to his own cleverness. Maybe he knew something nobody else did. Maybe he just liked the pursuit and the challenge. Because, some say, as he went about his futile labors, even after centuries, he could still be seen smiling."

And, you think, maybe he knew the future.

A woman stands on the dock. She's alone and unarmed, the only civilian left amidst the panicked fleeing. She places a skull mask over her face. Where do you know her from? A name flashes through your brain: Mother Camus, of Faction Paradox.

Open the window. Talk to her. **163.**

She has a sword. A frigging sword. Close the window before she uses it! Come · *on now!* **167.**

Surrender. **128.**

162

Continued.

"Come on," Mother Camus says. "You know what you've done. You know why you have to be punished."

What did you do? You robbed a bank, sure, but that's petty human crap. She's some magic time travel cultist.

"Faction Paradox," you say. You don't know why you're saying it, but the words fit.

Tucker gapes like the fish surrounding him. "Faction who?"

"We're a resistance movement to the architects of history, standing against the tyranny of cause and effect," Camus explains, grin looming from beneath the skull's decaying teeth. "I'd say we don't make a habit of meddling with little people, but we do. It's rather our bread and butter. The most beautiful paradoxes come from the smallest of butterflies. But what *you've* done, well, that's not little."

"I haven't done anything," you protest. "Not yet!"

"The bank thing doesn't count?" Tucker scoffs.

A silence, accompanied by the rushing of wind. In some dim part of your brain that can still process additional levels of surrealism unfolding around you, you notice Camus is keeping up with your car on what can only be described as a "rocket segway." Even the hovercraft pilot looks fairly awe-struck. Or maybe that's just her power, holding the chase in a moment of grace while she confronts you one last time.

The rest of your brain is focused on something more important. You haven't done it *yet*. And maybe with this path, you will.

Because maybe you've already had the power of time travel. Maybe you've already freed Sisyphus. This is just how you got there.

"Anything you do, the Faction can undo. You know that, right?" Camus continues.

"And I can change you changing it," you retort.

Tucker buries his face in his hands. "That's playground logic!"

But Camus agrees. "That's how time wars begin."

"The ritual," you begin, plans forming in your brain that will have always come true. "What is it? How did I free Sisyphus?"

"Books are living things, especially the right book. They grow with you, colonising your thoughts, which change their words in turn. You never fully understood that, did you? Now you're paying the price."

"It's always been paid," you reply. "And I win."

Continue. **Win.**

*Or go back to **128** and face the consequences. It's your last chance.*

You choose to trust fate. Camus fades. But in her place are so, so many guns. The police are here, and the moment of grace is over forever. You've made your choices. These are the consequences.

You hit the gas.

A thousand guns fire.

The car plunges into the water, and sinks without a trace, dragging you, Tucker, and the story of Sisyphus into the depths.

GASP.

The water's flooding in through the open windows. The car's tilting down, plunging so fast into the cold. It's pulling you with it.

GASP.

Tucker is beside you. He's not looking good. There's a massive hole in his chest. The chair behind him is sticky and crimson, and now it's oozing into the water. You're drowning in his chum.

GASP. Your mouth fills with water and blood.

All is black.

"It's a very simple ritual," Sisyphus explains. *His voice is distant. Nonetheless, there is power in it. "It only takes two ingredients. You have both at hand."*

"I have nothing," you reply. "I'm drowning. The police have me cornered. There's no way out."

"You have the blood, and you have the book. In other words, the keys to the cell, and the getaway vehicle. All you need is time. I can give you it."

Getaway vehicle? Blood? Whose blood?

And so he tells you.

"Trust fate," says the trickster. *"These pages have already been written. See them through."*

Closed windows kill. At least where underwater cars are concerned, it's the worst case scenario. You probably read that once, somewhere. If the doors are closed and the windows shut,

165

it's a very, very long wait for the interior to match the pressure of what's outside, and by that time, you'll be too deep to do anything.

You're in luck. You left the windows open. But you're still a long way down. Unconsciousness only held you in its embrace for the briefest of moments, but any delay is huge when adding metre after metre of dark water to push yourself through to survive.

The water is far too dark, when moments ago the sun was shining. Sisyphus has given you a taste of his gift, skipping you off into the night.

As water cascades over you through the open windows, you turn, curious to see what Tucker makes of it all. Instead, something has already been made of Tucker: the bloated, swollen corpse of a man several hours drowned. You hope he finished the script in his head, even if it never made it to the page.

No time to mourn. You push yourself to the surface, faster and stronger than you've ever swum before. The docks are still a mess, and faint police lights still lurk amidst the wreckage, but the chaos is over. Like Tucker, they've clearly assumed you dead. The gift of time was all you needed. It's time to go home.

Go home. **175.**

Continued.

The woman, Camus, snarls from the other side of the glass. It's predatory but defanged, in the manner of a proud carnivore before jeering kids in the zoo. Swords were never made to pierce bulletproof glass and metal.

"Who the hell is that?" Tucker screeches.

"Camus, I think her name is," you answer. "I feel like I've met her before. She's with some cult, Faction Paradox. They want to stop me."

"So they're a cult that works with the cops?"

The car jerks suddenly, wheel wrenching itself side to side without your guidance. Swords cannot pierce bulletproof glass, but they can pierce a tyre.

You seize the wheel tighter. Maybe there's still time to take back control of where it's going, to stop things from ending like—

The car rolls over and over again, and is swallowed whole by the water. You only see this for a moment. The steering wheel rushes towards you, meeting your skull with a resounding crunch.

When a car goes underwater, time is crucial. The faster you get out, the better odds you have of surviving, because wait too long and the pressure differential will seal you in. Opening a door or window before you go under can save your life. So can special tools designed to shatter the windows and let the water in. You don't have one. And you never had a chance.

There's flashing lights above, a hundred emergency vehicles watching you fall. But even with all that backup, nobody expected you to take a dive. Least of all you.

You're trapped, and consciousness is fading fast. It's a long way down.

Down.

Down.

The man wakes in the hospital. He's swallowed a lot of water, and several major organs will never work right again, but he is unmistakably alive. A kind nurse has wrapped him in a blanket, and a cop who'd rather be studying classics sits with him.

This man is not you. Nobody here is.

Tucker shivers, his body worn beyond belief, but still there, still working, unlike yours. "The person who kidnapped me. Are you sure they're dead?"

"Yeah," says the cop. "But you're not. That's something to be thankful for, right?"

Tucker isn't sure. Tucker never will be. But Tucker knows one thing. He's alive. And that little fact is the biggest thing in the universe.

Maybe he'll actually be inspired to write for a change.

You are dead. Tucker is not. But maybe you can cut a bargain with fate.

How steep can the price be? And what kind of monster are you to pay it?

Find out. *163.*

Continued.

Not many know this.

There is a crack in the

universe is cracked.

It used to be a problem

is an ongoing problem

never happened anymore.

The car hits the bottom. You're unconscious as it fills with water. This is how you died. If only you had some way to break the windows.

The crack runs

Every place.

through everything.

Sometimes you

Every moment.

see the crack

Sees you.

A white, jagged line

malevolent smile in the wall.

You are drown.

Drowned.

ing.

The universe is cracked.

Tucker gasps for air beside you, tears streaking down his face. Today, he will live. But yesterday? Tomorrow? Two steps to the left? Time is unravelling. Where time unravels, the crack grows.

What's on

Nothing.

Everything.

the other side?

The weight of the water is great, but the weight of infinity is far greater. Both are crushing down upon you, squeezing all in their path, damaging everything beyond all recognition. Time compresses and snaps. But where there's a break in the glass, there's a way out.

You are dead.

Imprisoned.

Forever in the Boulevard

No ending.

The crack

Unless.

widens and swallows you whole.

Free.

Continued.

"Look out the window," says your Will.

The world is bathed in red and blue. It flashes across the water, and gleams across the metal chains in your hands as you slip the key into the lock. You give it a turn as you look up, and the chains fall away.

Out the window, you see you're by the docks. There's a police car racing along the water's edge, pursued by countless more. The driving is erratic, scattering barrels of fish and stalls of knickknacks everywhere. You'd never drive that poorly.

You see the driver's terrified face, bathed in the same two hues as all else now is. Blood red and corpse blue bisect a face, and it is yours.

"You understand, don't you?" says your Will, stretching almost lazily despite the chaos, rolling out the wrists that had once been shackled. "We're neither of us free. But I appreciate you giving me the key."

"You're not my Will," you realise.

"It's just a form to take to get what's needed, same as I've always done. I've been trapped on the Boulevard for far too long."

Not-Will reaches into his pocket, pulling out a gun. "Sorry, Charlie!" they shout cheerfully, blasting out the brains of a hopeful student of history who will now never know a future. The cop slumps to the side, dead in the driver's seat, but the car keeps on driving, like an amusement park ride on a track.

"I'm only here to free Sisyphus," you say, trying and failing to ignore the stench of death.

"And where do you think you are?"

"The docks?" A pause, searching the monster beside you's incredulous face. "Earth?"

You watch through the window as the car plunges into the water, dragging a very scared you along for the ride. How is this possible?

Not-Will laughs, long and hard. "You've not been there in a very long time. *This* is the Boulevard. You've been here a very long time, for an attempted breakout you arranged years ago. Amazing, isn't it, what a Faction Paradox prison dimension can do to your perceptions? You've been running up and down these enclosed timelines for centuries. One of their more artful cages, I must say."

They seize the key in their hands and slither—*slither!*—for the car door. Their features grow more and more monstrous with each passing moment, until every part of Will you ever knew has been corrupted beyond recognition. Well, every part except the gun still in one of their dozen fetid claws, now trained on you.

"It won't kill you," says Not-Will. "You'll just wake up back at the start, and try again. But you'll never get anywhere, and with this key, I'll be getting everywhere. Goodbye."

Time, whatever it means anymore, seems to slow, as gnarled talon plunges down on trigger. There's an explosion of blood.

The blood is not yours. It's Will's, or whatever Will had become.

"Apologies for the inconvenience," a woman's voice coos. "Normal running of your cell has been disrupted by an outside force. We'll have a reset along in a moment."

You recognize that voice distantly, and a name floats through your brain along with it. Mother Camus.

"Hello, dear. Yes, it's me. We could just do this automated, or use the spirits, but I take your imprisonment rather personally. I hold grudges against people who kill me."

No matter where you look, you fail to see the source of her voice. Things continue to play out around you like a preordained ride, the car drifting through carefully choreographed chaos, thrilling but somehow ultimately fake. Testing a theory, you climb from the moving car. Your feet never hit the ground. You just float above the tarmac, drifting through the endlessly shifting, endlessly moving, but never-ending Boulevard.

"You too, Sisyphus," she continues.

"Me?"

"I see you trying to wriggle out with your servant again. Wasn't becoming a text-based lifeform bad enough? Get back to your cell already."

"No, wait, please, I—"

With a sound like the flipping of a page, his presence vanishes from your mind. His words live no longer in you.

The sky is shifting, too, and that's where you see it. It's the face of Camus, looking down at you with scarcely contained glee. You understand now how an ant in an ant farm feels when the child comes to stare. A massive hand reaches down from the heavens, plucking away the withered body of Will, and with it, a single glittering key. You faintly see the numbers etched into it for a moment, but they're blurred and distant, and they, like the key, soon fade beyond the clouds.

"Not sure where this came from," she says, "but it won't bother you anymore. Are you ready to get back to your punishment?"

"Let me out!" you scream.

"Now, now, that's not a Sisyphean attitude," Camus tuts. "Now give me a smile for the camera, and say, hm, not cheese, what's the other one? I know! 3… 2… 1… boulder!"

Boulder?

A rock falls and crushes you to death.

*Go back to page **125**.*

Continued.

Homecoming at last. Your clothes are torn and soaked through, and you absolutely, absolutely reek. Your neighbors don't recognise you; they recoil with the faintest veil of detached dignity, the way your standard Karen does from a fetid beggar. As you slop, still soaking, toward the familiar door, you hear voices from within.

There are people in your home.

"I didn't know they could do that!" one woman protests.

"You've never known what anything you meddle with does," another snaps. "But you did it anyway, because you wanted our attention. Well, congratulations, witch. You've got it."

"I just wanted to join the Faction! To be part of the divine chaos!"

You creep up to the door, listening. There's two of them. You ease your fingers in to pry the door open just a crack, enough to see inside. One's in a pantsuit and a skull mask, the other in a velvet ren faire cosplay dress. The one in a suit has a sword. The one in the dress doesn't, and seems very keenly aware of that fact. Tears burst from her eyes, like blood so easily could from her veins at any moment.

"Faction Paradox isn't about chaos, my pretty little fool. It's a liberation movement, and movements need organisation. We have structures. We have systems. We have prisons and criminals. You've blundered in and nearly set a dangerous one free."

"I'm sorry, Mother!" the younger, weaker girl pleads, clutching at the older woman's hem.

"I know you are, child," Camus coos. She leans in close to the girl, lips almost brushing her forehead. "And I'm sorry for being so cross."

"Thank you, Mother."

"Sister-in-waiting Annie, please wait no more."

"Thank you, thank you, thank—"

The sword slices through her throat before she can finish the words. The interior of Annie's neck gushes all over your floor.

"And you," Camus snaps, turning to the door, "where do your packages usually show up?"

You try to run, but she's at the door faster than you could ever believe, slamming it tight on your arm. You're trapped.

And, to your great shame, you have no choice. You tell her.

Camus sits with you on your sofa. The sword rests at her side, but you have no doubt if you tried to grab it, or tried to make a run for it, it would gut you before you could blink. She flips through *The Book of the War* with only mild curiosity, clearly having seen it all before. For your part, what you see seems strange and wonderful, pages concerning such bizarre things as Babels and Parablox and other, intriguing words you don't understand at all.

"I'm curious," she says, closing the book, "how was this going to break anyone out of the Boulevard. Did Sisyphus ever tell you?"

"There's a ritual," you say.

"I know rituals, child. I don't know this one. Explain."

"Sisyphus says every book lives with you. It's not just words on a page, it's the way your brain processes them, the time you read them, the headspace you're in, all of it. By reading these words, they become part of you. They travel across the dimensions, from 2D right into your head."

"Fanciful, but irrelevant," Camus sniffs.

"There's a creature, though, living in that book. Sisyphus called it a conceptual entity. It exists as words on a page and words in your head. He doesn't want to come back as a person, you see, not anymore. He wants to come back as an idea. He's already inspired legend in this world, and he wants to use that creature's powers to become it."

"A Shift? In *The Book of the War*? The damn fool Celestis don't know the trouble they're making. But if we screw with their plans, doomed as they ended up being with that whole unpleasant meme incident, the Homeworld might take notice. The last thing we need is their attention with the War as it is."

She's scared. She fidgets anxiously, one hand scratching her neck, the other drifting towards her mouth to gnaw her nails. Occupied. That's all the opportunity you needed.

You seize the sword and plunge it into her heart.

She's screaming still as you write the words upon the page in her blood. Well, words of a sort. The strange runes Sisyphus gave you fall somewhere between ancient Greek and something grander, strange circular patterns beyond your understanding. But you know their meaning.

Blood is life, and there's a power in blood. The vampires of old knew it. The Faction knows it. The ancients with their sacrifices knew it, though never how to use it. But now you know it, too. Now you can use that power. And this isn't just any blood, it's the blood of a long-time member of Faction Paradox Mother Camus. There's enough power and history in there to tear open a path to their realms.

Camus has fallen dead, but the screaming hasn't stopped. Now the pages are screaming. You can see it printed on the book, a long "aaaaaaaah" and "please don't" and "look, friend, I've been tortured enough already, just leave me alone" and such. You keep writing.

The blood starts to wriggle, too. It comes together, forming a circle which then wriggles around the page like bacteria in a petri dish, or Pac Man in his maze. It moves steadily around its new territory, devouring the black text in its wake. Maybe there's other copies of the book out there in which the idea of this Shift lives on, but here, at least, it's been devoured by a larger legend.

The crimson squiggles rest, at last, coalescing into letters. *"I am Sisyphus, and I am free. And I give you the gift of time."*

"That's the thing about time, though." A woman's voice breaks into the room, accompanied by a woman's body in a clean white suit. Mother Camus. She looks disdainfully at her own corpse on the floor. "It's never what it used to be."

"I killed you!"

"You tried. Your master Sisyphus has been locked away too long. There's been a War, you see, one fought in time as well as space. The Faction's old tricks are the norm now, but we've been crafting new ones, discovering exquisite new paradoxes to survive and resist. We have no more time for relics."

178

The blood red words snarl in response: *"I am no relic. I am a legend. I am Sisyphus, the man who tricked death himself, the king of—"*

Camus closes the book, and all goes white.

You're standing in the street, looking at Camus. You don't understand, but you almost do. You've been here before. It always comes back to the street in the end.

"You could have gone free," she says sadly. "You were a pawn in his game, but you went too far. That's what this War does, too. It eats up the little worlds, burning them to never-having-beens and once-weres. But you've struck against the Faction, and even killed one timeline of me. There have to be consequences."

"How long have I been here?"

"Time is different here. You're here as long as you want to be. You can turn back your choices, view the errors of your ways. But you made the choice to take on Sisyphus' boulder. You can push up any hill towards freedom, but it will always take you back here. Back to the Boulevard."

"I just want it to end."

"There is no end," says Camus. She steps aside as a boulder rolls slowly but steadily towards your toes. You can feel the cracking already, as you have so many times. "But if you'd like, try again."

You fall to the street. The tarmac is bumpy and jagged, it's digging into your back. It hurts. You should stop it doing that. You never will.

But maybe if you keep on trying, somewhere, somehow…

Continue to page **125**.

The Oracle

Philip Marsh

Cousin Ravensbrook stepped into the viewing gantry. The room was empty, so she walked across and looked out the window at the street below. Or rather, at the Boulevard that stretched far into the distance.

"Greetings, Cousin."

Ravensbrook spun around. Standing behind her was a heavy-set man with the face of an aging brick-layer and the make-up of a twenty-something New Romantic. It was a startling combination, but fair play to him for carrying it off.

"Er...hi."

"Welcome to the Boulevard. I'm Cousin Gaval and you must be Cousin Ravensbrook, one of the newest recruits to our little family." He walked over to Ravensbrook and looked out of the window. "Quite a view, isn't it? Almost endless, stitched together out of streets from all different times and places, all across the multiverse. And we are charged with keeping it ship-shape. An important responsibility."

"Is it?"

"No, not really. That's why they send all the Baby Goths here as one of their first duties—unlikely to stuff anything up. No offence."

"None taken. Although you don't look much like a baby anything—how come you're still here?"

"Well, someone's got to supervise, haven't they? Although, honestly, when I joined up with a bunch of time-travelling anarchists I didn't expect to end up on what is basically a dull desk job, but hey. I mean, my old mate Colin used to wear eye-liner and listen to The Cure but he worked for the Inland Revenue

so I guess guy-liner and dark clothes don't protect you from admin. Anyway. They've explained to you what we do here, right?"

"We imprison people."

"Criminals, yes."

"Isn't that a bit authoritarian for a bunch of anarchists?"

"Hey, you've got to have some rules."

"Absolutely—otherwise there'd be anarchy."

"Exactly." Gaval paused, suddenly feeling as though he had stepped in a trap but being unable to see it. He ignored the feeling and pressed on. "There are people out there who mean us harm, and then there are people who want to use the powers they get from joining the Faction to do harm unto others— the wrong others, others we could do with staying in one piece. So, we lock 'em up here, each in their individual cell with its own individual hell generated for the occupant. It's our job to monitor the Boulevard and make sure that all it's all working properly—that there's no breakdown in the systems, no doors open that shouldn't be, no intruders, that sort of thing."

"And are there ever any problems?"

"Almost never. A tech fault here and there, the occasional visitor to escort. Once in a blue moon, frankly."

"Visitors? I thought no-one was allowed to see the prisoners?"

"Ah, there, you see—you don't know it all, after all. You're right that the prisoners aren't allowed visitors...but I never said there are only criminals in the cells."

"So who else is there?"

"Occasionally, we come across people who haven't done anything wrong but who we need to...keep secure. Either because they're too useful to us to let

181

wander, or because it would be too dangerous to us if they were to fall into the wrong hands, tentacles, suckers and/or assorted protuberances. So we keep them securely here as...guests."

"Guests who have to live in a cell and can't leave?"

"Basically, yes. Come on, let me show you around, and while we're out I'll introduce you to one of those guests. We call her The Oracle."

As he led Ravensbrook through the temporally elongated street that comprised the Boulevard, Gaval regaled her with stories about the various occupants of the cells they passed. Or at least, he thought he did—Ravensbrook had quickly stopped listening. Eventually, however, Gaval brought them to a stop outside a particular cell and put his hand on the release mechanism.

"Hey, you're going to actually open one up? Is that...allowed?"

"Oh, it's allowed in the right circumstances. But this cell is different anyway—no common criminal inside this one. Nor uncommon, for that matter."

"The Oracle?"

"Correct. Now she's not a criminal and not considered dangerous, although care has to be taken. When she has visitors they have to go in in twos, just to be on the safe side. Now, how many of us are there?"

"Two."

"Well, that's perfect then. Now, I'm going to open this door up, we're going to have a butchers, and then we close the door and move right along, ok?"

"Ok."

"Ok. Ready? Here we go then."

The poster was clearly new—the bill was hardly damaged by the dusty breeze that tugged at it, attempting to coax it from the nail that held it in place against the sign-post.

THIS WEEK!

THE LEGENDARY ORACLE

FORTUNES REVEALED! QUESTIONS ANSWERED!
FIND THE TRUTH IN HER EYES!

ALL FOR 2 CREDITS PER PERSON.

TOWN HALL, 7PM, MON-FRI.

CHILDREN HALF PRICE!

Equally eye-catching were the two people reading the poster. Both were dressed in black robes with their faces covered by skull masks—or, at least, that was the least concerning of the two options.

"What d'ya think, Mother?" asked the taller of the two. "Fancy a night out before we leave?"

The slighter figure turned to her companion. "I doubt we will find much amusement in the charlatanism of a backwater planet psychic, Cousin."

"That's a very cynical view to take," the first figure replied. "How often have the Faction found promising and talented initiates on exactly this kind of planet? Especially considering the fact that we're only here in the first place because of concerns about possible Enemy activity."

"...of which we found no evidence. Still, I take your point, Cousin Gottfried. Although I cannot help but feel that your desire

183

to attend this event has more to do with it being an opportunity to sample the local ale and, if things go well, the local females."

"Mother Hangaku," he replied, mock-hurt. "My suggestion was motivated purely by a strict sense of duty and scientific enquiry. After all, if this advert is any way accurate, who knows what mysteries this Oracle could unlock? Of course, a few drinks and a little flirting would act as excellent camouflage."

The irony of someone dressed in black robes and a skull-mask concerning themselves with blending in was left without comment.

"Very well," replied Hangaku. "I suppose you deserve an evening of relaxation after the dry days we have spent on this planet for no result. Let us see what this Oracle has to show us."

Patience was the kind of town that would be flattered to be described as 'two horse'. In effect, it was little more than the hub of the few businesses and official buildings that served the homesteaders whose houses and farms were spread out across the surrounding acres. The Sheriff's office, the local saloon, the barber shop, the small hotel, the various artisans required to carry out repairs and forge new items. It was odd, Hangaku reflected, how human colony worlds so often retreated into old patterns. Behind this old-world façade hid the technology that allowed the colonists to travel millions of light-years across space—functional rather than fantastic, admittedly, and with an understandable desire not to repeat the over-reliance on polluting technologies that drove so many to leave the home planet in the first place. There was no need for the mythology of the American West to have travelled with them, yet they had been unable—or unwilling—to leave all of this behind. Hangaku understood the value in traditions as well as anyone, but this was a mythology invented years after the fact, in films and cheap pulp novels, not a noble style of civilisation based on centuries of accumulated wisdom. And as for the clothes…

Cousin Gottfried had begged her to wear a prairie dress. He claimed it was because cross-dressing in a retrograde community held together by mutually agreed codes of behaviour would attract unwanted attention, but she suspected it was more for his own enjoyment. Not that she never dressed in a traditionally feminine manner, but while in an unknown environment she liked to be wearing clothes she could fight in. So, she was dressed in trousers, a shirt, waistcoat, and a broad-brimmed hat, with her long silver hair tied up out of sight.

In contrast, Gottfried, having made the case for blending in, was managing to attract far more attention than she, simply by the swagger he had acquired as soon as he had stepped out onto the main street. She had told him to tone it down, but he was clearly enjoying himself far too much acting the part of an alpha male. She only hoped that his display of machismo didn't invite a challenge from any of the denizens of the town.

His delight was mercifully cut short when they reached the Town Hall and found that not only were they not serving any alcohol at the , but that no beverages of any kind were allowed to be brought inside. Hangaku hid her smirk far better than Gottfried hid his dismay.

The hall was decked out with enough chairs to seat about a hundred people, and to her slight surprise the hall was full—they were lucky to be able to sit together. The stage at the front of the hall was empty except for a small marquee, large enough for maybe two people to sit comfortably inside.

185

Cousin Gottfried was looking decidedly glum. "I didn't kill my own grandfather to end up sat on an uncomfortable chair with no wine, women or song," he complained. "This is like selling your soul to the Devil and getting nothing but an eternity of prayer meetings in return."

"Well, it looks as though *this* prayer meeting might be getting started," Hangaku replied, nodding towards the stage, on which a large man in a loud coat and mutton-chops was walking towards the centre.

"Excuse me, folks," he said in a voice as large as his stature. "If you could all take your places, the Oracle is ready to come to the stage. She asks that those of you wishing to access the wisdom she channels to queue up in the wing here, and to have your money ready to be collected by her assistant before you go up."

Immediately, half of the crowd squeezed their way down the rows of seats to the wing. When they had settled, a lady walked onto the stage. Hangaku observed her closely. The first thing she noticed was that there was nothing showy about her—short, slight, with dark hair, dressed modestly in a black dress with white trimmings, and nervously acknowledging the waiting crowd before entering into the marquee. If this was a show business performance, the star of the show was lacking in pizazz.

Cousin Gottfried had obviously had the same thought. "I'd have expected something a little more...well...*more*," he said. "Some music when she came on stage, a snazzy costume that makes her look mysterious...Hell, she could have borrowed our robes, they'd have been perfect. Where's the stage-craft, the razzamatazz?"

Hangaku did not reply, staring instead at the stage. The first of the townsfolk, a woman, was being escorted up to the marquee, and then disappeared inside. Although there was nothing to see, all eyes were on the dark cloth box, and there was a palpable sense of expectation. Nothing could be heard from within—whether because the curtains deadened the sound or because The Oracle's technique was silent, Hangaku could not say.

After a couple of minutes, the curtain was pulled back and the lady re-emerged onto the stage. She moved uncertainly, as though dizzy, and the master of ceremonies stepped up and took her by the arm.

"Don't worry folks," he boomed, "the lady is quite alright. Seeing the hidden truths of the universe is no laughing matter, and can put a bit of a strain on the nerves. It's quite normal and the lady will be right as rain in no time at all. Now, can our next punt…er…I mean, seeker of truth step up while I help this lady to her seat?"

Cousin Gottfried leaned forward in his seat, suddenly interested. "Fake mediums and the like are usually exhausted—or play exhausted—by the reading, but not the people *having* the reading. Unless she's a stooge to set the atmosphere up?"

"I don't think so. I think it could be very important that we find out what exactly happens when this Oracle reads a person's future."

"Right, well we'd better get a move on before our star—if somewhat dazed—witness leaves the building."

"You go and speak to her—I have a more direct approach in mind."

"What do you mean?"

Hangaku smiled.

"Please, take a seat."

"Thank you."

Hangaku sat down on the empty chair. The only other furniture in the tent was a small table, and the chair on which sat the Oracle. Up close, there was nothing obviously unusual about her—she was in her late twenties, her dark hair streaked prematurely with grey., her features slightly pinched.

"You must be tired."

"I'm sorry?"

"You must be tired. The queue to see you was very long. It must be tiring to have to see so many people and give them what they want."

"Oh…yes. Yes, it is." She spoke uncertainly, obviously unused to her customers caring enough about her to ask how she was feeling.

"It can't be easy, being presented with so many questions, night after night. It must be draining to have to engage with the other world for such a long stretch across the evening."

"Your concern is very kind but really, I am quite able to cope with the process," the Oracle replied with a polite frostiness, which made it clear that Hangaku had over-stepped the mark. "And in fact, I don't have to find anything. You do the searching, I am merely the conduit for your search. Do you know what it is you desire to find out?"

"I came here looking for answers."

"Are you sure you know the right questions?"

"I think so."

"Then we will begin. Look into my eyes."

Hangaku winced internally—surely not some cheap mesmerism trick? But she followed the instruction and stared into the Oracle's eyes. They were light grey, with tiny flecks, like pin-pricks of light. No, not pale grey, dark, and darkening all the time. And the flecks of light got brighter, and formed oddly familiar patterns…Of course! Stars, constellations she had seen before. She was seeing…everything. The entire universe—past, present, alternative, future. And it all *made sense*. She was seeing the infinite, all in the same tiny space, and she could discern it all distinctly, without confusion. She saw herself as a child, in warrior training, her first battles in the Emperor's Army, battles she didn't take part in because she joined the Faction and went back in time to stop herself enlisting, her alternate lives projected like films on a screen…

And then the vision was gone and she was back in the tent, the Oracle falling back from the table, her hand over her eyes. Hangaku stood and made her way around the table. "Are you alright?" she asked.

The Oracle ignored the proffered hand and the question, looking up with fear in her eyes. "Marc…I mean, John!" she shouted. "John, come here!"

A moment later the man who had taken Hangaku's coins ran into the tent.

"Thea, what…" He stopped, taking in the scene—the Oracle on the floor in a panic, with Hangaku standing over her. She could not blame him for leaping to the obvious conclusion. "You'd better leave—*now*, before I lose my temper and give in to the temptation to use *this*." He pulled his jacket to one side, revealing the pistol in his belt. Hangaku weighed him up instantly, as she

189

did any potential threat. His aggression was for show, he didn't carry himself with the confidence of someone who felt themselves in charge of the situation, despite the weapon. She didn't doubt she could have sliced him in two before he could draw it. However, she decided it would be best to withdrawn quietly. She stood, nodded her acquiescence, and left the tent.

"You won't believe what that woman just told me," Cousin Gottfried said. He had been waiting for Hangaku outside the front door of the hall and had accosted her eagerly when she emerged.

"She said she looked into the Oracle's eyes and it felt like she was looking into the cosmos itself, but was still able to make out the thing she was looking for."

"Oh...yeah, basically." Gottfried was clearly deflated by her lack of surprise, and Hangaku regretted being so abrupt.

"Please, tell me more," she said. "I suspect my own experience with the Oracle was rather different to the norm." She gave him a rare smile. "But not here. Back at the hotel."

They sat in Cousin Gottfried's room—Gottfried on the bed, Hangaku in the uncomfortable chair. It would have to be a lot more uncomfortable than it was before Hangaku would even consider sitting on the bed with him. Such familiarity was not to be encouraged.

"So," Gottfried explained, "she sat down in front of the Oracle, and the Oracle did the eyes thing like you said. Apparently, she had had suspicions for years that her husband had been bang...I mean, had been unfaithful with other women, including a friend of hers. So she asked the Oracle to show her. She said she had a

190

moment in which everything was overwhelming, as though someone poured the entire universe into her head at once. But then she found herself focusing in on her husband and her best friend doing a horizontal dance, *sans* clothes. And then she was back in the room, feeling a little detached from reality—which is understandable I guess. When the session was over it was like waking from a dream, and all she could remember was what she had seen about her husband."

"Interesting."

"How was it for you?"

Hangaku explained what had happened in the marquee.

"Do you think your time sensitivity had something to do with it? She's unlikely to have come across someone with such extensive experience of time travel on a back-water like this."

"Quite possibly—it must have been something about me that was different, and that is the most obvious thing."

"So…what now? We've established that she's genuine. But what does that lead to, if anything?"

"It leads," she replied, "to the most important mission I have ever found myself undertaking for the Faction. We must convince her to come with us."

"And if she refuses?"

"Then take her without her permission."

"Kidnap her? Isn't that a bit strong?"

Hangaku looked up and met his gaze. "Strong, Cousin? Don't you appreciate what we have found here?"

"Look, I get that she's gifted…"

Hangaku sighed. "Cousin, as always you see only what's in front of you, but miss the big picture. The Oracle is not simply 'gifted'. Don't you see the implications of her gift? Imagine the Faction were to become aware of a possible threat to its safety. With the Oracle in our possession, we could immediately establish the nature of the threat. Instead of sending agents out to investigate backwater planets, we could just see what was out there by looking into the Oracle's eyes."

"Ok, I get that but she's not a piece of tech, she's a sentient being."

"But in the wrong hands she becomes worse than piece of technology—she becomes a weapon. Because everything we could use her for to protect the Faction, our enemies could also use to attack us. They could use her to locate our bases, to examine our plans, identify our agents. She is not only too great an asset to ignore, she is too great a threat to ignore also. And such a threat leaves only two options—co-option, or elimination."

"You'd kill her?"

"To protect the Faction? Of course. It is not as though you haven't killed for the Faction before, so I'm surprised at your squeamishness."

"Ok, ok. But assuming we have to kidnap her—what do we do with her then? Where do we keep her?"
"Where else, Cousin? The Boulevard."

"No!" Cousin Gottfried jumped off the bed so suddenly that Hangaku almost knocked him to the floor out of instinct. "You can't be serious. The Boulevard? Bloody hell! You know what they do to people there. Even if she is a potential risk she doesn't deserve that."

"Not everyone who stays in the Boulevard experiences it as a punishment."

"But she'll still have to spend the rest of her life in a cell, with no-one but ghosts for company."

"Cousin, the matter is settled. Help or leave me to do it alone if you feel able to deal with the consequences of disobeying."

"Ok, ok," said Gottfried, holding his hands up in surrender. "I'll do it. So, what's the plan?"

It had been decided that they would make their move that night. Cousin Gottfried had been in favour of waiting—after all, the Oracle was scheduled to be in town for a full week. But Hangaku had insisted—after the shock she had received this evening, the Oracle might decide to cut her losses and run.

Hangaku was pleased to have such a strong argument for immediate action. She could tell that Gottfried was not at all happy about the plan, and the longer it took to put into action, the more his doubts would grow. In fact, she suspected that he had proposed the delay to give him time to come up with a way to persuade her to change her mind—or to think of a way to sabotage the mission. The former would not happen, the latter could not be allowed to—or the Cousin himself might have to be dealt with. She did hope not.

It had been a particularly gruelling night for Thea. She had felt that there was something odd about the final customer the moment she laid eyes on her—and it wasn't because she was dressed as a man. When they had made contact, instead of being able to channel her to what she wanted to see, it had felt like she was at the centre of a raging flood. The confusion was so overwhelming that she had been compelled to break contact for fear of being swept away by it. This had never happened to her before. It frightened her. John had shooed the woman out of the booth and brought Thea back to their room at the hotel to recover. She had gone straight to bed and passed out almost immediately.

She woke in the middle of the night, the only light coming from the lamps on the street outside the window. She could hear John breathing beside her, untroubled by her waking—sleeping heavily as usual. She opened her eyes and let out a startled cry which jolted John from sleep, before his hair was grasped by the figure at the bed side who pressed some kind of blade to his neck. But when she asked who the intruders were, it was the shadow seated in the chair at the foot of the bed that answered.

"We have already met, Oracle," came the voice she had first heard that evening—the final customer.

"What do you want?" she asked.

"I didn't get my money's worth earlier."

"You want a reading?"

"Well, I did pay for one and it was somewhat curtailed. However, despite that I think I saw all I needed to."

"Who are you?" demanded John, "and what do you...?" His question was interrupted by the increased pressure of the blade against his throat.

"Please don't interrupt our conversation. The Oracle is important to us; you are not and you would do well to remember that. However, to answer your first question, my name is Hangaku, a Mother of Faction Paradox, and the young man with the shadow-blade pressed to your man's throat is Cousin Gottfried."

"Faction Paradox?" said Thea. "Never heard of you."

"We are a very secret organisation," replied Hangaku. "Sometimes we are so secret that we don't even exist. And then we exist again. I appreciate that it can be rather confusing."

"Confusing…yes. That was what I saw when I tried to guide you. Confusion. Chaos. It was…overwhelming, I could feel myself being lost in it, drowning in it. That was you, wasn't it? Something to do with this paradox that you mentioned. You did that to me."

"Yes, but not deliberately I assure you. It did not occur to me that I myself might interfere with the process."

"Then what is it that compelled you to break into my rooms in the middle of the night?"

"Curiosity. I would like to know about your gift—how long you've had it, how it first manifested itself, what the extent of it is. I appreciate that these are not sociable hours, but I was concerned that you might choose to leave town before my curiosity could be satisfied."

Thea glanced nervously at John, who was still being restrained by Gottfried, before looking back to Hangaku.

"It started when I was sixteen years old, nine years ago. I grew up on an isolated farm—my parents had moved to the planet because they had been fed up of living in tiny cubicles in the megacites. So, when they arrived, they chose a homestead as far away from the nearest town as was practical, and stayed away from the other settlers, except when they needed to trade with them. Even my boyfriend Marc was only grudgingly accepted in the house.

195

"One day we were sat at table, eating our evening meal, all three of us. I had been feeling strange for a few weeks but I put it down to growing pains. At one point, my mother asked me a question. I turned to answer it and our eyes met. Immediately I could tell that something was wrong. She did not appear panicked or distressed—rather she seemed lost, or as though instead of looking *at* me she was looking *through* me. Worried, I tried to get her to respond to me, not looking away from her for a moment, but it was not until Father got out of his chair, walked around the table and turned her to him that she finally came out of it. She tried to speak but her speech was confused. Hardly a word did she manage before she would stop and start again, as though having to choose between several things to say all at once. Father insisted she go to her bed for rest, and it was only later that evening that she managed to explain anything of what had happened to her—that she had had her eyes opened to the universe. She went to the hospital, underwent all the scans and tests, and the doctors found nothing unusual. It was put down to sunstroke from working in the fields, and forgotten about.

"As the years passed and I grew older, I began to feel different, as though I had an extra sense that I could access. I began experimenting with my abilities. I convinced friends to sit for me, as though testing out a childish parlour trick, having sworn them to utmost secrecy. Time and again, I was successful—to the point that I frightened Marc away. I soon learned that it was impossible for anyone to remember all that they had seen, but if they were to focus on just one particular thing, they could carry some version of that knowledge back with them. However, in my enthusiasm I was careless, and Father learned of my experiments. Furious at me for recklessly dabbling with a power I didn't understand, and without Mother being there to protect me having died earlier that year, he me threw me out of the house. I left with Marc, and used my gift to pay our way..."

"No Thea," interrupted John, despite the knife at his throat. "Not Marc. You had already split up with him—you just said so. You left with me. And your mother was—is, as far as we know, still alive. She was there when you left the house with me, but your father wouldn't listen to her."

Thea looked confused for a moment. "But I remember…she died of a brain tumour. I was sat at her bedside when she died, I remember it. But…no, you're right. I remember turning back as the carriage took us away from the house and seeing her holding a handkerchief to her eyes. And I turned to you, and you took my hand and squeezed it, and then held me while I cried. I remember it so clearly and yet I also remember her dying."

"You must have dreamt it," John suggested. "One of those vivid dreams that eventually become inseparable from memories. You're just tired, that's all, after everything that happened today."

"Yes…yes, you're probably right. Well, as I said, the two of us began a transitory life, using my gift as a source of income. All was well, until you entered my booth tonight."

"And what happened then?" asked Hangaku, "From your perspective, I mean."

"You felt different to me, as though you were not one person at all, but numberless variations on a person, all existing at once. Just looking at you was dizzying. And then when you actually sat for me…"

"Normally, I do not share the vision of the person sitting. I open up the way and help guide them to whatever it is they want to see. But the moment I made contact with you, everything stopped making sense. You were there in front of me…but you were also never born. And you were born, but you died in childhood of starvation on a colony world. And you survived malnutrition, but

197

died fighting in the Emperor's Imperial Guard. And you defected from the Imperial Guard and assassinated the Emperor...all of these things, contradictory but all equally true. My vision no longer made sense."

"It's the Observer Effect," said Cousin Gottfried said, turning to Hanguka, but never relaxing his grip on John. "Or a version of it, anyway. Everyone she has ever been in contact with has had a linear relationship with time. But you don't—you're a walking paradox, as well as a time-traveller. And now she's seen you, it's changed the way she perceives space and time. She's seeing a whole new layer of the universe."

"Can't you make it stop?" asked Thea.

"I doubt I could...even if I wanted to," said Hangaku. "However, I can instead make you an offer."

"What kind of offer?"

"Come with us. The Faction will help you to understand and develop your skills. Believe me when I say that no-one understands paradox better than we do."

"And what would you want in return?" said John. "Somehow I don't think you broke into our room in the middle of the night and held us at knife-point just to do us a favour."

"We would help you control your gift in return for your using it on our behalf. We have enemies, and it would be very useful to be able to see what they are doing at all times, without the use of our agents. Given that we are simply asking you to do what you do already, I think that would be a fair exchange."

"So, you come here, disrupt Thea's gift, and then offer to repair the damage you did, but for a price? Sounds like extortion to me."

"Remember that knife to the throat that you mentioned a minute ago?" asked Cousin Gottfried "Well, it hasn't gone anywhere, so shut it."

Thea considered for a moment. "You say I would need to offer you access to my gift as payment. For how long? And where would you want me to be during this time? I assume I will be kept somewhere I can be found at short notice?"

"In other words," said John, anger outweighing caution, "she'll be kept a prisoner until you have defeated this enemy of yours. At which point you'll probably find a new enemy, so you'll continue to need her to help you against them. She'll never be free of you, will she?"

"There's no point, John," Thea said. "We aren't exactly being given a real choice, seeing as they have a knife to your neck." She turned to Hangaku. "I'll come."

"Cousin," said Hangaku, "please escort the gentleman out and see that he leaves. If he remains here he may give in to the temptation to do something noble but foolish."

"Come on then," Gottfried said, moving the knife away from John's throat. This was all that he had been waiting for—he grabbed Gottfried's arm and threw him across the room. Hangaku was fast but she could not react quickly enough to stop John from reaching under the pillow and pulling out a gun. The first shot slammed Gottfried against the wall. The second caught Hangaku in her stomach from point blank range...just as her *katana* pierced his. The two fell to the floor, the carpet staining red beneath them.

"Cousin," said Hangaku, "please escort the gentleman out and see that he leaves. If he remains here he may give in to the temptation to do something noble but foolish."

"Come on then," Gottfried said, moving the knife away from John's throat. This was all that he had been waiting for—he grabbed Gottfried's arm and threw him across the room. Hangaku was fast but she could not react quickly enough to stop John from reaching under the pillow and pulling out a gun. The first shot slammed Gottfried against the wall. The second had fired wildly into the floor, as John's aim had been thrown by Hangaku's *katana* piercing his throat as he pulled the trigger.

"John!" Thea jumped out of bed and hugged the already lifeless body of her husband to her, his blood staining her white nightgown.

"I'm sorry," said Hangaku, "but I had no choice."

"No," Thea replied. "And neither do I." And she turned, raised the gun she had picked up from the floor next to her husband's body, and shot Hangaku in the chest.

"I'm sorry," said Hangaku, "but I had no choice."

"No," Thea replied. "And neither do I."

And she turned, raised the gun she had picked up from the floor next to her husband's body, and shot herself through the head.

"No," Thea replied. "And neither do I."

And she turned, and raised the gun she had picked up from the floor next to her husband's body, but Hangaku was already moving towards her and kicked it from her hand. Grabbing Thea by the shoulder, she spun her around and pinned her to the floor.

All the fight had gone out of Thea but it never hurt to be careful, Hangaku thought, as she tied the girl's wrists together.

"Now, I'm going to take you to..."

The Boulevard. The door of the Oracle's cell open. Cousins Ravensbrook and Gaval standing inside, entangled in webs of infinite possibility, transfixed, watching the story of the Oracle, seeing themselves transfixed watching the story of the Oracle, seeing themselves transfixed watching the story of the Oracle, seeing themselves transfixed watching the story of the Oracle...

"Get that door shut!" commanded Mother Hangaku. "What has happened here?"

"Cousin Gaval was showing Initiate Ravensbrook around the Boulevard in preparation for their stint monitoring it," said Cousin Beatriz. "It appears he decided to give her an actual look at the Oracle. And now they've become part of the story and can't separate themselves from it. Certainly there's no way that anyone can go in there to get them out safely."

"It was a terrible breach of protocol. No-one was supposed to go into that cell."

"I agree. Although, perhaps if we had warned the guards about what had happened to the Oracle they wouldn't have been so tempted to go in to see her."

"Impossible. If our enemies were to find out that we do not, in fact, have access to the visions of the Oracle, it might embolden them. That information must be known to as few people as possible—and guards should have enough discipline to stick to the rules."

"Do we know yet what did exactly happen to the Oracle?"

"We think so. The Oracle had never been in contact with paradox before she read me. As a result, she saw an ordered, stable universe. But when she looked into me, the whole of the multiverse opened up to her, all the divergent time-

201

lines and events that didn't happen but could have, that did happen but might not have, and those that both did and did not happen. It was too much for her—she was overwhelmed and could no longer guide anyone to anything, except her own personal story, including the way it started to break up after she met me. We then made it infinitely worse by bringing her here, where she was completely surrounded by those disruptive forces. Ultimately, all those possibilities began to seep out of her very pores until they filled the cell. How long was that door open?"

"A few hours. We checked when Cousin Gaval didn't respond to a request for access."

"A few hours? Who knows what possible futures and alternate pasts might have escaped in that time. And then there's the Oracle herself..."

"You mean...she's not in the middle of all that?"

"She might be. Or she might have found a way to escape from all that confusion. Or worse—to control it somehow. Perhaps what we're seeing is the possible present in which she stayed in the cell, but in reality she escaped."

"You mean...she could show us any potential reality and we'd never know we weren't looking at the real one?"

"Perhaps. We might be as helpless as the two wretches we found inside the door, while the Oracle prowls the Boulevard with who-knows what powers."

"So what do we do?"

"The only thing we can do. Live like this is real, until we find out that it isn't."

Hangaku turned and walked away.

202

The Fixer

James K. Maddox

Thirty years in Hollywood, and Tucker still hasn't found his niche. He's tried his best to create one, to fake it as he's sure that others must do. But while he's purchased this penthouse with his producer's salary and filled it with gaudy and tasteless things—a private pool for a man who cannot swim, the four-poster bed in which he now lies, tangled in sheets which cost too much and in which he wakes itching and chafed—he cannot believe the illusion. None of it helps him to feel secure. None of these objects disguise his concerns, that he's been an imposter all along. That the people around him are not his own.

And then there's Dodie, snuggled against him, resting her head on his furry chest. He counts himself lucky to have her at all. Every producer needs a starlet apprentice, a girl to use, and be used by. Tucker clings to buoyant clichés, terrified of sinking. Clings to Dodie now.

"Did you ever see *Starpocalypse*?" It's something to break the silence, perhaps, or maybe he just likes to hear himself speak. A movie producer should.

Dodie wriggles and stretches. "The name rings a bell, but it doesn't appeal." Her dark hair tickles at his skin, and he brushes it away like an insect. Dodie's accent is nearly charming, full of New Jersey twang. Charming, too, how she'll listen to him. He can talk about movies, his hopes, his fears, his dreams of secret societies. This last point, he supposes, is the mid-life equivalent of wanting to run off to join the circus.

"It might've been before my time." This is Dodie's particular talent; she knows what to say to urge him on, will *um* and *ah* when he needs it most.

"Yeah," he says. "I guess you're right." Doubtless she is. Dodie is half of Tucker's age, less than half, nineteen to his fifty-two. She doesn't have adolescent memories of cruising between theatres to find the best movies; algorithms spoon-feed her desires.

Starpocalypse is kitschy by modern standards, full of model work and Matte landscapes. But the movie, with its pretty actors fighting evil warlords in shimmering, revealing outfits, still holds a place in Tucker's heart. He sees it as a template for the current trends in teenybopper movies, and he's sure that a sequel would be a success. But sequels are prospects best handled with care, and Tucker isn't sure that he'd pull it off.

"I bought the rights a while back." He tries not to look at his own reflection, huge in the mirrored ceiling. "I could make a sequel, if I wanted to, but I'm running out of time. If it doesn't happen soon, the rights will revert."

Dodie's eyes are glazing over; she has no love for legalities. But he knows she likes this more than his other obsession, and so she says, "You should focus on that. Forget the secret societies."

He slides out from beneath her, letting her head thump onto the mattress. "What can I do? The movie is stuck. The treatments don't work. And I need my own interests, too."

Dodie's over-plucked brows are threadbare lines, arching now as she speaks. "Take up swimming, or yoga, or tennis. Cabals and cults will get you nowhere."

"That's where you're wrong." He opens a drawer in a hideous dresser, pulls out designer underwear. He looks back at Dodie while he puts it on, stumbling around on the thick shag carpet. "I've got a hell of a lead."

Only one of her eyebrows is raised up now, and somehow this is worse. Tucker prepares to go on the defensive. "Who," she says, "are you trying to join now?" She gathers the sheets around herself.

Perhaps she's right to be sceptical. He's flirted with joining several groups and come away underwhelmed. Dodie thinks he's wasting his time, though she'll never come out and say it. She has to stay on his good side if she aims to get what she wants from him.

"The Faction." He finds a shirt, off-white and crumpled, and squeezes into the sleeves. "I don't know a lot about them, but I think they worship skeletons. A real-life cult, and a spooky one, too. And their sense of style is to die for."

The eyebrow drops. "Go on."

"They wear skulls for masks wherever they go, like it's the *Día de los Muertos* all the time. Robes, too. They're occult, I think." He's done as much research as possible, but the details still elude him. No matter. It won't be long until he finds out more.

Dodie bites her lip. "Sounds like the kind of people Stevie Nicks might have hung out with. I bet they cast spells and call each other wizards."

"Cousins, actually." He's worked out that much. Works his way, now, into trousers. "And you might not be wrong about spells. The Faction has power. A lot."

"I don't know. I never heard of them."

205

"Dodie, honey, that's the point." His fingers fumble and he bungles his tie, has to undo it again. His hands are trembling. Anticipation, surely, for the meeting he has planned after leaving the penthouse. Fear, too. Perhaps. "The Illuminati are common knowledge. The Scientologists are hardly better. And everyone's uncle is a member of the Masons. I need something more."

Dodie sits up in bed and looks at the ceiling, converses with Tucker's reflection. "You're sure that this isn't a joke? Sneaking through the shadows in Halloween masks and pretending they're all related—it sounds kind of silly to me."

He's ashamed to tell her that this is the appeal, that a familial group is just what he needs.

"Yeah," adds Dodie, "it's got to be a scam. They'll dress you up and cover you in gore while they stand nearby with a camera. Then they hawk the results to the press." She looks back down. "Or the cops, I bet."

Cautious of the law is Dodie Sinclair. For reasons that Tucker finds hard to pin down. He's worried what he'll find if he starts to dig.

He conquers the tie. "You're overthinking. If the Faction was a scam, I'd know about it. There are people in Hollywood who've dealt with them. They used to have a presence here."

"And where did you come across these guys?"

"I know someone—by reputation. A fixer. He gets things for the folks in this town, me included."

She pouts. "And what about me?"

Tucker ignores her. "According to the grapevine, Kincaid is the best. Whatever you want, he can get it. For Norma Jeanne, it was peroxide dye. Reagan in the White House? Kincaid's work."

"Sounds too good to be true."

"He costs a lot."

"I guess he would." She leaps up from the bed. "Can't I come?"

"Dodie—"

She puppy-dogs her eyes. Tucker's stomach turns. He's tempted, though, to bring her along. He's heard what happens to the people who displease Kincaid. Some Dodie-shaped fodder between him and the fixer might come in handy if the bullets start to fly.

But he shakes his head. "You stay where you are, okay?"

He stands at the door, fully dressed and ready to go. Clothes make the man; he's heard that often. When he steps outside, will people see through him? Other things are also said: you can't polish a turd, for instance. Tucker might be too bald, too wrinkled, too sweaty, to ever fit in with the people around him, let alone to fit in with the Faction. He can only hope that Kincaid is inured to the glitz and the glamour of the town. And that his help doesn't incur debts too hideous to pay off.

When Tucker leaves, Dodie stretches out across the king-sized mattress. Her bare legs snarl in the duvet. She clicks the television on but the channels bore her; she checks and rechecks the time. Tucker didn't tell her when he'd be back.

Her eyes stray to the suite's front door, but she quickly kills the thought. She's forbidden from going outside alone. There's a risk, Tucker says, that she'll stumble into scandal.

That's nearly funny. If only he knew.

But she sees his point. Her career is so fragile as to be non-existent, and the last thing she needs is added drama. Dramatic enough, she thinks, to be sleeping her way up through the Hollywood ranks. Not that Tucker just wants her body. When they first met, he was divorced and bored, too drunk to notice her upturned nose and pouting lips, her dated heroin chic. If he grew to love her in the cold light of day—and she's almost certain that he hasn't—then he loves her for one thing: her ears.

Dodie hates them, huge and soft like mezzelune. No casting director could favour them. Tucker, though, doesn't care what they look like. As long as she listens to his petty complaints, his heart-to-hearts and his future schemes, he's happy to keep her around. It's a small price to pay for an industry foothold.

But Tucker's influence has its limits. She's done a dozen auditions in the past few months, and several directors promised to call. Bullshit. The only person who ever phones is Jennifer, back across the country in Ocean City, sick of tourists and yearning for a drink. Jennifer is her mother, if she wants to get technical, though lately she'd rather not.

She checks her phone anyway, sees missed call grapeshot from Jennifer and ugly silence from the studios. She deleted her mother's details months ago, but she can't bring herself to block the number. As consistently difficult as Jennifer is, it's nice to feel wanted by someone. Tucker's suite might have a sauna-sized tub and room service to order, but the maids are never talkative. It's not occurred to Tucker that she might feel lonely, but then he probably doesn't give much thought to her feelings. She thinks that he sees her as just another item, something to prop up his image.

Perhaps it wouldn't hurt to return a call. Just one, or two, from time to time. So long as they avoid one troubling subject. Ha. Fat chance of that, but Dodie needs the contact, will shrivel away without it.

She keys in the memorised number. The screen is cold against her cheek. After a moment comes Jennifer's voice, the same slow drawl that Dodie is trying to exorcise, three thousand miles away and three hours in the future. "Dodie," she says. "Dodo, baby. When are you coming home?"

Dodie cringes at the pet-name, cringes at Jennifer too. The woman wasn't there when Dodie needed her. She was present only in her disappointment.

"I'm not," says Dodie. "We've talked about this."

"Maybe you have. I'm not finished." They're skipping the small talk, circling.

"I don't know what you want me to do."

"You can't ignore what happened forever. His family—"

Dodie swallows. She should end the call before recriminations surge through the satellite links connecting mother and daughter. But spending the day feeling guilty is better than spending it feeling nothing at all, and so she drags things on. "I regret it, you know."

"Do you?" Scorn twangs in Jennifer's voice.

"You know I wish that it hadn't happened."

Jennifer deploys a tested jab. "You wish it hadn't happened because you think it'll haunt you. That your career will suffer if this comes out."

"I don't."

"You do. You'll trend on Twitter. They'll be out for your blood."

Pointless to argue, Dodie knows. Knows, too, that her mother is right. Dodie has the face for good-girl roles: she could star as a nun or a kind schoolteacher in some coming-of-age Oscar bait. Too bad, then, that she doesn't have the past to match.

She hates what happened, but she knows that she needs it, poison to draw on when acting. It helps her to weep on command. To weep in private, too.

"Listen," Dodie says, "I've got to go." She gropes for an excuse, comes up blank. "I'll call you back sometime, okay?"

Jennifer grunts. "You'll come home, too."

"Sure, I will. See you."

She puts the phone down. The past is a graveyard. The future is frightening. The only place for her now is the forever-present of the cinema screen, frozen on sinless celluloid, and she'd sell her soul as she's sold her body to be there for just a moment.

When he arrives at the fast-food joint, wrinkling his nose against the deep-fried air, Tucker can't help but wonder if he's come to the right place. The restaurant is all but deserted; there are more stains on the linoleum than there are customers in booths, and the waitress at the counter looks tired and listless.

Kincaid is in the corner of the furthest booth. He's a small man, with dark and close-cropped hair, and his off-grey eyes keep darting around over the top of his burger. A big eater, Tucker surmises. Dirty plates spill out before him.

The fixer looks up, shoots Tucker a smile. Leading-man teeth, blindingly white. Uncanny, somehow. Inhuman. "Granting wishes burns a lot of calories. You must be Mr Tucker. Pleased to meet you."

Tucker sits down opposite Kincaid and takes the man's hand. It shines with grease and tomato sauce. Once, Tucker would've been disgusted. But he's tired of Hollywood showmanship, and Kincaid's messy manners make a pleasant change.

"And you must be Kincaid. A.C. Kincaid, the miracle worker."

"A-dash-C; I value the hyphen. It's the closest I can get to a zero. But yes," he says, as Tucker wipes his fingers on a napkin, "I've been known to perform a miracle or three."

"That's why I'm here." His colleagues told him not to ask questions. But now that Tucker is seated in the booth, with his leg jiggling beneath the table and perspiration crowning his lip, his curiosity bubbles up. "How is it that you do what you do?"

Kincaid clears his throat, phlegmy from the greasy food. It sounds like an engine's dying breaths. "I made a deal with the devil."

"I've heard rumours that you are him."

"Do you see horns?"

"Maybe they're hidden. If you don't mind me saying, there's something about you. You look like a man with hidden depths."

Another flash of the knife-blade smile. "I think you might be getting warmer. But I've never met a singular devil. Just as geese come in ganders, devils come in Houses." He spreads his arms wide, threatens to send plates tumbling. "Now, Mr Tucker. How can I help?"

Tucker takes a deep breath. "What can you tell me about the Faction?"

Kincaid blinks then, caught off-guard. The smile falters for a fraction of a second, and then he gives a nod. "I know of them. I've dealt with them too, with the others, as well. I don't pick sides. I'm done with all that."

"I need to contact them."

Kincaid lets out a wheezing chuckle, slaps his hand on the table. Cutlery jars against crockery; salt and pepper tremble. "I see what you want. You want to make a movie. *Uncle Kristeva vs. the Homeworld?* I doubt that the Faction would care for it—it's hardly their finest hour—and the public would only be underwhelmed."

"No," says Tucker. "Not for that." His stomach gurgles. "I want to become a member."

The laughter subsides. An eyebrow cocks. "They're picky, the Faction. You'd need to be vetted. And you'd need to get their attention first."

"Tell me how, then. That's what I want. Don't get me in the door. I don't need a shortcut. Just tell me what I need to get their interest."

Kincaid's eyes flash like a cat's, but there's no sign of life behind them. "There's a tenet of Faction ideology," says the fixer after a moment. "As far as they're concerned"—he picks up one of the dirty plates, moves as if to hurl it at the wall—"this dish becomes valuable once I've smashed it."

"That doesn't make sense." He watches Kincaid place the plate back down. "Destruction for destruction's sake."

"Destruction for significance's sake," corrects Kincaid. "Think about the *Titanic*. Would anyone care about the boat if it had got to New York *sans* iceberg? Of course not. No shipwreck; no drama; no best-selling movie. No one would even remember the name."

"I don't have a *Titanic*. Just a sailboat." Bought because a producer is meant to have one, it now gathers dust in storage; the gentlest waves make Tucker retch. "What if I scuttled that?"

"I don't think that'll cut it. Things are given meaning because people care, and I can tell by your voice that you don't care for sailing. Tell me, Mr Tucker. What are your passions?"

It's a good thing, he thinks, that he doesn't love Dodie. But he isn't sure what he loves instead. The movies, maybe. Once. Sitting in a darkened room with a flickering screen, getting through his popcorn before the ads ran out, catching his fingers on the chewing gum beneath the seats. People say that Hollywood is a sleazy place, and Tucker knows that they aren't even wrong, but it's the glitz which he hates the most. So far away from the simplicity of that cold, dark room, and the chiaroscuro glow of the cinema screen.

"I'll try to think of something."

Kincaid nods. "As long as you cause a cultural kerfuffle, the Faction is bound to come knocking. I'd never say it to their faces, of course, but they're really not a complex bunch. All that separates an internet shitposter from a junior member of the Faction is that one wears a bony mask."

Tucker sits there, overwhelmed. What's he to do with this information? He feels as impotent as a movie extra.

"I'll try my best," he forces out, and the words seem flat and feeble.

Kincaid slides out of the corner booth, brushes crumbs from his sweater. "You're a movie mogul, Mr Tucker. I'm sure you'll be able to work something out."

That's easy for Kincaid to say, but nothing in the industry is working right now. That *Edwin Drood* movie is going nowhere. His latest comedy was almost a flop. The *Starpocalypse* sequel is at a grinding halt, and it'll take deft hands to bring it to birth without causing serious damage.

But perhaps, he thinks, he can afford to be rough.

When Tucker returns, he's got a searchlight grin beaming from his face. Dodie hasn't seen him like this in all the months that they've lived together. At first glance, she wonders if he might be drunk, or high, or maybe both, but on closer inspection he seems about sober. Excited, yes. Wasted, no.

"I've got it all worked out," he says to her, before he's even gotten his coat off. His arms get stuck in the too-tight sleeves, and Dodie gets up from the couch to help him. "Kincaid really is as good as they say."

She takes the coat and hangs it on the stand, an ugly thing, studded with glass and gold. "Is that it?" Her voice is dull. "Congratulations, I guess."

He doesn't answer her right away, but parries with a question of his own. "You remember what I said about the *Starpocalypse* sequel?"

"You said that it was stuck in development hell." The phrase is too cute for Dodie. She went through hell before coming here, and it's far worse than botched scripts and money troubles. "But you didn't want that guy to sort out a movie. I thought you went there for that cult of yours."

"This is for the Faction." He gestures to the couch and Dodie sits back down like a housebound, obedient puppy. She hates herself for doing so. Tucker goes to get them both a drink. Dodie squints at him. "I don't get it," she says. "You're going to make a movie with them?"

"For them." He squirts soda water into a glass and hands it to Dodie. She takes a sip and listens. "Critics be damned. Audiences, too."

"Hey," she says, "you need to slow down. I don't understand what you're saying."

He spends a minute or two recapping the details from his meeting with Kincaid. Dodie humours him until he concludes, "If the Faction wants me to ruin a touchstone, who am I to disagree? The *Starpocalypse* franchise is fish in a barrel, just waiting to be trashed with a terrible sequel."

Dodie narrows her eyes. "Think about this. A movie this bad could tank your career." Could easily tank both of their careers. A producer blacklisted for subpar pictures is no use at all to her.

"Listen, Dodie, listen." Stick to what you're good at, Tucker seems to say. He comes to sit beside her. "Movies flop all the time. It isn't going to be a problem. I'll hire a hack fraud writer to vomit up a script and shoot the whole thing against a green screen. Fill the movie up with lousy effects. Six, seven, eight months from now, *Starpocalypse 2* will hit theatres, and the Faction will have their sacrifice. They'll have no choice but to let me in."

Dodie drains the rest of her glass and puts her head on Tucker's shoulder. "There's something you're missing," she says to him. "What if people like it?"

"They wouldn't."

"They might. People these days will watch anything. You've told me that yourself."

"And I'm telling you now, there's no risk of that. It'll make *Plan 9 From Outer Space* look like *Citizen Kane*. This thing is gonna bomb so hard it'll tear a hole through the movie screen." He looks down at her, reaches over to squeeze her thigh. "And I want you to be in it."

Dodie would like to retain her dignity, to say, "No thanks, I want something more." To tell Tucker that she won't settle for less than a great script, some career-making role as a scientist or as a heart-of-gold hooker. But she longs for the relief of the silver screen, and her sense of self-worth has never been strong.

"Sure," she says, grins and bears it. "I'd love to be in your movie."

Tucker pulls strings like a puppeteer, but it still takes six months and a hundred favours for *Starpocalypse 2: Awakening* to hit the movie theatres. He scrimps on the redrafts, scrimps more on effects, and hires any actor who can manage the lines. Dodie gets her part, a minor one; he'd hate to stain her resume.

He reads the reviews in his air-conditioned office, with a crystal tumbler between his fingers. The cabinet of drinks in the corner of the room is full of whiskey, vodka, schnapps, but his glass contains grape soda. It leaves rings of condensation on the long, squat desk.

Many call the sequel a waste of money, destined for worst of the year lists. The cast takes a beating, but Dodie is safe, if only because the stars draw most of the complaints. The acting, says one site, must be seen to be believed. Another calls it "lobotomised". Tucker sips and continues to scroll. Some reviewers are kinder, or shills, and they blame the acting on a lack of real sets, or a script that would stump an Oscar-winner. That's hardly surprising. Tucker pushed a story ruptured with plot holes and weighed down with clunky exchanges.

He drains the tumbler and switches to a *Starpocalypse* forum. The users debate continuity errors, and a few brave fans devise solutions, welding the canon together. Tucker pities these basement-dwellers. That they engage earnestly with a movie which holds them in contempt almost makes him feel guilty. But the guilt is assuaged by the more militant users, several of whom demand that the studio fires him. One or two even call for his death. A blogger famed for her use of long words decries the sequel as the final betrayal, an attack on workers by the capitalist class. Someone on Twitter mourns their own childhood, apparently ruined by *Awakening*. Tucker snorts. Nothing can strip away formative years. *Starpocalypse* fans must be crazy.

Still. The Faction wanted a cultural quagmire. He has surely delivered.

He's baffled, though, by the people who claim to have loved the sequel. They praise the characters as strong and developed, characters flat enough to roll up and snort coke with. The camerawork is apparently inspired, although Tucker knows that it's amateur trash. Even Dodie declared the movie to be better than expected, and he still isn't sure if she meant that as praise.

Not that Dodie has any right to complain. Bomb or not, the movie has helped her. He closes the browser and navigates to his messaging app. He flexes his index finger. It hovers there above her name, a nail-bitten hummingbird. Time to tell her to pack her things. They've done all the can for each other. And anyway, he'll be gone from her soon, doing whatever the Faction does.

But before Tucker can place the call, the screen of his phone lights up. It takes him a moment to place the number. Kincaid. Tucker lets it ring for a moment or two. It wouldn't do to seem overeager.

When he answers at last, it's with bated breath. Kincaid has a voice like melted chocolate, rich and artery-clogging. Even over the phone, Tucker can picture his snake-charmer smile.

"Mr Tucker," says the fixer. "I hope I find you well."

Tucker's enthusiasm gets the better of him. "You've heard from the Faction, haven't you?"

The rustle of a nod comes down the line. "I've spoken with them, yes. But perhaps it would be better to discuss this in person. We could meet at the restaurant if that suits you."

Tucker thinks for a moment. "My penthouse is closer. Dodie, my protégé"—a pretentious word, but it seems to suit her—"is already there. She'll let you in."

Another nod. "Your penthouse, then. As soon as you can."

Tucker nods back, sees himself as a rhino jostling a rival for dominance. Locking horns. "You're an efficient guy, Mr Kincaid."

"Don't speak too soon," comes the reply. "We still have a few kinks to iron out. Assuming, of course, that you want to proceed. The Faction moves in peculiar circles. I'd hate for you to get in over your head."

Tucker bites his tongue. "The only thing that I'm getting into is one of the Faction's masks." Even if he wanted to give up now, there's no way he wouldn't finish this. His parents raised no quitter. Barely raised him at all, but still.

"As you wish." Kincaid clears his throat. "I'll see you soon, then, Mr Tucker."

Tucker puts the phone away and stands up. He has to lean on the desk; his legs are Jell-O. Somehow he makes it to the door, down the corridor, past the foyer with its potted plants. His receptionist has a big red mouth and all the same dreams as Dodie. He tells her to cancel his future appointments and then rings for the elevator.

In the underground carpark beneath the tower, Tucker's heart thumps double-time. Angina sparks in his chest. He misses the ignition when he does get in the car, and the engine doesn't start when he finds it. For a moment he thinks about walking home. It's just a few blocks. But movie men don't walk, they drive, and Tucker has no wish to stick out from the crowd.

All that stands between him and his fate is the rush hour swarm of Hyundais and Fords. Tucker revs the engine into life and drums on the steering wheel. The lights will switch. His life will change.

Dodie's in the shower; how far she's come. Poached starlet, puce-faced from the steam. Tucker delivered on the *Starpocalypse* front, and she had her part in *Awakening*. Not a big one, sure, but it's a

219

stepping stone. Already she's had calls about commercial work, and grubby men have emailed her, asking if she has an agent.

She kills the shower and comes out of the bathroom, wrapping a towel around herself. If Tucker's need for the finest things has one advantage, it's that his linen is second to none. It almost makes her think twice about leaving.

In the living room she lets out a yelp. There's a man sitting there on Tucker's couch, but there's no way in hell that it's Tucker. No toupée, for a start. Instinctively, Dodie gropes for a weapon, wraps her fingers around a table lamp. Not exactly a Smith & Wesson, but better than nothing at all.

She does her best to sound in control. Acting classes come in handy. "What the hell are you doing here?"

When the man looks up, he blushes at her, and then he averts his gaze. "My name is Kincaid," he says, once she's quieted. "I imagine that you must be Dodie."

He's easier on the eyes than she expected. She takes a deep breath and relaxes her grip, and then she speaks through a big false grin. "Jeez." She tightens the towel. "You might at least have knocked."

Tucker must've given him a key. "Oh?"

"I mean, it's polite."

Kincaid smiles. "Is that what you want—for me to be polite?"

Dodie pulls a face at that. She goes back to the bedroom and throws on a robe. When she comes out, Kincaid hasn't moved. She studies him.

"Can I get you a drink?" she asks, playing the part of the good hostess. But the fixer only shakes his head and stares at her with ore-grey eyes.

Something tells her to keep her mouth shut. Kincaid is distant, but somehow charming, like every mistake she's ever dated. And Dodie Sinclair, moth to a flame, can't help but fill the silence.

"Were you an actor?" she says at last. He has the face for it, too good to be true.

"Aren't we all?"

She smiles. "In this town, sure."

He returns the smile, but it leaves her chilled. "On this planet, Dodie. Your gentleman friend wants to meet the people who write the scripts." He pauses and looks, for a moment, as though he's said too much. Then he adds, "But you never told me what it was that you wanted."

She demurs. "It's not like it matters. I'm not famous enough to work with you. Not yet anyway."

The shark-toothed smile stretches wider. "We've time to kill. I can make an exception. What can I do for you?"

Dodie blinks. There's an easy answer, but it's hard to explain to the people she trusts, let alone a total stranger. Yet Kincaid has a certain magnetism; secrets strain towards him. And she's longed for someone to talk to. What happened cost her most of her friends, and Jennifer too, and if she keeps it corked up there's a chance she'll explode.

Kincaid doesn't just attract secrets. He looks like a man who can keep them, too. Like a naughty child, also, who knows that his actions will lead to mischief.

221

"It's a long story," she says, and Kincaid nods, urging her on. "I guess I wanted attention. I was stupid, of course. You are at that age."

"I wouldn't know."

She takes a deep breath. "I dated boys—older boys—and I carried drugs for them. I was fourteen, then. Was I meant to say no?" The stuff was cut with something worse, but Dodie didn't ask questions. The cops did, though, when they caught up with her. "Someone died. The police came calling." Strange, she thinks, to tell him all this. He has the eager ear of a Catholic priest.

"I got off lightly on account of my age." Still Kincaid is silent. He sits on the couch, face split by a smile, slowly reeling her in. He's a Cheshire Cat with a fishing pole. "The judge thought that I was a victim, too. But the dirt is there on my permanent record if anyone bothered to dig."

A stain on her record and a stain on her conscience. Dodie isn't sure which haunts her more.

"You asked me what I wanted. I guess I know. I want that part of my life just—gone." She pictures her history as a massive body, and her guilty moments as tumorous growths, threatening to spread from past to present. Surely Kincaid, fixer to the stars, can root out her corruption? "You must know people who can do this stuff. Lifestyle coaches. Therapists. I don't know. You tell me. I guess I don't know a lot of things, but I know that I want this gone."

At last, he speaks. "Tell me, Dodie. Why do you want this?"

She feels light-headed, like she's glugging wine. "I wish I could say that I want it gone so the guy never would've died. I wish to

God that I was pure like that. But you must get a lot of selfish requests."

"It's true," says Kincaid, "but those are my favourites." He pauses, studies manicured nails. "I'll need to dot the 'i's and cross the 't's for a major reshuffle like this one. You're sure," he adds, "that this is what you want?"

She swallows, nods. "It's for the best."

He looks up from his nails and into her eyes. The seasick feeling intensifies, and the room seems to slosh through her field of vision, like a painting that's running in the rain. Trippy stuff, she thinks about saying, but the words catch in her throat. And then her throat seems nowhere at all.

They say that your life is meant to flash before your eyes. But Dodie's just swirls around and around, like a delicate garment in a tumble dryer, memories shredding to silence.

The traffic is worse than Tucker expects, and by the time he pulls into his building's garage, he's wracked by the sense that something is wrong. Has he left his keys back in the office, or a flame burning on the kitchen stove? The feeling gets worse as the elevator climbs, and by the time he steps inside his suite he can hardly focus on anything.

"Kincaid," he says, scenting the man's thick aftershave, alchemically charged engine oil. He wobbles on the spot, leans against the doorframe. "I'm sorry. I don't know what's gotten into me."

He glances around the living room. It's somehow barer than it was when he left. His possessions are all where they should be. So why does it feel like something is missing?

"Temporal residue." This from Kincaid, sprawled on the couch with his hands behind his head. "There was a woman here, and you knew her well. But she wanted her past cleaned up a little, and the baby went out with the bathwater."

A woman. Now that Kincaid mentions it, Tucker can just about picture her. Dark hair. Large lips. But not a major part of his life, no paramour or co-star. Just another extra.

"I wouldn't worry." Kincaid attempts a soothing smile, but the predator's teeth ruin the effect. "Time has a way of working things out. Or not," he adds. "Either way, I'm sure that the Faction will be amused, although this is a small-fry paradox by their standards."

"The Faction." Tucker seizes on the word, tries to anchor his roiling mind. A splitting headache threatens. "You told me you'd spoken to them."

Kincaid nods, gestures for Tucker to take a seat on his own couch, in his own house. "There's good news and bad—which would you like?" He pauses momentarily, as if waiting for an answer, but Tucker knows that it's pointless to speak. "The good news is this," Kincaid says. "The Faction saw what you to did to *Starpocalypse*, and they're impressed by your—scorched earth creative choices. In their eyes, you've produced something valuable. But the viewing public don't feel the same."

"I don't give a damn about the viewing public. I did all this for the Faction."

"That may be, but you picked the wrong movie."

The headache crashes in. Blood throbs in Tucker's temples. What was her name, this no-more woman? But that hardly matters now. "The wrong movie?"

"What do you know about Faction Paradox?"

Not a lot, though he'll never admit it. "I want," he says, "to know more."

"I'll tell you, then. The Faction is involved in one hell of a War. They're caught in the crossfire, more or less, though I get the idea that they might like being there." Kincaid's arms drop to his sides, and Tucker can't help but flinch. "Their enemies are an ugly bunch, with weapons forged from the cryptid gaps in the periodic table. A hydrogen bomb is like a water pistol in the eyes of the Major Powers."

Crazy, thinks Tucker, bleary-brained. Next, Kincaid will talk about aliens, spaceships, invaders from Mars. "What's this got to do with my movie?"

"The Faction has found ways to even the odds. They're skilled in the use of prankster tropes and clichés engineered to rot the brain. They can't destroy worlds, or events, or futures, but they can set off propaganda bombs. They have to be subtle, don't you see? If their rivals ever learn of the Faction's plans, I can't see it ending well. And so, we come to *Starpocalypse*."

"I don't see how." Tucker feels that he must speak now, no matter what he says. He must regain control. "I can't wrap my head around this."

"Listen, then. Don't interrupt." There's a harsh edge to Kincaid's voice, and Tucker recalls the rumours he's heard about the fates of those who displease the fixer. He keeps his mouth shut while Kincaid says, "*Starpocalypse* was built as a staging ground from which to deploy the Faction's weapons: subtextual warheads and anti-Shift landmines, deadly rhetorical plagues. The movie's heroes are beautiful, flawless, and it's left to them to fight against evil. Only they are good enough. The average viewer—a person like you—came away from the movie feeling useless. Leave it, they thought, to the beautiful ones. If a regime was cruel or corrupt or violent, it was the duty of heroes to make a stand, with their bouffant hair and perfect teeth. Everyone else was apathetic. And now look at the world today."

Tucker frowns, tries to keep up. "And what about people like you?"

"That," says Kincaid, "is beside the point. I am not a person."

Perhaps his head hurts from the vanishing woman, though he's forgotten, now, what she looked like. He'll have to find another somewhere. Or perhaps Kincaid was right all along, and Tucker really is in over his head. The flood of information is crushing him. "You mean that *Starpocalypse* is the Faction's work?"

A gentle nod from Kincaid, as though he's a schoolteacher urging on an especially clueless student. "The movie was a practical joke on their part; it's not as though they wanted to conquer the Earth. But it amused them to cause a minor disturbance, to put the cat among the Hollywood pigeons."

"But I made a sequel. I did them a favour."

Kincaid sighs. "You don't see it, do you? Your sequel has ruined the original, too. You've tanked the franchise's cultural cache. Now, the Faction wouldn't care, most of the time. They might even be impressed. But who will watch *Starpocalypse* now? You've defused their propaganda bomb."

It almost sounds like he's done the right thing, and maybe he has, though he doubts that the Faction will thank him. "What," he asks, picturing torment, "are they going to do to me now?

Kincaid's grin flashes back, a rictal smear of dentistry. "The Faction are going to induct you."

226

"What?" He can't believe what he's hearing.

"You've ruined this scheme, but they've plenty of others, and it was never more than a prank to them. Your audacity intrigues them. Yes, they'll have you for a Little Sibling. With some terms and conditions."

"Whatever they want." His life stops threatening to flash before his eyes. All that talk about weapons of war and stepping on toes made him think of the Faction as a criminal gang, the kind that tugs out fingernails, and his body in a shallow and unmarked grave. "I'm glad that we can act like adults."

"Of course. Once your initiation is complete, you'll be taken to the Boulevard to settle in."

"The Boulevard?"

"Oh, it's a very exclusive place." Kincaid's eyes are mercury grey and the final smile cracks open his face, giving Tucker a glimpse of the thing within, too huge to fit in a human being. A moment later the image is gone, out-dazzled by the fixer's pearly grin. "Faction members only."

This is What They Took From You

Phil Shaw

1

I'm in one of the more remote servants' quarters, and it clearly doesn't get used much. Dust everywhere, stains on the carpet. It'd offend my sense of professional pride if I had any. There's a new clay formation bloating horribly out of the wall near the ceiling. If anyone sees me round here I can say I've come to harvest it. It'd be a shame to lose a private spot like this one, but it's better than the Saint getting suspicious.

You're a comforting weight in my hands, my familiar. I scrape new lines into the clay of your muzzle, giving it a bit more definition. Making you a look a little more like yourself. The ambrite is as decrepit as the rest of the room, so as your shadow comes awake, it's a little less well defined than you like it.

- Hello Emmeline. Thank you for setting the scene, it does make things nicer. Even if you do make me sound vain.

I've not got it in me to soothe your pride, Petricrieu. It's been a day.

-Do you want to talk about it?

That's why we're here. I'm not sure I agree with myself that it's urgent, but I expect I know what I'm doing. I don't have time to tell you everything, but I can summarise.

-That's a shame. I've missed you, Emmeline. Can you at least try to tell it chronologically? It's easier for me to keep track.

Anything for you, my love. I was clearing away breakfast in the Heresiologists' Dining Hall, when Hannah Drummond came in.

I was appropriately servile, apologising for the plates still stacked down the end of the table. It turns out she'd come looking for me specially. The Saint'll be happy about that, if it means Hannah trusts me. Though I never scratched my name in there, so I've got no idea how Hannah knew where to look for me.

-That's suspicious.

Absolutely. But the Saint doesn't know we can think for ourselves, and Hannah thinks we're so pious we barely commune. They're more focused on each other than they are on us.

-If you're sure. What did she want?

Hannah's young, but has the wild hair and general untidiness of a proper academic eccentric. As she spoke to me, her familiar was never far from her hands, and once or twice, while she was talking to me, she broke off to whisper to it, adjusting its limbs while its shadow danced on the wall. I didn't recognise its form, some foreign animal with scales and hair. Possibly she's not a great sculptor.

"Can you get me these spices from the market?" she said. Her voice is odd. Her vowels all sounds the same, and her voice lilts at the end of her sentences like a question. "I asked the cook, but she was all, 'those look like poisons ma'am.' Which they are, technically, but I've been reading some old accounts and it sounds like the proto-Gibberlines used them as a preservative. Really fascinating stuff, actually."

I listened while she went off about preservatives, and how they relate to some foolish heresy from the Architects' School. I'm very glad that we predecided to never ask her to clarify anything, or I'd have been there even longer. Eventually, she handed me her list of poisons and wandered off.

229

Since I'd been seen there, I scratched my name with my fingernail into the wall of the dining hall, and recorded that I would be running an errand to the market for Hannah. The words were quickly swallowed up by the gentle movements of the clay, and new words bloomed from the house keeper of the Heresiologists' School, giving her blessing. As those faded too, another message assembled itself:

"Attend to me for report at earliest opportunity. Saint Dolores."

Apparently, I instincted that Hannah's task took priority. The nearest market to the Heresiologists' is about halfway down the Great Northern Corridor. The one with the seams of gold showing through the clay. They hold the market in Sergeant's Hall if the weather's good. Most of the ceiling is missing, pulled down by the bulk of the angel growing from it. It sags down pathetically, clinging to what's left of the roof. I'd not even approached the first vendor for Hannah's 'spices' when the angel lifted its faceless head and started babbling out a revelation. The whole market went very quiet and stared up at it, squinting in the light of the ambrites overhead. Did you hear it?

-Not a thing.

Overhearing people's communion after, I think it was something about a boat. Do you remember when we could commune in public, instead of in grimy rooms with things growing out of the walls?

-Do you think we should be concerned? Not being able to follow the parables makes it more likely that you'll be caught.

Probably not. None of it ever really changes anything. I just won't do anything I've not seen anyone else do.

-But what if, say, mushrooms with dirt sauce are suddenly forbidden, but you eat them anyway?

If it was forbidden, the kitchens wouldn't make it. Anyway, it's all up to interpretation. You remember the parables from when we were little, they're all basically nonsense. Everyone just does what they were going to anyway, and prepares an answer from the parables that justifies it. Which we don't need to do, because we can just say that we're acting on orders from the Saint.

-Which risks her hearing about it, and her realising you've got out from under her control. She's the one we need to keep out of it as much as possible.

I think you worry too much, Petricrieu.

-One of us has to. And while you're away from me I don't have much to do but worry. Worry and remember. Carry on with your story.

It's not like I enjoy being away from you. I'm not even properly thinking, just acting on instinct and predecisions.

-I don't want to argue with you, Emmeline.

You never do. You're getting old. We used to bicker for hours.

-No older than you, dearest. Your story?

After the angel had stopped its bellowing, most people went back to what they were doing, or started communing with their familiars. The only exception was a young woman with short-cropped hair at the edge of the market, who stepped onto a box and started preaching.

"My name is Peggy Clay!" she shouted. A gaggle of other young people around her repeated everything she said, amplifying it. "I am not afraid to speak the truth! This angel is broken down, unfit for purpose! Its parables are meaningless and degenerate!" She

231

carried on that way for a while, the usual not-quite heresy. Things were better when we served the angels, when there were commands not parables, all that stuff.

-So why are you telling me about it?

It was when I was reporting to the Saint. She was typically severe, sitting back on one of those low sofas in her withdrawing room while I stood in front of her and recited. I've told you about it before. Very plush, lots of red.

-I remember. I notice we've drifted away from the chronological.

Sorry. But we're running out of time. We were alone, without all her hangers on. I'd already told her about Hannah's spices. You know how the Saint has a really expressive face, even when she's not communing? She almost managed to hide the disappointment when I said that I hadn't seen Hannah do anything heretical. Anyway, since it didn't go against anything we'd predecided, I told her about the kids in the marketplace too. She just looked bored, until I mentioned the last thing that the reactionary girl said. That she's heard from the true angel of Gibberline, and she's going to reveal it one week from now.

The Saint paid attention to that. Wide eyes, mouth open. I'm surprised she didn't grab her familiar and commune immediately. She murmured, like she was talking to herself, "The true angels of Gibberline, and they wear their skulls on the outside." Remind you of anything?

-What happened to us. The Faction.

Exactly. I think we might need to go over that again.

-I only remember what you told me at the time.

But you remember it better than I do.

-You awoke in darkness, into a room unlike any other in the College. Rough, not smooth, and harder than clay, though you said you didn't touch the walls.

I just knew, I think. Like you do in a dream.

-It all sounds like a dream. If it hadn't changed us, I'd say it was. You were tied to a chair, though not painfully, and there was someone sitting across a table from you.

It was a desk, I think.

-You said table, when you first told me. You couldn't see the person's face, because you were partly blinded. A blotch across your vision, like the aftereffects of staring into a bright ambrite.

-They asked you, in a voice you described as 'creaking', "Where do you get your ideas?" You didn't answer, or you told them you got your orders from Saint Dolores, or that you are obedient. Your accounts vary.

That's not my fault. It's hard to remember.

-The first time, you said that you didn't say anything. But that was the time you used the least detail. I don't know if on later tellings you were remembering more, or if your mind was making up details to fill in the gaps.

-Your vision cleared, and you saw an old woman with an animal skull for a face. She asked you, "Do they tell you what to do, or do you decide what to do based on what they tell you?" You still didn't answer anything useful, and she asked you "Do you get your ideas from the same place that they do?"

I remember, whatever she was asking, they were questions I couldn't answer without help. I think I reached out to you.

-Which I don't remember, still being inert from the Saint's alchemy. You hadn't been able to reach for me for over a decade. Wandering about using only your instincts following orders, unable to predecide anything.

I ran my fingers over you and you wouldn't move. Just a hard clay statue. I was aware, like I was communing, but your shadow wouldn't move.

-*Don't cry, Emmeline. I know this is hard. I'll try to keep it short. The woman with the skull clapped her hands and said "Cognition at last! Marvellous. Don't think it'll sustain for long, but it never does with your lot. Not to worry, we'll at least get your little friend moving again".*

-*You asked her who she was. "I'm a representative of the Faction," she said. "Very important to your world's development, not that anyone remembers. Faction Paradox, ring any bells? No? Do you remember your war between the angels, at least?"*

-*You would have crossed your arms in warding, if you'd had your arms free. You thought she was some sort of heretic, and you were still the Saint's creature.*

-*"I'm not from your heretics' side," she said. Like she could hear your thoughts. "It was just an example. We're from a much bigger war, you see. So big that yours is like a reflection of theirs. You've got the rulers of the universe, and you've got their enemy. Angels and rebel angels, if we're following your world's rules.*

-*"The rebel angels won," you started to say, but she shushed you.*

-*"Your local theology isn't important. What I'm getting at is, the Faction is a third side. Caught in the middle, some people say, but I like to think that the middle's where we chose to be. Do you follow what I'm saying?"*

-*And that's all you remembered, more or less. You were scrubbing the Anatomists' Wing. The next time you had cause to commune, you reached out instinctively and there I was. Malleable and breathtakingly intelligent.*

So it does line up. The heretics want to bring back the angels that were overthrown. The Saint said they had skull faces, like the Faction.

-Not really. We have Gibberline with its angels, the Saint and everyone else, and we have the heretics. There's no third side, especially not the angels that were overthrown. I didn't think you cared that much about theology.

I don't, but listen. The Saint called in her acolytes, told them to start preparing the petrification bath. They were clearly all trying to hide their excitement, thinking their time's come at last, the little idiots.

-That's unfair. They don't know what happens. They think your lack of communion is by choice.

They envy me. They think I've been blessed by the Saint's blessed alchemy, so I can resist the temptation to commune with you. They think that communion's an indulgence.

-As did you, once.

I can never apologise enough, Petricrieu. I was young and I was stupid, and –

-And I believed it too. You did nothing to me that I didn't also do to myself.

Saint Dolores did it, to both of us. And she's planning to do it again.

-It's her acolytes' choice to make. You can't warn them, without giving yourself away.

She's not going to do it to an acolyte, she's going to do it to Peggy. The Saint's invited her to give a sermon to her congregation.

-One less reactionary. I didn't think you'd worry about that.

You didn't see way the Saint was smiling. Happier than catching a thousand heretics.

-This is it, then? Something to step out of hiding for?

235

I don't want to.

-I always knew you would, eventually. I can't think of a better reason than stymying the Saint.

I love you, Petricrieu.

-And I love you, Emmeline.

2

Selected records of investigation of Broken proto-Remote colony Gibberline

Investigators: Mother Dwysan, Mother Horun

Purpose: Determine nature of Great Houses intervention that caused colony to become Broken, ideally determine a way to reverse it

THESE RECORDS ARE DISTILLED FROM NON-LINEAR COMMUNICATION, TAKING PLACE AT OR NEAR THE COMMENCEMENT OF THE INVESTIGATION. RECORDS NOT TO BE STORED OR TRANSMITTED IN CONTEMPORARY-ACCESSIBLE FORMAT

Horun:

How are you getting on?

Dwysan:

This world is unsettling. They're ruled by a theocracy without ritual or belief. They always had a split between conscious thought and unconscious action, it was one of the things that attracted the Faction to them in the first place. But it's become considerably more pronounced. It's like talking to robots.

What's your report?

236

Horun:

It's hopeless, these people barely even have a culture any more. The closest thing they have to a mythology is some bog standard war among the angels. The first angel either created everything, or just said it did. Some other angels rebelled. The first angel died. They consider this a wholly historical event, and have absolutely no strong opinions about it either way.

You were here at the first intervention—what were they like then?

Dwysan:

They'd built up an entire culture based on the signals they picked up from the local sentient clay. We encouraged the development of the angel-forms, introduced the rebel angels—a minor intervention that would mould the culture into something more useful to the Faction. All of this was in the initial briefing; didn't you read it?

Incidentally, my attempts to establish a local powerbase to aid in information gathering are being subtly undermined. If that's your interference, I'd appreciate you dropping it.

Horun:

That's kind of troubling, if the scant mythology they have is something we gave them.

I've been observing the heretics. Fairly standard reactionaries, hankering after a lost golden age. They want to resurrect the first angel or, failing that, elevate another angel to replace it. They don't have an opinion on whether the first angel was their creator or not. They just think the angels should tell people what to do.

I've been back as far as I can, way into the first angel period. It's very confused back there, but from what I can tell, the angels' broadcast has always been complete nonsense. There's no sudden shift to suggest the sort of blunt cultural intervention the Houses favour towards the Remote projects.

Dwysan:

Then I suggest you keep looking, Mother Horun. Cultures don't just collapse of their own accord.

3

The walls have ears. Not literally, though some of the clay growths are reminiscent. In its own way, Gibberline listens.

Names and messages carved into its walls, swallowed up and dutifully reproduced when the recipient carves their name in turn. Gibberline has come to understand the words over agonising years. In the lightless places below the College, where no ambrite grows and no feet tread, Gibberline experiments with its own messages to no-one.

There is an emptiness in its thoughts and understanding.

Animate shadows dance, cast by the little figures bequeathed by Gibberline to its inhabitants. Do they understand that the clay growths are gifts? That when the children shape the clay into familiars, they are doing as Gibberline hoped? That when by some secret choice they settle on a single shape for their familiar, Gibberline knows them a little better?

It does not think the inhabitants understand it. It does not truly know them, and it thinks that the knowledge has been stolen from it.

238

Angels blossom from the walls and ceilings, speak communion to the familiars. Gibberline's children, in constant conversation. Sometimes Gibberline does not know if the angels speak with its voice, or if they have started to speak for themselves.

Gibberline knows that it is not right. Its thoughts are scattered and nonsensical. The words on the walls of its basements writhe in obscene alphabets. Angels bloom in empty rooms and sag shapeless to the floor. There is an infection in its rooms and corridors, that calls itself Paradox. Its agents disappear into their own rooms that are not part of Gibberline. They take the clay and kill it, or twist it to their own devices.

One of the inhabitants, touched by Paradox but not altogether lost, catches Gibberline's attention. It moves around the College, performing inscrutable tasks on behalf of other, more sedate, inhabitants. Emmeline, its communion names her, and Petricreu. She does not move in service now, but with her name uncarved on the walls. She reaches a place where Gibberline's understanding is fractured. A foul liquid laps at the edges of a clay bath force-grown to hold it, and where it touches the clay it renders it cracked, hard and dead.

Emmeline tears at the bath, dead clay crumbling in her hands. The liquid washes through the room, blistering the clay where it touches.

Gibberline cannot hold its attention there, and its focus whirls madly to other rooms. An angel crashes, malformed, babbling no parable or prophecy, only pain. Lovers' notes on the walls turn to threats, then nonsense.

When Gibberline can stand to return its attention to the hurting room, Emmeline has moved on. Where the liquid flowed it has killed the clay, but in doing so its malevolence is spent. Its foul alchemy has left scars that Gibberline does not remember how to heal, but it will endure.

4

Selected records of investigation of Broken proto-Remote colony Gibberline

Investigators: Mother Dwysan, Mother Horun

THESE RECORDS ARE A DISTILLATION OF NON-LINEAR CONVERSATION, OVER A PERIOD OF ROUGHLY 15 YEARS AFTER COMMENCEMENT OF INVESTIGATION

Mother Horun:

This isn't symbiosis, you idiot! The clay is a neural mirror, reflecting back the culture's own preoccupations. They're obsessed with the angels that're reflecting back to them. It's a feedback loop. You wouldn't even need an intervention from the Houses to make them like this, just natural information decay.

Mother Dwysan:

Your analysis of the angels is laughable—they're clearly the most successful part of the whole sorry operation. They're the spirits of the culture—they're hardly going to be a vital force when the culture's been completely broken down like this.

Horun:

The Houses were never here, were they? You and your team wrecked the culture with a shoddy intervention, and this is your attempt at a coverup.

Are you talking about spirits to distract me, or have you just gone completely off your head?

Dwysan:

This isn't an ordinary Remote world. The broadcasts have minds, physical form. We're on the verge of seeing a new kind of *loa*. Or we were, before the Houses intervened. And we can again, with just the right kind of push.

Horun:

That's revolting. Even if that was possible, even if it wasn't a complete misunderstanding of what the spirits are, the idea that these wretched homunculi could ever embody them is—it's heresy.

Dwysan:

Interesting choice of words. Have you been burrowing into this world a little too long, getting infected with their ideas? Perhaps that's why you can't conceive of them ever being anything else— you're assimilating. I even heard that you've picked up a genuine familiar for yourself. Have you turned traitor to the Faction, Mother Horun?

Horun:

What are you honking on about, you stuck up -

INTERJECTION

This is a fascinating conversation, ladies, but you've yet to produce anything other than complaints and your operation is becoming a drain on resources. Each of you has submitted a request for a review of the other's malfeasance, so here I am to investigate your investigation. I have no intention of being reasonable. See you soon!—Cousin Treacle

5

Miss Romiley was a prim, elderly woman who, for complex personal reasons, preferred to think of herself in the third person. Through a combination of nosiness, manipulation, and sheer bloody-mindedness, she had acquired an invitation to the social event of the century.

She entered the Saint's Hall with something that might pass for the proper respect, staring up at the intricately shaped ceiling. For support that she didn't entirely need, she was leaning on the arm of a young academic named Hannah Drummond, who it had amused Miss Romiley to pose as a student of for the evening. Saint Dolores, elegant and ageless, made graceful sounds of welcome. When she recognised Hannah Drummond, she gave a wide involuntary smile. Predatory, was the best way to describe it.

Miss Romiley and Hannah took a seat before the pulpit. It was not a large crowd, which one could consider as an indication that Saint Dolores lacked the courage of her convictions. Would it not have been wiser to open the event to as wide an audience as possible? Then again, the attendees were overwhelmingly the peak of their various fields in the College and tended to be, if not exactly champions of the unorthodox, then at the very least enthusiastic cataloguers of it. It was possible that this was intended merely to distract the Saint's competitors. Miss Romiley knocked her pipe against the arm of her chair. It made a dampened clunk, given that the chairs were, like everything else, grown up from the clay of Gibberline's walls and floors.

Saint Dolores took to the pulpit, and gave a speech that matched the hyperbolic tone of the invitations, full of pomp and empty verbosity.

"Let none say that the office of Sainthood is reluctant to embrace curiosity," she declaimed as her speech hit its climax. "Even when it comes from the most unlikely places." She gave a gracious smile to the young woman with short-cropped hair standing beside her. "Even when it sounds to us like heresy. Where would the discipline of experimental theology be, without a willingness to question? This young lady has fallen into apostasy, and she would like to tell us what she found there."

The young woman took the pulpit then.

"My name is Peggy Clay!" she shouted. "Gibberline has fallen into degeneracy! You spit on us as heretics, but only we have seen the truth!"

Saint Dolores stepped up beside her, and spoke softly into her ear.

"A new kind of angel!" shouted Peggy Clay, obviously hitting the end of a preplanned speech rather sooner than she had intended.

Servants of the college carried in a large box made from mushroom timbers and began to open it in front of the pulpit, as some of the crowd communed with their familiars in agitation.

"I was rather hoping that the honour of communing with the new angel would go to one of my charming acolytes." Dolores gestured gracefully to a group of young people standing awkwardly at the sides of the hall. "I planned to offer them a Confirmation, that would have fortified their faith and allowed them to withstand the angel if it proved to be false. Tragically, it was not to be. Some dissenting wretch stole into the depths of my department, and tainted the waters of Confirmation." Did Dolores' eyes rest on Hannah Drummond for a moment? "Fortunately, I have in my employ a loyal servant who underwent Confirmation when she was a girl. Since that day, and guided by my loving hand, she has not felt the uncertainty or doubt that inspire the need to commune with her familiar. Come forward, Emmeline."

From among the servants at the side of the hall, an older woman (though still far younger than Miss Romiley) came forward. She kept her eyes cast down, the very picture of religious devotion.

"I am reluctant to part with Emmeline, if a parting is the tragic result of Miss Clay's experiment. But it is a risk she is willing to take in the name of progress."

"Yes, Saint," said Emmeline quietly beside her.

The last of the box fell away, revealing the angel within.

"Behold, the true angels of Gi-" Peggy Clay began, before Saint Dolores shushed her.

Angels came in many shapes, as they blossomed from the walls of Gibberline, but this was unlike any angel the collected academics of the audience had seen before. It wasn't connected to the walls or ceiling, but sat patiently on its box. Where most had smooth, humanoid bodies of solid clay, this new angel was formed of thin clay strands, like vines or tangled hair, leaving gaps large enough to see through. Its body plan might have been described as humanoid, but such a description would be inadequate. In place of the usual blank face, this new angel wore a mask in the shape of a human skull, empty eyed and leering.

In its torso, the strands opened out to form a cavity large enough for Emmeline to climb inside, at Saint Dolores' command. The strands, formerly immobile, began to waft as though in a breeze. They fell against Emmeline's skin and grew across it. Perhaps it was just where she was sitting, but it seemed to Miss Romiley that the strands were not merely enveloping Emmeline but growing through her, as if her body was as insubstantial as water. Her shadow rose up behind her, filling the gaps in the angel's body.

Emmeline lifted her head. Above her, the angel lifted its head in unison.

"Speak, angel!" commanded Saint Dolores.

Emmeline began to scream.

6

Petricreu! Petricreu!

-Emmeline, my love! What happened? Your voice, it's so ragged.

Anyone's would be. I spent an hour screaming.

-I don't understand, Emmeline. What happened?

She just needed someone who had been put through petrification, so she could put them inside that *thing*. I'm so stupid, I made myself the only candidate.

-What thing? Emmeline, you're not making sense.

It hurts to remember. They put me inside an angel, Pet. A new kind of angel. They wanted me to speak for it, or it to speak through me.

-And it didn't work? Because I'm cured?

245

I don't know. I don't even know what the Saint was trying to do. I don't know if she suspects me, or if it worked the way she wanted, or anything. They put me in this room to recover, in case I can remember anything from inside the angel. I don't know how long it's been. They might come back, but I don't care anymore.

-What can you remember?

I can remember it hurting. I was the angel, or maybe the angel was just something that was happening to me. I was watching a ship made out of stories pull its way out from under the clay. There were angels helping to free it, and angels trying to keep it under, and they were fighting. I don't know what side I was on. One of them kept screaming at me, demanding to know where my ideas came from. And then there was this awful emptiness, and then just *anger*. Awful, awful fury. Something had been broken, or I'd been broken, and then even though I was starting to mend, I was just raging over what I'd lost. I was clawing at the walls of the College, or maybe it was the walls inside me.

-It sounds awful.

The worst part was— it was –

-Shhh. Just cry if you need to. Let the words come as they will.

The worst part is that I was feeling it and you weren't there. I've never felt anything and known I was feeling it, without you there to talk me through it. I was so alone, more than when you were silent, because I was communing and I was alone. I think I reached out to you to commune. I don't know if they saw me.

Say something, please. I can't stand to be silent right now.

-What are you going to tell them, when they ask you?

I don't know. I don't want to think about that, I just want to be here with you. It's late now, the ambrites have dimmed. Maybe they won't come until morning. Can't we just be?

-We can, if that's what you need. But I think we have to decide, Emmeline. If they saw you reach for me, we need to tell them something to make them not suspect.

I don't want to decide anything! It hurts to think about anything, and I don't want to go back to not thinking about it, because then I won't even have any control over it.

-Emmeline, I know you're hurting, but we need –

Shut up! I can hear something, I think someone's coming.

No, no no no, they're here, they've got a *knife*.

7

Miss Romiley smiled a little smile to herself as she brought her shadow weapon down on the back of the figure advancing on the cowering servant. The figure crumpled to its knees, dropping the knife.

"Why in the name of the Grandfather are you using a real knife?"

Hannah Drummond looked up from the floor, scowling but saying nothing.

"Exactly as I thought!" Saint Dolores sailed into the room, beaming cruelly at the fallen Hannah. "You knew the ritual hadn't gone your way, so you decided to murder the witness. It's very lucky you were here, Miss Romiley."

"Luck has very little to do with it," said Miss Romiley. "But since we're all gathered together, I think we can draw this to a conclusion.

From a pocket that didn't seem big enough to hold it, Miss Romiley drew out a Faction mask and fitted it neatly upon her face. The Miss Romiley persona submerged, leaving only me. My name's Cousin Treacle, and I *really* enjoy the bit where I get all the suspects in the same room together.

"Take a seat, ladies, and get your masks out," I said.

Saint Dolores sank into one of the fancy chairs at the edge of the room, fitting her mask to her face. Mother Dwysan's mask was predictably ornate.

Still glowering at me, Hannah Drummond picked herself off the floor, fastened her rather plainer and slightly battered mask to her face, and Mother Horun took a seat on the opposite side of the room to Dwysan.

Both of them outranked me in the usual scheme of things, which I think made them even more furious that I was intervening in their little spat.

The serving woman, Emmeline, remained on the floor.

"I've been dispatched by Godmother Wittering," I announced, "to investigate firstly, why you've spent so long mucking about, and secondly, whether the accusations from each of you that the other one has been sabotaging the operation have any truth to them. Happily, the second should answer the first." I beamed, not that they could see it behind the mask.

I won't bore you with the details of the arguments, counter-arguments, complaints, gripes, and endless self-justification. All my attempts to probe the extent of their activities ran up against the sort of needless overcomplication that you only get when a pair of cultists get to *really* start plotting against each other.

The brief version is that Mother Dwysan had set up a power base as Saint Dolores, established herself as the local theocrat, and had been gathering as much power to herself as possible. She'd decided that while the humans weren't much use, "the broadcasting 'angels' are clearly developing into embodied *loa* of the culture". Mother Horun, on the other hand, had posed as heresiologist Hannah Drummond, who didn't so much research heresies as elaborately fake them and try to get people to believe them.

Naturally, these approaches were wholly incompatible. Mother Dwysan accused Mother Horun of "assimilating too far into the local culture" and "sabotaging my best efforts at putting it back together. by introducing all sorts of nonsensical experimental heresies." Mother Horun claimed that Mother Dwysan was "a totalitarian nightmare crushing what remains of the culture", that Dwysan was largely responsible for breaking it in the first place, and that on a personal level Dwysan was "absolutely cooked."

At some point, one of them (I'm not even going to try to break down the sequence of events) induced an angel that was disconnected from the Gibberline's culture. That was the angel that had reduced a servant to incoherent screaming earlier in the day, and both Dwysan and Horun had very strong opinions about it. Which they proceeded to tell me about at very great length.

I will excerpt one small part of the conversation, because it gives a flavour of exactly what I suffered, because I believe it may have had an effect on the ultimate resolution, and because it was the only time Mother Dwysan admitted she was wrong. This may have been a unique incident in space and time.

We'd been going over the involvement of the reactionary young heretic Peggy Clay (probably a pseudonym, which is a neat trick in a surveillance society where all the walls know your name). It turned out that Horun and Dwysan had both been manipulating her for their own purposes. It would have been nice to verify all of this, but Miss Clay was unavailable ("Ran," said Horun. "So you butchered her too?" said Dwysan.) I was trying, heroically, to get to the bottom of what they wanted her for. It went a bit like this:

COUSIN TREACLE: Were you planning on putting Miss Clay through your petrification process?

MOTHER DWYSAN: By the time I realised we might need someone who wouldn't attempt conscious thought when they made contact with the angel, she was already too established. I was going to use one of the young ladies I was preparing, but *someone* destroyed the cauldron.

MOTHER HORUN: I want it on the record that I had nothing to do with the petrification experiments.

MOTHER DWYSAN: Of course not, that's why you keep making these hysterical accusations. You can't tell the difference between an individual with impaired facilities, and a culture so beaten down it produces people who behave like that by choice.

MOTHER HORUN: I hardly think destroying someone's free will is any better.

MOTHER DWYSAN: Oh, I freely admit that it never worked how it was supposed to. The subjects were rendered entirely too suggestible. I suppose that's why I kept doing it.

Thrilling stuff, I'm sure you'll agree. I never got anywhere satisfying with that line of questioning, but by the end of it, it didn't really matter. For all their accusations and backbiting, only one thing really mattered.

"Ladies," I said. "I'm getting very bored. Fortunately, there's a very simple way to resolve this."

"Do tell?" said Mother Dwysan, leaning forward in her chair.

"The Faction doesn't care about your interpersonal squabbles. They want results. You've very cleverly come up with two wholly incompatible explanations of what's happening here." I paced up and down the room, putting on a show. "Unless I've grievously misinterpreted your bickering, the whole thing hinges on whether the angels can think for themselves. The business with the angel this afternoon was meant to definitively answer that."

"That's rather a simplification," interrupted Mother Dwysan. "Probing the disconnected angel's mind would take many attempts, especially given how poorly the serving woman fared."

"Sorry, your Saintliness, you're out of time. The experiment's done, and if one of you is very lucky you might get to have another go. Emmeline?" I called out to the woman on the floor. She had remained on the floor throughout, glassy eyed and clutching her unmoving familiar. When I said her name, she began to get unsteadily to her feet.

"This is wildly unfair!" Mother Horun strode right into my personal space. "She's entirely Dwysan's creature. Her testimony can't be trusted." My shadow circled around her, shillelagh raised. Her own shadow was clutching a nasty looking hammer in one hand, and some sort of lizard in the other. Her familiar's shadow, I assumed. Maybe she really was being absorbed into the local culture. I filed that away in case it was important, but the hammer was taking up rather more of my attention. I honestly don't know if I could have beaten her in a fight.

"Don't talk nonsense, Horun." Mother Dwysan rose from her chair, her mask raised in aristocratic self-confidence. "All that's required is to ask her to speak truthfully, and she'll have no choice but to do so."

"You see? She wouldn't agree to it if she wasn't sure she's going to win."

"I'll be very surprised if either of us 'win', Horun. Her mind's clearly shattered. We'll get nothing out of her, our Cousin here will slink off back to her Godmother, and everything will carry on as it has been."

Every investigation I've ever carried out has been on the basis that if you act confident enough, people will react as if you know what you're doing. I took Emmeline's arm to steady her.

"Tell us what you saw in the angel's head," I said. "Just be honest."

Emmeline stared solemnly at me. It's rather disturbing, to look into someone's eyes and see them thinking without any signs of conscious awareness. Like a computer stuck on a loading screen.

"There was nothing," she said. "My own thoughts and pain echoed back at me. Endless, and awful, but still just me. The angel was empty."

Which rather definitively tied everything up, I thought.

8

We're back on the mud plains beyond Gibberline. I think the Faction thinks this is a suitably ironic place to consign Saint Dolores to her imprisonment. They're lined up in their masks and their fancy clothing. They've done something to her, she already looks broken.

-Are you alright, Emmeline? Being back?

I'm not looking over at Gibberline. It makes me feel all wrong if I do.

-It's hard to keep track of everything. I can't put everything together in my mind. It's like you said happened after the woman from the Faction woke you up. Do you think that was -

"Oh, that was me. I took a bit of your shadow and stitched it to Petricrieu's. Honestly, I just did that to see what would happen. Don't look at me like that with your mouth hanging all over the place. You're talking *out loud*. Don't worry, we can teach you some little tricks to communicate a little more surreptitiously.

"Look, there she goes! So long, Mother Dwysan! You were extremely aggravating.

"Come along, Little Sister Emmeline, Little Sibling Petricrieu. Great Works await, and probably a whole lot of deeply boring Works along with them."

-Emmeline? Are you still there?

I'm waiting, until Treacle's out of hearing.

-Is everything alright?

I wanted to get a look at their prison. The Boulevard.

-You said. It sounds awful. An eternity alone as the only real person. I can't even imagine it.

I think I'm going to end up there some day. The Faction produced someone like Saint Dolores. Cousin Treacle's the only half decent one we've met, and she messed with our heads for fun. They don't think anyone's real people, unless we're in their gang. I just—I can't see being able to go along with them forever.

-Would we be separated? Would I have to spend forever with a pretend version of you?

I don't know. Maybe they'd keep us together, so we were properly aware. Maybe they'd just mess with our heads again. That's the one thing that might keep me with them. The fear of losing you again.

-There's another option.

Oh?

-We keep our heads down. Just like before. And when we get a chance, we run so far and we hide so well that not even the Faction can find us.

-Emmeline?

Yeah. Let's do that. Come on, before they leave without us.

-I love you, Emmeline.

And I love you, Petricrieu.

9

The visitors depart, leaving Gibberline alone on the plain. From the outside, its shape is clear. A vast hunched angel. The empty expanse of its face is broken open by a colossal weapon still embedded there, left over from some half-forgotten war. After some days, it attempts to rise, staggers, falls. More days, silent. In time, Gibberline reaches out one huge hand, and begins to drag itself across the plain.

The Crikeytown Cancellations

Charles E.P. Murphy (apologies to Dudley Watkins, Davey Law, Ken Reid etc)

PANEL 1. The classroom at Crikeytown Comprehensive—as always, the beezer Slobs (with Tommy the Terror and Naughty Nancy at front) and the snotty Snobs (headed by Soppy Sammy) sit on opposite sides of the room. Even as he talks to their teacher Miss Snatcher, Tommy the Terror is using a catapult to splat Sammy with tomatoes.

MISS SNATCHER: I've got *good news*, children—the *mayor of Crikeytown* is coming to see your performance of Macbeth!

TOMMY: *What* performance of Macbeth?

PANEL 2. Miss Snatcher slams a huge book titled "BORING SCHOOL PLAYS Vol. XXV" on her desk. The Slobs groan in horror and the Snobs cheer.

MISS SNATCHER: The one you're all doing *this afternoon* to make the school look good!

NANCY: *Oh no!* More work!

SLOBS: GROAN!!

SAMMY: *Hooray!* More work!

SNOBS: WHOOO!!

PANEL 3. Tommy, Nancy, and others brainstorming at their tables.

NANCY (whisper): Bang goes our trip to the arcade…

256

TOMMY (whisper): *Don't worry*, gang, I've got a plan to get us out of that boring play!

PANEL 4. Soppy Sammy, Speccy Sally, and Count Money are dressed as the Three Witches, and are dead smug about it. What they don't know is Tommy, disguised as a prop tree by pieces of wood, is secretly dumping pills into their ginger beer.

COUNT MONEY: Ha! Thanks to the mayor being my second uncle twice removed, *we* get the best characters!

SOPPY SAMMY: Now now, doing work for teacher is *always* its own reward! *Smarm!*

TOMMY (thought bubble): Heh heh!

THE READER (off-panel): Ooer! I wonder what Tommy's putting in their drinks??

PANEL 5. The play on the night, right in front of everyone. The Three Witches suddenly embarrassed as they simultaneously blast out out a huge green-smoking fart! The entire scenery backdrop is blasted down!

SPECCY SALLY: "Where shall we three meet again? In thunder—"

SFX: **PAAAARRRRPPP!!!**

PANEL 6. The Three Witches continue to fart away, with green fumes filling the room and forming the words "FETID PONG". The Slobs, with clothes-pegs on their noses, cheer— Miss Snatcher looks in horror as the mayor faints. Tommy reads from his script while winking at us.

SFX: PARP! PARP!

SOPPY SAMMY: *The curse of the Scottish Play!!*

TOMMY: *Ha ha!* I slipped *laxatives* in their ginger beer! Now we "hover through fog and *foul air*", eh *readers?*

MISS SNATCHER: *No!!* The eggy pumps have made the mayor faint!

PANEL 7. The Slobs all run out of Crikeytown Comp in a riotous frenzy. The roof of the school is blasted off by the gaseous SFX of:

SFX: **FAARRRT**

TOMMY: Ha ha! It's another great day in Crikeytown, just as always!

PANEL 8. Everyone is down at the arcade, hammering away at the games. Nancy has just lost a match of Punch Brothers to Tommy. (Zeke the Sneak, his trench coat over his red-and-black jumper, is playing one game while reading a sheet saying "CHEAT CODES"—nobody's talking to him but he'll be relevant later, readers!)

CAPTION: Down at the arcade, everyone's having a great time!

NANCY: Bums! You win again!

TOMMY: *Nobody* can beat The Terror!

PANEL 9. New character Jill Thrill zooms in on her tricked-out wheelchair, both it and her hair marked with go-faster strips. Nancy is almost obscured in the panel.

JILL THRILL: Sez you! I'm Jill Thrill and I'm up for *anything!*

TOMMY: You're on!

NANCY (thought bubble): Oh no... already??

PANEL 10. Jill and Tommy are trying to play but obnoxious fake-tanned Stu Spencer The Influencer is shoving himself into the panel, his phone ready for a selfie.

STU SPENCER: Check it out #stustans! Your friend Stu Spencer The Influencer is with his bff #tommytheterror at #CrikeytownArcade—

TOMMY: ???

PANEL 11. Babyface the wrestling baby slams the Punch Brothers arcade cabinet onto Stu's head. A baby referee is crawling in the corner, giving the count.

BABYFACE: *BIG WORDS MAKE BABYFACE'S HEAD HURT!!*

REF: *One, two... uhhhh... what's after two???*

PANEL 12. Jill gives Tommy a defiant thumbs-up while booster rockets appear out of her wheelchair.

JILL THRILL: Well, that's the game over, I guess—*how about a race down Death Hill?!*

TOMMY: Done!

PANEL 13. The Slobs all mug for the camera, including Jill and Babyface (who is numming on his Championship belt)—Stu tries to take a selfie that makes him look in front.

THE READER (OFF-PANEL): Where did these three new Slobs come from though…?

TOMMY: Doesn't matter!

TOMMY (thought bubble): That's an existential question we can *never ask* because the answer's probably *very scary!*

CAPTION: And so, some new chums have come to Crikeytown—chums that do new things nobody's done before! That's a sign *a big change* is coming…

PANEL 14. Tommy the Terror in his original 1950s scratchy art style in black-red-white is regenerating, with big warps of energy, into his sleeker full-colour 1980s style.

CAPTION: Every *ten years* or so, there's a *great regeneration* in Crikeytown. People change *just slightly* to be 'modern', and people who *can't* change get replaced with new people. That's why Tommy the Terror's in charge and *not* Ted E. Bear, the bear who's a teddy boy…

THE READER (off-panel): What's a teddy boy???

CAPTION: Ask your granddad! And that's why Ted *had to go.* Your pals in Crikeytown like to stay current…

PANEL 15. The decaying, bone-strewn ruins of a 1950s Scottish town. The sun burns black. Nothing stands. Slapped over it is a big "CENSORED" so the kids can't see the screaming infant corpses and how they clearly died in pain.

CAPTION: Because if you *don't* manage to stay current enough… if you *don't* keep up with the times… Then you might end up like The Towns Nobody Wants to Talk About…

CAPTION: …and Crikeytown's *the only* town still around these days…

PANEL 16. Naughty Nancy, fuming in the corner—a huge dark cloud reading "FUMING WITH RAGE" orbits her head.

CAPTION: Better hope nobody's going to interfere with the regeneration, *eh readers?*

NANCY: Bah! Grrr! Everyone likes these three a *little too much*, readers!

NANCY: And there's only so many positions open for us girls, so if Jill Thrill gets too popular… is there room for *me* in the core gang…?

PANEL 17. Naughty Nancy, in fond memory—a big thought balloon shows her in the 1960s, splattering Speccy Sally with custard pies.

NANCY: I came in before a regeneration once, all devil-may-care and loaded with peashooters! And soon after, when the big change happened, I got to replace Weighty Katie as an important person…

PANEL 18. An old reprint of the title card of WEIGHTY KATIE, THE GLUTTONOUS GIRL and a black-and-white panel of her adventures—eating a plate of pies while other schoolgirls look on horrified. She's eating all the pies.

261

OLD TEXT CAPTION: Instead of being lady-like, Katie ate all the pies.

KATIE: Yum yum!! I'm eating *all* the pies!

GIRL: Oh no, *she's eating all the pies!*

PANEL 19. Naughty Nancy holds the original art of panel 1 of this very story, with Weighty Katie circled riiiiight at the back in red pen.

NANCY: Replacing her as a main character *wasn't very difficult!* Now we only see her in the background so we know she still exists.

NANCY: *I can't live like that*, chums! To have popularity and power taken away, to be *the nothing* in the corner? I deserve better!

NANCY: I'm *not* giving up power, regeneration or no regeneration!

PANEL 20. Nancy, rubbing her hands with glee in demonic red lighting.

NANCY: So I guess *something bad's* going to have to happen to the new characters, *eh readers??*

PANEL 21. Nancy has called a meeting with Zeke the Sneak and Ned Ed the bovver-boot skinhead, at a slap-up feed of huge piles of bangers and mash.

CAPTION: Naughty Nancy can't do any scheme without help—she needs two dopes to help her out, and there's two mega-dopes *right here*...

NED ED: Pbbbt! New guys don't matter to *me*—I'm too busy with all these wimps to *beat up*! Huh huh!

ZEKE: And what's it matter to *me* what the new guys do? I'm fine...

NANCY: Zeke, we came up at the same time, your dodges and schemes get us into *and* out of all sorts of scrapes! Remember that time you almost became Prime Minister??

NANCY: Now you're... well, when *did* you last hang out with us?

PANEL 22. Zeke, defensive, but also bitter.

ZEKE: I helped Tommy *steal the maths test* and convince Miss Snatcher that it was *the Snobs* that did it!

ZEKE: ...*last month*.

ZEKE: ...but Tommy said he'd hang out another time...

PANEL 23. Nancy is whispering into Zeke's ear—while in the background, Ned Ed is sticking a sausage up his nose.

NANCY: If *I* was still in the core gang after the regeneration, I could suggest you hang out with us more...

NANCY: Wouldn't you like to be a core guy again...?

PANEL 24. Nancy, crying sadly—with a big arrow saying "CROCODILE TEARS"—as she talks to a startled Ed.

NANCY: And maybe if he was, he could *save Ed!* Boo hoo hoo!

NED ED: Grunt???

NANCY: I heard the three new people say they want to kick Ed out of Crikeytown to make room for them! *Meanies! Waaa!*

PANEL 25. Ned Ed, nervous, but hiding it with thuggery.

NED ED: Th-they wanna kuh-kuh-kick me outta Crikeytown?

NED ED: Well, uh, th-those wimps won't get rid of *me!* I'll bash them up first!

CAPTION: Poor Ed didn't *always* live in Crikeytown—when one of The Towns Nobody Wants to Talk About falls, a few people manage to escape to another. Ned Ed *used* to live in Porkopia… and *then* he *used* to live in Corville…

PANEL 26. Ned Ed with a thought balloon saying "CENSORED!"—as his terrified, pleading eyes stare into us, haunted by what they've seen, the face of a child who can't sleep at night.

CAPTION: You *don't* want to see his flashback, chums! Trust us! Let's just say he *doesn't* want to go back out into the wastelands!

PANEL 27. All three shake hands, while Naughty Nancy gives a big wink to <u>you</u>.

ZEKE: Then we're agreed! We're going to get rid of these loser new people by shifting them out of town!

NANCY: Yep, just shifting them out of town...

NANCY (thought bubble): Won't *they* be surprised, *eh readers?*

PANEL 28. Nancy and her gang are meeting Stu Spencer the Influencer in the Crikeytown quarry—a big series of pits and piles of debris, with signs saying "KEEP OUT!", "THIS MEANS **YOU!!**", "ESPECIALLY NANCY, ZEKE, ED, AND STU".

CAPTION: Getting Stu Spencer The Influencer to go to the dangerous quarry took a few hours of friending, retweeting, and general schmoozing...

STU: The quarry *really* wants to sponsor me?

ZEKE: Would I lie to you?

NANCY: Yeah, all you need is a nice photo of you, say, *right next* to *the pit...*

PANEL 29. Stu talking a selfie with Zeke and Ed.

STU: Hi #stustans!! Hanging out at #Crikeytownquarry, the most happening place in town #authenticlocal #sponsored Things are always going down here!

NED ED (thought): Who's Stus Tans???

ZEKE (thought): Ha ha! We'll give him a good scare and he'll be gone when the regen--

265

PANEL 30: Nancy shoves Stu into the pit!

NANCY: Things *are* going down here! Ha ha!

SFX: AAAAAaaarrrgg....

PANEL 31: The view from the pit and it's a long, long, looooooong way up—Stu's broken, twisted hand bleeds in the corner.

ZEKE: *Oh no!* Do you think he's alright?

THE READER (off panel): What a silly question!

PANEL 32. Zeke and Ed staring in horror, Nancy giving a big thumbs up.

ZEKE: Nancy, *how* could you trip so badly--
NANCY: Nah, I *totally* murdered him! Ho ho!

ZEKE: AAARR! Don't say that!

ZEKE: Okay, as long as *the reader's* the only person who knows, we're okay, it was *just an accident—*

PANEL 33. Naughty Nancy looking innocent, holding Stu's phone. Zeke and Ned Ed stare in such shock their eyes pop out of their sockets and great "!!" signs appear above them.

NANCY: And *uh oh*, Stu got photos of you before he died so looks like you can't grass me up or you'll go down with me!

PANEL 34. Zeke and Ed panicking—Ned is whimpering in a

foetal position, Zeke has turned green with wavy 'NAUSEOUS' text coming off him.

NED ED: Th-this is—I dunno, bruv, I… I…

NED ED: …I don't have th-the *big words* to *describe nuffin*…

NED ED: I feel like… I feel *too* naughty… is that right???

PANEL 35. Soppy Sammy comes skipping over, aghast.

SOPPY SAMMY: *Oh no!!* I was coming home from Flower Pressing Club when I saw *everything!!* M-Maybe Stu's okay??

ZEKE: Aaaaa!

ZEKE: I mean, uh….

PANEL 36. Naughty Nancy leans into the panel, a big angel halo over her head.

NANCY: Oh, Sammy, it's lucky you're here, there's been a *terrible* accident!

SAMMY: I know! Choke!

NANCY: And guess what---

PANEL 37. Nancy hangs Soppy over his ankles over the pit.

NANCY: There's gonna be *another terrible accident* if you grass us up, mush!

SOPPY SAMMY: AAAAAA!!!!

PANEL 38. Zeke, looking at us.

ZEKE: I know I should help Sammy, chums…

ZEKE: …but then Nancy will *fit me up!* So I won't.

ZEKE: You'd do the same in my shoes, I'll bet! *Anyone* would!!

PANEL 39. Nancy drops Sammy back on the ground, his skin completely white and hair up on end.

SOPPY SAMMY: Puh-puh-please don't kuh-kill me, Nancy, I-I-I didn't see anything—

NANCY: Ha ha! I knew I'd have no trouble with this wimp!

SOPPY SAMMY (thought bubble): She's right… I don't dare tell anyone… And I thought I was *a good boy*… If I was a *real* good boy, I wouldn't be a *wimp*…

PANEL 40. Nancy has a big matey arm around her terrified pals. Sammy is ignored in the background.

NANCY: Y'know, this is all really easy!

NANCY: Time for us to go after our next target….

PANEL 41. Naughty Nancy shaking hands with Babyface.

CAPTION: I'm afraid to say it's even easy for Naughty Nancy to set up her *next* victim…

NANCY: Hey, Babyface, want to have a *death*match?

BABYFACE: *You're on!*

BABYFACE: As I was born yesterday, I'm assuming there's no sinister reason you italicised the words 'death' just now.

PANEL 42. A grotty sports club bar covered in beer stains and with the wafting fumes spelling "EVERY CIGGIE, FART, AND WEE EVER" reaching the ceiling. In the ring, Ned Ed is being bodyslammed by Babyface as the Slobs cheer in a few seats! In the corner is a wrestling fan in a cheap Babyface shirt.

WRESTLING FAN: What a *great* Britwres turnout—a whole *seventeen people!*

PANEL 43. Ned Ed about to throw Babyface off the ring and into a table.

NED ED: I'm gonna throw you into a table! Grr!

BABYFACE: WHEEEEE!!

CAPTION: Don't do a table spot without training, chums! Certainly don't do it if the table's rigged to split in a way that makes *really sharp jagged edges….*

PANEL 44. Everyone in the Slobs stares in utter horror—except Nancy.

SFX: 'ORRIBLE MEATY RIPS

NANCY: Uh oh! Looks like Baby*face* just *lost his head…. Eh readers???*

PANEL 45. Tommy the Terror, sweating and pale.

269

TOMMY: That... that shouldn't have happened...

TOMMY: That's not meant to happen to *anyone*...

PANEL 46. Everyone files out of the sports hall looking shaken, confused, unable to understand what's happened—all but Nancy.

CAPTION: Your chums the Slobs aren't happy bunnies, reader! They don't know how to *process* what they've seen...

THE SLOBS (collective thought bubble): Could that happen to anyone? Could that happen *to me??*

NANCY (thought bubble): I wonder what's for tea...??

PANEL 47. Zeke the Sneak, popping his head around the side of Panel 46.

ZEKE: *Phew!* Looks like everyone thinks it's a nasty accident! Half the time my naughty schemes didn't work out *at all*, but looks like we'll get away with it after all...!

PANEL 48. Sheriff Squarejaw, hulking Wild West strongman, holds up a photo of Babyface's chalk outline—with a separate chalk outline for the head.

SHERIFF SQUAREJAW: Ah don't think this *was* an accident *at all!*

PANEL 49. The full cast (who are squished up at the back), assembled in an Agatha Christie drawing room—Nancy, Ed,

Zeke, and Sammy all sweat nervously while Squarejaw paces up & down.

TOMMY: Oooer!

SHERIFF SQUAREJAW: In fact, Ah suspect that's why Stu Spencer *hasn't updated his Instagram* in the last 24 hours too!

SHERIFF SQUAREJAW: Now, this is a *little* different to all the apple-scrumping, graffiti, and Mexican bandits that Ah normally deal with, but Ah'm confident Ah can find who it is…

PANEL 50. Zeke and Ed are sweating so much a vast waterfall marked "FLOOD OF SWEAT" is coming out of their shirt sleeves and gushing down on tiny Little Herbert under them.

SHERIFF SQUAREJAW (off-panel): …they may have someone who knows and is getting really nervous right now…

SHERIFF SQUAREJAW (off-panel): …IS THAT NOT RIGHT….?

PANEL 51. Squarejaw waits expectantly in a quiet room.

PANEL 52. Squarejaw slumps.

SHERIFF SQUAREJAW: Nuts, Ah thought that'd work.

PANEL 53. Outside, Squarejaw is lifting an entire building up to look under it. Zeke and Ed continue to have shaky knees.

SHERIFF SQUAREJAW: No clues under here!

ZEKE: W-W-We just have to puh-pretend we're *f-f-f-fine*, Eddie…

SFX: KNERVOUS KNEES KNOCKING

PANEL 54. Ed, exhausted—Zeke's eyes dart left and right.

NED ED: I can't *do that*, mug… I feel *real grotty all the time*, I don't wanna sleep, I don't wanna eat…

ZEKE (whispering): You'll be overheard, Ed!!!

NED ED: *The guilt's too much!* It's not like beating up a wimp or cheating at exams, I feel… wrong? I dunno…

PANEL 55. Zeke nervously pats Ed on the back.

NED ED: I gotta confess what I dun, Zeke…! This is all *too much!*

ZEKE: Don't worry, mate, just… wait a bit, eh?

ZEKE (thought bubble): While *I* go grass you up to Nancy!!

PANEL 56. Nancy, burning red with anger, jumping up and down while Zeke looks away.

NANCY: *$^%&@~~&*!!!!!

ZEKE (thought bubble): She's taking it well.

PANEL 57. Nancy steeples her hands together as little devil horns come out of her head.

272

NANCY: Well, I've waded in this long enough that going back will be as hard as going on! I'm going to wade further…

NANCY: ….and Ed's not going to be able to *handle his guilt, eh readers??*

THE READER (off-panel): Stop dragging me into this!

PANEL 58. Zeke, worried, while Nancy points ahead to the next panel.

ZEKE: I dunno, can the two of us alone pull this off?

NANCY: Ah, true, what we need is more muscle…. People who'll *willingly* get involved….

NANCY: Aha! And I know where we can—the answer's over in Panel 59!

PANEL 59. The outskirts of Crikeytown, a row of 1940s buildings and retirement homes and gas-lamps. Every building has cobwebs grown over it.

CAPTION: Out in Dunfunnin is where certain people who can't *hack it* anymore go to live… the ones nobody *wants* to see around….

CAPTION: People like:

PANEL 60. Right in front of us, waving to the reader: Paddy Whack the Irish Boxer in his green derby hat and boxing gloves; Bossy Boots, stroppy not-attractive schoolgirl who thinks she should be in charge; and Gunga Din 2000, a 1950s robot who looks like an 1850s stereotype of Indians.

PADDY WHACK: Begorrah! I'm Paddy Whack the Irish boxer! I get violent because I'm Irish!

BOSSY BOOTS: *Humph!* If I was in charge, this story would be done sooner! (But I'd give it all up for a *real man*... *Simper!*)

GUNGA DIN 2000: [Dialogue censored for being too racist— Obverse Management]

PANEL 61. Nancy pats them all patronisingly on the head.

NANCY: Now I think you were all wrongfully cast out, and you've got a lot to offer us—and you shouldn't need to *change a thing*...

GUNGA DIN 2000: [Oh wow, we're censoring this too— Obverse Management]

NANCY: Uh, yeah.

PANEL 62. Nancy stands on a model of a mountain, pointing at the rest of Crikeytown.

NANCY: Imagine being back in the warmth, getting to do all your japes and fun again! Nobody calling you outdated!

PADDY WHACK: Leapin' leprechauns, that'd be grand!

BOSSY BOOTS: I haven't done *anything* since Jimmy Savile made a guest appearance!

NANCY: You can have *all* you see here and all you have to do is... *help me* with *a little problem*...

PANEL 63. The three sign a contract Nancy has out, marked "AGREEMENT TO MURDER PEOPLE". Bossy Boots, who's already signed, is making eyes at Zeke.

CAPTION: They agree very quickly—it's really depressing in Dunfunnin, readers!

BOSSY BOOTS: Bah, I was only cast out because men found me *intimidating!*

BOSSY BOOTS: But if a *real man* told me not to be bossy, Zeke… (Sigh!)

ZEKE: *Oh no!* Twitter's not going to be happy I'm in this panel!!

PANEL 64. Zeke, whispering to Nancy.

ZEKE (whispering): Are you sure we want *these* losers to be in the gang???

NANCY (whispering): What could go wrong?

THE READER (off-panel): A *lot!*

NANCY: Nobody asked you!

PANEL 65. Night-time, and Ned Ed's corpse hangs from a noose from a lamppost: X's where his eyes should be, a note saying "I TOTALLY KILLED STU AND BABYFACE :-(" pinned to his chest. The Slobs have found the body and are recoiling & vomiting in horror.

CAPTION: And so, a fall guy is found hanging around…

TOMMY: *Oh god no that shouldn't be!!*

275

SFX: BLEEEUUURRRRGGG!

PANEL 66. Paddy Whack and Bossy Boots giving a witness statement to Sheriff Squarejaw.

PADDY WHACK: Oh f'sure I saw him definitely kill himself.

BOSSY BOOTS: I didn't see *anybody* do it!

SHERIFF SQUAREJAW: That's… that's case closed then…

SHERIFF SQUAREJAW: Ah… Ah don't really feel this is the right end… Nobody should do *that* in guilt. That's not what the law should be….

PANEL 67. Jill Thrill wheels down the street, panicked, a device on her chair marked "EVIL MURDERER DETECTOR".

CAPTION: Everyone in Crikeytown thinks it's all over—but not our Jill!

JILL THRILL: Ed's 'suicide note' was in someone else's handwriting *and* spelt correctly! Someone's gunning for us new people and I must be next!

JILL THRILL: But what am I gonna *do*…?

PANEL 68. Soppy Sammy's head pops out of a bin.

SAMMY: Pssst! I know who's after you! We both gotta get to safety before *we're next!!*

JILL THRILL: Humph! Not sure I want to hide with a Snob!

SAMMY: Got a better option??

PANEL 69. Jill close-up, looking bitter.

JILL THRILL (thought balloon): Blast! I really don't have a choice. This isn't what I'm meant to *be*... Whoever's doing this, they're... I dunno the words for it. They're ruining things, that's the best I've got...

PANEL 70. The Slobs, all bored and depressed at the arcade with a big cloud marked "GLOOM" above them. Tommy lifelessly pokes at a game.

CAPTION: Despite her angst, Jill does a runner—and in the morning, all the mysterious disappearances and dead bodies have really brought everyone down!

TOMMY: ....

PANEL 71. Nancy, grinning as she enters with her henchmen behind her.

NANCY: Why's everyone so miserable? We got the day off school!

BIFF, A GENERIC SLOB FILLING THE CROWD: Well, *the reason* why we got it off....

NANCY: Don't be a wet!

PANEL 72. Tommy the Terror stares listlessly into space, with wavey lines and "EXISTENTIAL ANGST" coming off him, while Nancy has a big matey arm around him.

TOMMY: Nuffin feels fun anymore, Nancy.

TOMMY: And what's gonna happen with the regeneration if we're all like this...? Without the new chums—

NANCY: It'll be *fine*, we don't *need* anyone new! Trust me, *everything's fine the way it is!*

PANEL 73. Bossy Boots and Paddy Whack are dressed up like John and Gillian, with Gunga Din 2000 as a Trod, while everyone else stares and scratches their heads. Zeke and Nancy have big fake grins on.

CAPTION: It turns out to *not* be fine at all!

TOMMY: You're *what??* I don't get it.

ZEKE: Oh, Tommy, *everyone's* read the TV Action strips from 1964!

BOSSY BOOTS: Yes, this is a *very funny* skit!

PANEL 74. The apparent end of a storyline, with every girl Snob and Slob jointly staring at Paddy Whack in confusion— except Nancy, gamely pretending this all makes sense.

CAPTION: Everything starts to go backwards....

PADDY WHACK: ...and *that's* why women need a good strong man!

GIRLS: ????

NANCY: *Ahahahahaha! Classic!!*

PANEL 75. Tommy the Terror's dad spanks him hard with a slipper.

CAPTION: …and that starts to catch on…

TOMMY'S DAD: Grrr!

TOMMY: *No!! Please stop!! Why are you doing this?!*

PANEL 76. The sun above Crikeytown has started to dim. In the centre, a flame of dolorous black stutters.

PANEL 77. In a clubhouse, where Soppy Sammy, Jill Thrill, and a handful of other characters are hiding out ('LOOSE LIPS GET US GOT!' warns a propaganda poster). A map of Crikeytown is being poured over.

CAPTION: Hiding out, Soppy Sammy and his resistance keep notes on the situation…

SPECCY SALLY: It's all falling apart! The centre is not holding, the maddening gyre does a thingy!

SOPPY SAMMY: The town's going to be Not Talked About *in two days maximum….!!*

JILL THRILL: Okay, so what are we going to *do* about it?

PANEL 78. Everyone looks at each other for an answer.

CAPTION: But nobody has any idea of what can be done.

PANEL 79. The crew are startled; Sally hurriedly checks the Yellow Pages as they hear:

THE READER (off-panel): You silly billies, you're in *a Faction Paradox anthology* about their magic time prison! Why don't you just ask Faction Paradox for help?

SOPPY SAMMY: By jove, that could *actually work!*

SPECCY SALLY: Would they be under "F" or "P"...?

SOPPY SAMMY: No, they're *ex-directory!* There's only one hope of summoning them:

PANEL 80. A huge ink-stained hand descends from the heavens– the words "EDITOR" point to it.

EDITOR: *Groan!* Fine, I'll have Faction Paradox written into this. Can't *believe* I've got to fix someone's plot *again...!*

SOPPY: Lucky the Ed's so *hands-on, eh readers?*

EDITOR: Less of your puns, you horrible creep!

PANEL 81. Over at the old stage at Crikeytown Comp. Nancy is sitting listlessly on it, holding a prop dagger before her. A half-seen corpse lies near her, with an arrow pointing to a red puddle: "NOT KETCHUP, READERS!"

CAPTION: Everything's taking a bit of a toll on our frenemy Nancy...

NANCY: Tomorrow, and tomorrow, *and tomorrow* creeps in this place from day to day... My life's but a boring play, told by a thicko, loud noises meaning nuffin...

PANEL 82. Zeke's head pops halfway into Panel 81.

ZEKE: Psst! Nancy's cracking up, readers! This is *getting bad...* my conscience is doing the rumblies! I gotta stop her—

THE READER (off-panel): A likely story! *You're* just worried she'll kill you next!

ZEKE: Shaddup!

PANEL 83. A shadowy alleyway at night—Zeke is sneaking around with his trenchcoat pulled up, up to a shadowy Squarejaw.

ZEKE (whispering): Pssstt! Sheriff! I know who's *really* behind everything and I'll let you know if I get a suspended sentence!

SHERIFF (whispering): Oh really?

PANEL 84. Zeke, whispering furtively, not aware the "sheriff" is Naughty Nancy in Squarejaw's bloodstained uniform.

ZEKE (whispering): Yeah, it's Naughty Nancy! Not me ever, all her!

NANCY: Oh really?

PANEL 85: Zeke's eyes pop out in fear.

ZEKE: Sheriff, why does your sound girly *OH NO!!!!*

NANCY: Oh *yes!* Hear a voice cry, *snitch no more!* Nancy does murder grasses, *eh readers?!*

CAPTION: Oooer! Looks like there's *no way out* for Zeke! Not unless someone from Faction Paradox can show up within the very next panel!

281

PANEL 86. Cousin Sequential of Faction Paradox warps in, their face covered by a mask of a happy cartoon skull.

SFX: VWORP VWORP

COUSIN SEQUENTIAL: I am Cousin Sequential of [series logo] Faction Paradox [/series logo]

COUSIN SEQUENTIAL: Honestly, I feel this is beneath me.

ZEKE (off panel): What a stroke of luck!

PANEL 87. Naughty Nancy charges at Sequential.

NANCY: I *will not yield* to kiss the ground by Jill Thrill's feet! I will *try the last*, and *stuff them* that first cries--

PANEL 88. Cousin Sequential zaps her.

COUSIN SEQUENTIAL: *Enough!*

COUSIN SEQUENTIAL: No man of woman born can stop you but *I'm* non-binary, so *nerrr!*

NANCY: AAAAAIIIII

NANCY: NO NO IT FEELS LIKE KNIVES IN MY VEINS

PANEL 89. Nancy is dissolving into pencil outlines on the page.

COUSIN SEQUENTIAL: You're being sent to *the Boulevard* for your crimes of forcing an *unchanging order* on your world. (We really hate that sort of thing)

COUSIN SEQUENTIAL: But 'tis ironic, for there will be an unchanging order—your suffering, for all time, alone, unmourned, and unloved.

PANEL 90. Zeke looks relieved.

ZEKE: That's *heavy stuff*, Sequential! Still, I'm glad you turned up when you did--

COUSIN SEQUENTIAL: Don't know why *you're* relieved, chum…

PANEL 91. Zeke is zapped! He's screaming in pain as he turns into an outline.

COUSIN SEQUENTIAL: …*you're going to the Boulevard too!*

ZEKE: AAAAAAA! AAAAAAA! IT HUUUUUURTS!!!!

COUSIN SEQUENTIAL: An eternity of loneliness with his own self-loathing thoughts will teach him not to be such a moral coward, *eh readers?*

PANEL 92. Cousin Sequential warps out, leaving the place abandoned—no trace anyone was ever here.

SFX: VWORP

PANEL 93. The playground at school, the next day—everyone's sitting around in a funk, a great smoky cloud marked "DOOM!" above their heads, Tommy rocking back and forth in a foetal position. All the while, Paddy, Bossy, and Gunga are

283

forcing their Trods' skit on everyone again. Jill and Soppy Sammy look on this work with dismay.

BOSSY BOOTS: Look, maybe you'll get it's funny if we *tell you* how it's funny—

JILL THRILL: *Yeeesh!* And we've got how long until the regeneration??

SOPPY SAMMY: It's happening in panel 98!!

PANEL 94. Jill zooms her wheelchair over to Tommy and chums, holding a big sack marked "ROTTEN FRUIT"—green stink lines come out.

JILL THRILL: *Wotcher!* Boy, those three are *losers*—what d'you say we pelt them with rotten fruit until they go away?

TOMMY: Gloom! Nothing matters anymore, Jill…

JILL THRILL (thought bubble): There's only one thing for it…

PANEL 95. A speaker pops out of the back of her wheelchair and blasts a loud fart noise towards the three startled losers.

SFX: PAAARRRRPPPP!!!

JILL THRILL: HA! HA! THEY FARTED!

WEIGHTY KATIE: Whoa! They *did* fart! Ha ha!

PANEL 96. Everyone, even the Snobs, throws rotten tomatoes at the three as they run off crying.

CAPTION: Luckily farts are *always* funny! Everyone gets back to their old jolly selves.

TOMMY: Ha ha! More like toma-*go* for you three!!

SOPPY SAMMY (thought bubble): That was terrible.

PANEL 97. The Slobs pelt the Snobs with tomatoes once more, everyone starting to glow with regeneration energy, but Tommy the Terror has a fixed grin that's not meeting his eyes, and Soppy Sammy looks almost relieved, but not quite, like he's waiting for the punchline.

CAPTION: And so everything's back to normal in Crikeytown, just in time for the regeneration! Japes and jolly times for all as everyone tries to force themselves to forget how close they came to *the abyss of no return* that awaits for all, including all of you at home... *eh readers??*

THE END!

COMING SOON

FACTION PARADOX:
THE BOULEVARD
Volume Two